THE BATTLE FOR CARNILLO

BOOK II
The Estorian Chronicles

The BATTLE
for CARNILLO

Nikki
Tate

With illustrations by
E. Colin Williams

sono**nis**
PRESS

WINLAW, BRITISH COLUMBIA

NATIONAL LIBRARY OF CANADA CATALOGUING IN PUBLICATION DATA

Tate, Nikki, 1962-
    The battle for Carnillo / Nikki Tate.

    ISBN 1-55039-127-5

        1. Title. II. Series: Tate, Nikki, 1962- Estorian chronicles ; bk. 2.
PS8589.A8735B37 2003   jC813'.54   C2003-910442-7
PZ7.T2113Ba 2003

Sono Nis Press most gratefully acknowledges the support for our publishing program provided by the Government of Canada through the Book Publishing Industry Development Program (BPIDP), The Canada Council for the Arts, and the British Columbia Arts Council.

Interior illustrations and map by E. Colin Williams
Cover and interior design by Jim Brennan

Published by
SONONIS PRESS
Box 160
Winlaw, BC V0G 2J0
1-800-370-5228
sononis@netidea.com
www.sononis.com

Printed and bound in Canada
by Houghton Boston Printers.

Distributed in the U.S. by:
Orca Book Publishers
Box 468
Custer, WA 98240-0468
1-800-210-5277

The Canada Council | Le Conseil des Arts
for the Arts | du Canada

For Alex—
Yes, Alex, this one really, truly is for you . . .

And for Needa—
In Memoriam

ACKNOWLEDGEMENTS

There are so many people to thank and I'm always scared I'll forget someone important. If you are that person, I am sorry! Dani, I must start with you because you are the most forgiving and supportive person I know. I would have wasted away to nothing by now if it hadn't been for all those delicious meals, smoothies, and desserts you prepared during the struggle to finish this book. I'd also like to thank you for your keen eye and excellent junk-shop scrounging—without your help, Dominique would have spilled a lot of aurum-curare. Freda, without your wise insights this story could not have been told: thank you, thank you, thank you. Jim, as always you make everything beautiful! Diane, you are an extraordinary person and a fabulous publisher—just how lucky can an author be? Dawn, your eagle eye is much appreciated: in a sick and twisted way, I love the way you make those pages bleed! J.A.Z., thank you for your patient work on all those drawings. What a pleasure it has been to visit the streets, taverns, and prisons of Carnillo with you.

Most important of all, I'd like to thank all the readers who have encouraged Dominique in his journey so far.

NT

*May I rock you to sleep with a tale; may I wake you
with a tale.*

Rwandan storyteller's opening refrain
—From *The World of Storytelling* by Anne Pellowski

*The boys gathered around the fire as the old man
spread his arms wide. The story was about to begin.*

—Traditional Estorian story opening

*When the story stick was raised, the villagers fell quiet
and began to listen.*

—Traditional Campriano storyteller's opening gesture

Once upon a time . . .

1

THE FOOTHILLS

It was when he travelled that Owen the Small
felt most at home.

—Traditional Estorian story

"Don't shoot!"

The leranon banked sharply and soared back down the canyon away from the two riders, its leonine tail arched sideways to help the great beast keep its balance in the air.

Dominique held his breath. *Fly faster!*

Amana lowered her bow and arrow. "Why did you shout?" The Campriano girl turned in her saddle and glared at him. "I had a clear shot!"

A thousand answers careened through Dominique's head. Because the horse-lions had once given him shelter. Because they had treated his wounds. Because they were beautiful. But Amana was in no mood to listen to Dominique's explanations, even if he had been able to find the right words.

"Don't you Estorians have stories about those monsters?"

"Well . . . yes . . ."

"And?"

Dominique swallowed and looked down at the ground. Fine, wispy grasses sprouted here and there between the rocks. His horse, Dust Storm, tugged the reins through Dominique's fingers and put his head down to eat.

Yes, the Estorians told many stories about leranons, none of them good.

When he awoke he was a prisoner in the leranon cave, surrounded by stones wet with the blood of innocent victims, the air filled with the cries of lost souls . . .

"The stories might not be quite . . . might not be . . ." He faltered as Amana began to laugh. ". . . completely accurate—"

"Every Campriano child has heard about the evil nature of leranons. We have lots of stories about the horrible things they do to people. There's one story about a herder who was captured. The leranons corrupted his mind and he never thought clearly again after that, not even well enough to look after his sheep."

"Yes, but..." Dominique stopped again. If Amana thought the beasts could corrupt people's minds, she'd hardly believe his story of leranons who fed him and gave him shelter and gifts in exchange for as much as he could offer them: a story. What good was telling her the truth if she wouldn't believe it?

"'Yes, but' nothing," Amana was saying. "There are only two things to do with leranons: cut off their horns and put them to work, or kill them."

"Cut off their . . ." Dominique grabbed the front of the saddle, dizzy, sick. He closed his eyes and thought of the young leranon, Kyrie, and the excited expression on her face when he had prepared to tell his story. How could Amana talk so blithely about killing these gentle creatures? No wonder the leranons had bristled when they initially mistook him for a Campriano.

"Next time," Amana warned, "don't interfere. A leranon horn is worth a lot at Carnillo markets."

"Why?" he asked weakly, immediately regretting his question. He did not want to hear any more about the fate of leranons at Campriano hands.

"Do Estorians know nothing from nothing? There's not a Carnillian soldier who would go into battle without first drinking tea made of powdered leranon horn. It makes a warrior braver. Stronger. Camprianos have been hunting leranons and selling the horns to Carnillian soldiers for hundreds of years."

"Have you ever . . ." Queasy now, but wanting to know, he tried again. "Did you . . ."

Amana followed his gaze to the bow and arrow she still held in her hands. "Killed one? Is that what you want to know?" She aimed the arrow tip back down the canyon. "That would have been my first."

Dominique wrapped his arms around his stomach. He could not imagine how awful he would have felt if she had found her target.

Amana put her arrow back into the quiver and slipped the bow over her shoulder.

Please, Dominique wished silently, *please stay away from us.* If only the leranons could hear his thoughts: maybe they would be safe as he and Amana travelled away from the Misty Mountains toward the foothills and, beyond that, the distant city of Carnillo.

"Is that a shack over there?" Amana pulled Brimstone to a halt and peered over the horse's head toward a dark dot tucked into the fold of a hill.

Dominique shaded his eyes with his hand and squinted. "Maybe—unless it's another one of those boulders." Though the path they'd been following away from the Misty Mountains had widened and become much easier to navigate, every so often the two riders had skirted boulders so large Dominique had not been able to see over them as he rode past.

Amana stood up in her stirrups and leaned forward, the muscles in her slender arms tensing as she shifted her weight. "I don't think so. We haven't seen any of those big rocks for a while." She sighed and settled back into her saddle. "That might be a roof, but I'm not sure what's over there. There's never been a reason to cross the valley. I've never made this trip so *slowly* before," she added pointedly.

All afternoon they'd been travelling south, heading for a distant bump in the foothills that Amana called Sleeping Rabbit, the place where she usually stopped for the night on her way back to the city. The hut, if it was a hut, was on the opposite side of a wide valley nearly due west of where they had stopped. Dominique squinted harder, but the lump refused to become clear.

Amana turned and reached behind her to undo the leather cord lashing the sturdy saddlebags closed. She pulled out a spyglass and lifted it to her eye. "Out of the way, yes . . ." She lowered the glass and grinned. "But that *is* a roof—so we'll be safe."

An icy shiver ran up Dominique's spine and he felt a sudden urge to wallop Dust Storm and race across the valley toward the shelter. He knew exactly what Amana meant. One way or another they had to be under cover by nightfall. It was the only way to be sure they'd escape the breath-drinking incubus that plagued the region east of the River Epilobium.

"Have you ever seen one?" Amana asked, tucking away the spyglass.

"An incubus? Yes." Dominique nodded, exhilarated and terrified by the feeling of his breath sliding in and out of his body. He exhaled, slowly, savouring this simple pleasure. How could he ever have been so naive as to assume that one breath would follow another without effort for all time?

"Really?" Amana slapped the outside of the saddlebag and flicked the leather strap through the buckle. "And how did you survive an attack like that?"

Dominique's delight in his ability to breathe evaporated, replaced by a sense of panic that pushed in on his chest as he now struggled to inhale. He stared across the valley at their destination so he didn't have to meet the challenge of Amana's gaze.

"Liar," she said, practically spitting contempt.

"I jumped into a yagabono pit," Dominique blurted out.

"Oh, how disgusting!" Amana said, pinching her nose shut.

"Yes," Dominique agreed. "Rotting mudfowl eggs wouldn't have smelled so hideous!"

Still holding her nose, Amana made a rude retching sound.

"Exactly!" Dominique said, and they both laughed.

If only it had happened that way, Dominique thought. In truth, he had been rescued from certain death by three leranons who had managed to hold the incubus at bay and then fly him off to safety. He shuddered, as unhappy about the half-truth as he was about being reminded of one of the most terrifying nights of his life.

"We should go," he said, waving his hand in the direction of the smudge on the hill.

Amana eyed the trail they had been following and then nodded her agreement. "Yes. We don't have time to waste admiring the view."

For the briefest moment Dominique felt something like kinship with the Campriano girl, but she was quick to put him in his place.

"If we could ride faster," she said, turning Brimstone

downhill, "we could get all the way to the cave near Sleeping Rabbit."

What could he say in his defence? It was true that he didn't ride nearly as well as Amana. Why should he? *His* people, the Estorians, were storytellers, not horsemen. She had made allowances, yes, but she couldn't seem to resist reminding him of how much faster she was able to travel on her own. Again Dominique wanted to drive his horse forward at a gallop, this time to prove to the girl he was not a liability.

"Come on—we won't have the light for long," she said, though her voice was gentler now. She checked back over her shoulder to make sure Dominique and Dust Storm were following, but Dominique was too annoyed to appreciate her concern.

They rode on beneath the wide blue sky, the sun now directly ahead, sweat darkening their horses' necks. Dominique squinted at the distant cabin. It was still going to take a while to get there, even though the grassy foothills made for much easier going than the steep, rock-strewn trails of earlier in the day. He tried to make himself comfortable, but no matter how he shifted in the saddle, his backside ached. The sun's descent toward the top of the hills seemed to speed up as the burning disc slid down the sky.

"Whoa!" Dominique clutched at the saddle when Dust Storm slipped on a steeper part of the trail, startling a wild tonneck. The sturdy creature bolted from its hiding place in the tall grass. Propelled by its heavily muscled back legs, the animal bounded away, zigzagging across the grass. Dominique's thoughts bounded off like the fleeing creature and then kept on going. They raced away from his troubled journey all the way back to his clan, the clan that had cast him out for failing to tell the right kind of stories, the Stories of men.

When Dominique had lived with his own people,

before they banished him for a year and a day, his job had been to take care of the captive tonnecks. Thinking of the plump animals behind the stick bars of their cages reminded him of his mother's cooking. Oh, what he wouldn't give for a helping of roast tonneck. As he rode along behind Amana, his mouth watered and he wiped away a bit of drool. With each day that passed it seemed less and less likely he would ever share another meal with his mother and sisters. It felt as if a stone had lodged in his throat and he had to swallow hard several times to make it go away.

"Amana?" he asked, his voice croaky, strange to his own ears. "Do your people eat tonnecks?"

"Of course we do. Roast tonneck. Tonneck stew. Fried tonneck. Dried tonneck." She neither slowed down nor turned around.

"Tonneck smoked over green chickling boughs— that's my favourite," Dominique said dreamily.

"What?!" Amana spun her horse around and Dust Storm's hooves slid in the loose dirt and gravel as Dominique was forced to bring him to a quick stop. "You mean your people eat tonneck?"

"Of course we do."

Amana rolled her eyes. "I should have shot that one."

"Why didn't you?"

"I thought you were probably some kind of tonneck-lover, too."

"I *do* love them—fried up with wild onions and peska root!" Dominique thought she might be angry and braced himself for another of her verbal onslaughts. But none came. Instead, she shifted her bow slightly and squinted across the undulating foothills.

"I won't let another one get away!"

At this, Dominique smiled and reached forward to pat his horse's neck.

Amana turned and started off again, as easy in the

13

saddle as if they were just starting out and not nearing the end of a very long day.

Dominique scanned the grasses—not just for ton-necks, but also for Navina, his kasyapa bird. She was in her element here, darting from one clump of grass to another, hanging upside down, feasting on the ripening seeds. She had eaten so much since leaving the barren, rocky slopes of the mountains that Dominique wondered how she was still able to fly. But fly she did, swooping and soaring, her iridescent blue-green wings braced against the breeze. She never strayed far from the horses, but Dominique still worried about losing her. He would never find her if she disappeared into the wild, and he feared she would never return to him if she was called away by another kasyapa.

Distances were strange in the foothills. For ages the odd shape on the far side of the valley remained indis-tinct. The riders' shadows grew longer, rippling across the undulating grass as they slid along at the horses' feet. Dominique's thoughts began to wander. What if Amana were trying to trick him? His heart thudded in his chest as he tried to think why she would lead him into a trap. Surely she would have killed him by now if that had been her intention.

Uneasy, Dominique planned an escape route—a full gallop back the way they had come. Glancing back over his shoulder, he was surprised at how steep the path was—it was so deceptive, riding down into the valley. His horse was tired. He'd never outrun Amana. Or her arrows, he thought glumly.

Then, suddenly, the roof of the hut appeared and his doubts dissolved. Dominique felt a surge of excitement as he realized that the roof of the shepherd's hut even had a squat stone chimney.

"She knows it's a good place to say," Amana said as they halted the horses in front of the stocky building. She pointed at Navina, who perched on the chimney, preening.

"Hello?" Amana waited for a reply, but Dominique knew from the untrampled grass around the building and the bright green moss growing over the mud walls that nobody had used the hut for a long time.

The sun caught the brilliant red crest atop Navina's head. When a breeze ruffled the feathers it looked as if she wore a flaming crown. Dominique frowned. The only story he knew about a flaming crown was one in which a young prince stuck his head too close to a potter's kiln. His hair caught on fire and he was left with terrible waxy scars all over his face and neck. He wondered if Amana's people, the Camprianos, had a story like that, too.

Amana dismounted and disappeared around the back of the hut, leading Brimstone behind her. A moment later, Dominique heard her shout, "Oh, no!" followed by a string of curses that would have shocked even his uncle, Sethka.

CHAPTER

2

INCUBUS

So long was Aggerita's story, the evening never ended.

—Campriano Recitatorium tale

Dominique hopped off Dust Storm and took a couple of tentative steps. He walked as if he still had a horse between his legs! He led his mount around the corner of the building and gasped. Though the walls and sod roof seemed solid enough, someone—or something—had torn huge holes in the wooden door.

"Some fool has ripped down the planks!" Amana swore and kicked the wall. The baked dung and mud was as hard as stone, and Dominique bit the inside of his lip so he didn't burst out laughing at the sight of Amana hopping around on one foot, howling. Her shrieks set Brimstone dancing at the end of her reins.

Noticing him watching, Amana drew herself up straight and approached the hut again, Brimstone's reins held firmly in her hand. Amana stuck her arm through one of the gaps in the door.

"We'll have to fix those," she said, all business. "But it will be a good place to stay. See—there's even a stall at the back for the horses. It's a bit low—I suppose it was for the sheep—but it will do. And look, there's water over there."

Someone had built a low stone trough across the stream, though the hole meant to let water in was plugged with a thick mat of weeds. Most of the flow trickled around the trough until Amana poked the weeds out of the drainage hole, and fresh water gushed in to fill the stone receptacle.

The horses drank, noisily slurping the water over their bits.

"Wood to fix the door and fuel the fire—then we can eat," Amana said, shooting Dominique a look that clearly said *Get to work!*

She was right, of course, about how much they had to accomplish before dark, but that didn't make her superior attitude any easier to take. When Brimstone lifted her head for the last time, water dribbling in twin streams off her chin, Amana led the mare into the gloomy recess of the sheep barn that made up the back half of the hut.

"They'll be safe in here tonight."

Dominique removed Dust Storm's saddle and bridle and led him into the shelter. Then he helped Amana gather many armloads of grass for the hungry horses. Once the animals were comfortable, Dominique and Amana set to work to secure the shelter against marauding creatures of the night. For each order Amana snapped at Dominique, he grumbled back a retort under his breath. *Snapper-crab. Louhilli-hilli. Indio-hag!* Swearing at Amana only made him madder. If he hadn't been so terrified of the incubus he might have stalked off into the foothills to try to find his own place to spend the night.

"A good enough meal can end a war," Dominique said, one hand resting comfortably on his tummy, the other reaching lazily along the dried dung wall behind him. The sun had long ago dipped behind the hills, surrendering the valley to darkness.

"We've been travelling too long when a meal of rice and beans tastes as good as a palace feast," Amana said, tugging a wooden comb through her hair.

The familiar comfort of a fire crackling in the hearth and the satisfaction of a full belly made Dominique yawn.

"This is much more comfortable than the cave at Sleeping Rabbit," Amana said, working through a knot. "It was a good day, in the end."

Dominique nodded. Amana had told him that with a long ride the following day they could reach Carnillo. The horses were sound, and tonight they had good water and plenty of feed. The shelter was snug and safe, and, Dominique thought happily, they hadn't seen any more leranons. Despite everything, it *had* been a good day.

The Campriano girl smoothed her hair and pulled it apart into three strands. Reaching up and working behind her head, she began to wind her hair into a thick blond braid. Dominique had watched this performance for the past two nights in the damp caves they had used for shelter, but the quick, strong movements of Amana's hands still surprised him. Watching her made him conscious of his own thick tangle of curls. He twisted his finger into a trailing strand and absently stroked it against his cheek.

"Your hair's almost as long as mine," Amana said. "Though not nearly so clean."

Dominique untangled his finger and scowled. Why did she always say just the thing to annoy him? "Well, your hair is—"

In the stall at the back the horses snorted. Amana's hands stopped mid-braid and Dominique's mouth froze around his unfinished sentence. The horses shifted back and forth, and Dominique jumped when one of them whinnied, a shrill call that seemed unnaturally loud in the small space.

Something clunked against the back of the hut, and then a *whoosh* outside the front door brought Dominique's head around with a snap. Navina's sharp *peep* in his ear set his heart thudding even faster. They had patched the door with sticks and slabs of bark collected from a stand of nearby trees, but now the barrier seemed hopelessly flimsy. It quivered and Dominique shrank back against the wall.

Hair forgotten, Amana's half-finished braid slid across her back. She and Dominique scuttled backwards into the corner farthest from the door, crouching to stay below the level of the windowsill. The shutters, closed and latched, clattered and rattled before the wind.

In the stall, the horses grew more agitated, kicking and pawing. Amana glanced nervously at the partition. The hut was divided floor to ceiling by a solid stone hearth and chimney, but to either side of this the mud walls ended an arm's length below the ceiling beams. The horses churned up the dust on their side of the wall, sending clouds of filth into the air. The particles hung suspended in the firelight like smoke or fog.

Shadows thrown by the crackling flames swayed over the rough walls, caught in the haze of dust, and pushed into every corner. Another *whoosh* outside shook the loose boards of the door, and Dominique gasped and held his breath as if he might protect it from the swirling attacker outside.

"Incubus," Amana whispered. Firelight reflected in her eyes, making them seem huge. She reached for her bow and plucked an arrow from her quiver. In one smooth movement she lifted the bow, placed the arrow to the string, and eased it back, aiming right at the wooden door.

"Don't waste an arrow!" Dominique shouted. "It's no good for an incubus!"

The air inside the cabin swirled, lifting dried leaves from where they'd settled in the corners and tossing them into the middle of the room. There they danced in tiny whirlwinds, spiralling up and falling back, directed by an unseen hand.

"Watch out!" Dominique screamed as a dark tendril, wispy, nearly invisible, squeezed between cracks in the door and swept through the inverted cones of whirling leaves and dust. The horses squealed and a powerful kick rattled the door at the back of the stall.

"No!" Dominique shouted. If the horses broke the door down, the incubus would get in!

Amana spun around and hauled herself up the dividing wall, aiming her arrow at the panicky horses.

"No!" Dominique screamed again. He threw himself forward and snatched up the saddle blanket he'd been sitting on. Flapping it in front of him as if fanning flames, he beat at the air as the leranons had once done to protect him. The great *whooshes* of the blanket bent the incubus tendril back and forth, sending it twisting and turning through the whirlwind of leaves.

Dominique flapped the heavy blanket harder, sweat pouring over his face, down his sides. Behind him, the horses squealed and churned up the dust until his eyes wept from the grit and smoke, and his lungs nearly burst from the effort of pounding at the air and at the dark shape writhing around the room, until finally, with a sickening screech of rage and pain, the tendril withdrew.

Dominique lunged toward the door and covered the hole with the blanket. "Help me!"

From where she stood beside the fireplace, Amana

raised her bow and arrow and aimed at the door. "Watch out!"

Dominique shrieked as she let the arrow fly. The arrow tip pierced the blanket and buried itself in the wooden door.

"Stand back!" Amana reached for another arrow.

Dominique didn't wait to be told twice. He collapsed backward and out of the way as Amana shot three more arrows in quick succession, neatly pinning the blanket to the door.

The fire flickered and nearly went out as if someone were choking the flames. It gasped and then, with a *whoof,* roared back to life.

The horses still moved uneasily but no longer seemed determined to break down the door. Dominique wanted to stand and see that Amana was all right, but his lungs felt filled with water or smoke and he doubled over with a bout of harsh coughing and choking. He struggled to swallow and found his throat raw.

"Don't move!" Amana whispered. Her voice, too, sounded hoarse. She coughed and wiped her eyes. "You saved us. It's gone. It can't get past the blanket. They need air—open air."

Gradually, as they sat, panting, side by side, leaning against the wall, Amana and Dominique breathed more easily. Neither of them could tear their gaze from the square of blanket tacked to the door by four arrows. The howling wind outside eventually abated until it was so quiet they could hear only the crackle of the fire and the horses munching their grass.

"Shall we stoke the fire?" Amana whispered.

Dominique nodded. If they kept the fire burning all night, they'd survive. He reached up and touched Navina when she fluttered back down onto his shoulder from where she'd hidden up on a ceiling beam. "We could tell each other stories," he said before he could stop the words from coming out of his mouth.

"Yes," Amana said, surprising him with the speed of her reply. "Yes, we could."

Dominique closed his eyes, leaned his head back against the wall, and sighed, the exhalation full of relief and something close to joy. The Campriano girl had listened to his stories during the two evenings they'd spent in the caves, and she didn't seem to care that the stories Dominique told were those he had heard many times before—the Tara stories of the women, the travelling stories of the men, and the myths and legends all Estorian people knew as well as they knew the changes of the seasons and the direction to travel at the start of each migration.

"You can tell me the story of how you found the kasyapa bird," Amana said. "I'd like to hear about that again."

Dominique ran his thumb lightly over Navina's beak and the bird pushed back with a gentle nudge. "Then you can tell me how you came to know Lord Emberto. I'd like to hear about *that*."

"I suppose you would," Amana said, picking up her braiding where she had left off.

Amana knew plenty of stories herself, and not just the unsophisticated lies he'd always been told were the best that the Camprianos could manage to tell. Amana's people might not have the Estorian men's power to receive Stories of Truth from Beyond, but Amana was a good teller, even so.

Being a girl *and* a Campriano, Amana was doomed never to hear tales from Beyond, just like he seemed to be. But Dominique took more comfort than he might have expected in the knowledge that he and Amana would have stories, even if they weren't the best kind of Stories, to keep them company through the long night.

3

A PRISONER IN NAME

Long might you suffer, long might you cry . . .
—Ancient Estorian song

At first light, Dominique and Amana prepared to leave the cabin. Amana wiped the tips of her arrows on her leggings before slipping them back into her quiver, and Dominique followed her outside with the saddle blankets and bridles.

Neither of them said anything as they worked quickly to ready the horses. They had slept very little, barely keeping their fear at bay by telling one story after another until it was nearly dawn.

"Navina!" Dominique shielded his eyes from the bright sun already searing the tips of the mountains.

"Hurry," Amana scolded.

Dominique kept calling as he mounted Dust Storm. "I know, I know." They could not risk being caught out in the open that night.

Amana's mouth snapped shut, but she let him stand

in the stirrups with his hands cupped around his mouth as he shouted, "Naaaah-veeee-naaaaahhh!"

With a big sigh of relief, Dominique sank back into the saddle as the bird swooped overhead and then away again. The sun rose higher, bathing the valley in the sharp, clear light of morning.

Amana trotted ahead, her mouth set in concentration. Once they were underway she beckoned for Dominique to ride beside her.

"You can't just ride into the city," she said, not slowing down to talk.

"Why not?"

Dominique had finally mastered the art of rising and sitting with his horse's trot so he no longer slammed into the saddle with each step. But it was still hard for him to talk and ride at the same time.

"Because according to my dream I'm supposed to be bringing back a prisoner—"

"I'm not a prisoner," Dominique insisted.

Amana flicked her braid and refused to say anything more. How could she persist in thinking he was her prisoner after all the stories they had shared the night before? They still echoed in his head. He'd told her about how he'd been led to Navina's nest by the dying kasyapa. Amana had told him how she'd been sold into the Tellers Guild even before she was born.

Lord Emberto had come to power when Amana's mother was still pregnant, and she had sold him the right to own her unborn baby. When Amana was born not long after this agreement had been made, she acquired the title of First Teller Born. In accordance with tradition, Amana had been raised in the Recitatorium and enjoyed special privileges at Emberto's court. The story of how Amana had come to work at the palace and tell stories to Emberto and the other court members was as strange as any Dominique had ever been told by his own people.

But Amana apparently didn't think that sharing some of their stories had changed anything. Dominique tried a different approach. "I'm travelling just like you," he said, feeling the heat rise in his neck and his cheeks turn red. It was ridiculous how she made him defend himself.

"It's not up to me," she said finally. "In Carnillo an Estorian is considered little better than a dog. A particularly stupid dog."

"But how would anybody—"

"Where is your story stick? Your arrows? And you look different."

"What do you mean?"

"Most Carnillians have much darker skin than you do—and dark hair." She eyed him silently and his flush grew hotter. "And your nose is wrong—too small, too straight—and your chin is pointy, not round, and your eyebrows aren't heavy enough."

"Like you!" he said. "Your skin isn't so much darker than mine. And your hair—"

"I consider myself to be a Campriano," she said slowly, as if explaining something obvious to a very young child. "I live in Carnillo. My mother is half Carnillian, half Campriano. But my father is a Campriano teller—a great teller whose ancestors were Camprianos. Camprianos have fair skin and light hair."

"So why couldn't I pretend to be a Campriano?"

"Because there aren't many of us any more. Not so you can see, anyway. For hundreds of years our people have intermarried with the Carnillians, had children. Only a few, those who left the city for a time—like my father and his parents before that—" She stopped abruptly. "It doesn't matter. You are not a Campriano— you know that. I know that. How would you ever learn all our stories?"

Dominique had no answer, but he wasn't ready to give up. "But I had a—"

Amana put her hand up to stop him from saying anything else. "I know what you are going to say about your vision, the way you saw us as equals—"

"Yes! We approached the city gates side by side!" Dominique was shouting. She could not tell him what he had or had not seen in the Cave of Departure. "I know what I saw, and you told me that you had seen the same thing in your dream."

"I will tell you this," Amana said, her long braid bouncing against her back as Brimstone trotted on. "Visions or no visions, any Estorian who dares to assume he is equal to a Campriano won't live long on the streets of Carnillo. Not if people know who he is. Believe me, you are safest with me—as my prisoner."

Dominique swallowed hard and bit back the words he longed to hurl at the girl. *You speaker of false stories . . . liar . . . pig-dog.* But he said nothing. The Estorians had always said the Camprianos could not be trusted. Not ever.

"You know I would have killed you when I had the chance if it hadn't been for—"

"I know what you are going to say," Dominique interrupted, mocking her. But he didn't finish the sentence. He didn't need to. Amana had spared his life because he had a kasyapa bird. In her dream vision, Amana, Dominique, and the bird had stood before the walls of the city. In the dream, Dominique had been very much alive.

"If I bring you in as my prisoner, we will not be questioned by the guards. We can use the name ring that you found—we can say you are a petty thief that I am returning to the city. Lord Emberto will know what to do with you. He was the one who said to bring him . . ." She broke off, leaving the thought unfinished, and urged Brimstone forward even faster.

Dominique glanced down at the wooden name ring

he wore around his ankle. It was identical to Amana's, except the symbols carved into its surface were different. He had found the ring in his travels and put it on without knowing what it was used for. How would Amana use it to get him into the city?

Dominique sighed and grabbed hold of the korval, the hollow knob at the front of the saddle. At this speed, his legs could not maintain the exhausting pumping as he pushed himself up and down in the saddle. Instead, he hung on grimly, half in, half out of the saddle as they made their way out of the wide valley and into the last of the hills before they reached the salt marshes and, beyond that, the sea.

The lack of sleep the night before and the gruelling pace Amana set soon had Dominique gritting his teeth and singing the Curse of the Festerworlds song under his breath.

Long might you suffer
Long might you cry
Long might you wait
For peace tonight.

When, at last, the horses trotted over a final low rise, Dominique gasped.

They stopped above a wide expanse of windblown grasses growing in a glittering marsh. This salt marsh, unbroken by tree or building, stretched all the way to the distant horizon. There, Dominique could just make out the darker blue of the sea. He scanned the horizon and, in the southwest, spotted a short black line dividing the marsh from the sea.

"Carnillo," Amana said, following his gaze.

To Dominique, the city seemed impossibly far away. His arms, back, legs, and empty belly ached. All he wanted to do was get off his horse and have something to eat.

Amana glanced at the sun, at the distant city, and then back at Dominique.

"We'd best eat here," she said, "as long as we are quick. There will be no more stopping for many hours." She waved her arm at the only route across the marsh, a narrow white road built atop a steep-sided berm.

Dominique nodded and smiled in agreement. One way or the other, they'd make it across the marsh before nightfall. He jumped from his horse before Amana could change her mind. Dust Storm shook his head and neck and immediately stretched down to snatch a mouthful of sparse grass.

MUMBINO-GUMBINO

"What if I don't share my bread?" the child asked.
"Then you shall eat alone," the wise queen replied.

—Campriano tale

". . . and the great yellow worm retreated into its den, dribbling blood from the gash in its side," Dominique said. He jabbed at the thickening mix of rice, beans, and spices with his stirring stick as if he were spearing a vicious worm.

Amana poked at the crackling fire with a long, green stick. "Be careful!" she said to Dominique as the pot tilted sideways.

He reached out to catch it. "Ow!" He pulled his hand back before he was singed.

"You Estorians shouldn't tell stories and cook at the same time," Amana said, deftly sliding her stick under the low side of the pot to level it. With lunch no longer in danger of sliding into the flames, Amana rocked back on her heels and said, "We have a story about a great worm, too."

The rice and beans sizzled. The water Amana had added had nearly all boiled away. Dominique poked his stirring stick toward the pot, but Amana took it from him.

"Don't stir any more," she said. "Let it get brown on the bottom. That's how I like it."

A gust of wind made the flames jump. Dominique squinted as smoke swirled around him. He was so hungry it took every bit of self-control he could muster not to pluck the food from the flames. He didn't care if it was brown on the bottom. It was stupid to wait. Hadn't Amana been hurrying them along all morning?

Annoyed that Amana knew a worm story, too, he couldn't even bring himself to keep going with the tale of Great Yellow One, even though it was one of his favourites and would have helped to pass the time.

Amana leaned over the pot, poked her dagger under the edge of the concoction, and lifted it up to peer underneath.

"Perfect," she said and pulled the pot off the fire.

None of the women and girls in his Estorian clan were like Amana. She really scared him sometimes, though it was hard to say exactly what it was about her that he found so intimidating. She was sturdy and a little taller than he was, but not unreasonably so. It was more the way she always moved with such certainty and confidence, the way she was unafraid to strike out—fire an arrow at her own horse to save them from an incubus or stab someone she knew nothing about. Self-consciously, he touched his fingertips to his shoulder. She hadn't thought twice before she had stabbed him with her dagger on the very day they met. He wondered if her hands ever shook, whether she was ever tongue-tied. He doubted it.

As she sliced the slab of food neatly in half she kept talking.

"In our story it isn't a Soldier of the Dark who slays the worm. In our story it's—"

"Clio," Dominique interrupted, anxious to get hold of

the food. He had heard plenty about the princess warrior since he had started to travel with Amana. Those stories about the great Clio seemed to be the ones she liked best, and Dominique grudgingly had to admit that she did tell them rather well.

"Yes, Clio," Amana said and handed Dominique half the mass of rice and beans, now brown and crispy on the bottom, still barely moist on the top. As usual, it was the smaller half.

"This isn't as big as—" he started to complain. "Ouch! Ahhh! Hot! Hot!" Dominique tossed the steaming rice-and-bean cake from one hand to the other.

"Where's your knife? Your dagger?"

Amana stood motionless, balancing her half of the meal on her own dagger blade, the fingers of her other hand poised in mid-air, ready to break off a piece to eat.

Dominique juggled faster, his fingertips burning with each toss. "Oh, no!" he exclaimed as his meal dropped into the dirt.

Amana's portion was still perched on the blade of her dagger. She nudged the shallow pan well away from the flames with the tip of her leather boot and flipped the food back into the pan.

"No wonder Estorians don't let their men near the cooking fires."

Dominique's ears burned. He bent down to pick up his food, but the rice crumbled and fell through his fingers in even smaller chunks. Navina swooped down and pecked at the food on the ground.

Amana shook her head and sighed loudly. "That wasn't meant for your bird." Then she sliced her portion in half and pushed the pan toward him. "Here. No need for a prisoner to starve."

Glancing at Amana, Dominique caught her quick smile before the girl became her stern self again and commanded, "Eat."

But her prisoner comment, though made half in jest, brought up the whole problem of getting Dominique into Carnillo.

Dominique stared at the food, his gut twisting with anxiety.

Amana might not deign to share her plans for what they'd do when they reached Emberto's palace, but Dominique had secrets of his own. He knew he could never tell her that he wanted to help Ieranons held captive in Carnillo or that he was looking for his father, Boris Elnedo.

"Are you not hungry?" Amana asked, slicing off another piece of the thick rice-and-bean cake. "Because if you do not want it—"

"No. I mean, yes. I am hungry."

And he was. But the anxiety in his belly fought against his desire to eat.

Upset though she'd be if she knew he wanted to help the gentle beasts she hated so much, he could not imagine what she'd do if she learned they shared the same last name: Elnedo. He had lied at the Cave of Departure about that, too, when he had told her he was a Bertolescu. It was the mention of that name, Roman Bertolescu, the name of the leader of his clan, which had nearly got him killed.

"Eat," she said. "You will need all your strength."

Dominique nodded and retrieved his dagger from his deerskin travelling sack. How could it possibly be that they both had the same name? Dominique frowned and cut off a bit of rice cake the way Amana had. It had bothered him ever since she'd told him her name. He flipped his blade sideways and balanced the mouthful on the tip.

As he chewed, his thoughts again returned to the city on the horizon. Questions he had managed to ignore during the journey through the hills now spun in relentless circles in his mind. Would he find news of his father there? And if he didn't, what then? Would he find any leranons? If he did, would he be able to help them? Would the Carnillians know he was an Estorian? What would they do if they found out?

According to Amana, the walled city was protected by armed guards at each of its twelve gates. It didn't sound as if it were that easy to come and go. How would he escape again if Carnillo did not provide the answers he sought?

Dominique sighed. It was easier not to think of the future.

"Well?"

He stared at Amana. She had been speaking to him and he hadn't heard a word.

"So," she repeated, "at the end of your story does the Soldier of the Dark get rewarded with gifts from the king and a lovely new wife?"

His mouth full, Dominique nodded. Amana knew a lot about stories and, strangely, many of the Campriano stories were similar to those his own people told. During the long night before, Amana had often known the gist of a story Dominique had been telling. And, just as often, he had recognized parts of stories she had told him.

"How do you learn your stories?" he asked.

"What do you mean?"

Dominique thought a moment, not wanting to mention the sacred Estorian Stories from Beyond. "Where do your stories come from?"

Amana shook her head. "We all have stories. Do you mean the real stories? Like the ones I tell to Lord Emberto?"

Dominique almost put his hand up to stop her from continuing. Was she going to say that she heard Stories from Beyond?

"I learn stories at the Recitatorium."

"Recita—what?"

"Recitatorium. That's the place where all the young tellers live, where we learn to tell stories. The best are taught directly by the Grand Teller."

"You live away from your family?"

Amana wrinkled up her nose. "Where else would I live? We train for hours every day and often the palace performances are at night."

"Don't you miss your family?"

Amana shrugged and flipped her braid over her shoulder. "I see my mother. And my brothers and sisters. I take them silver kinnels every week. How do you think they buy food?"

Dominique had no idea what to say. What kind of strange people sold their unborn children and then saw them only once a week? Even stranger was the fact that Amana seemed quite happy with this arrangement.

At least the Camprianos didn't hear Stories from Beyond. They were not the kind of story that could be taught at any retica . . . "Retica—?"

"Re-ci-ta-to-ri-um," Amana said, exaggerating every sound and bulging her eyes out.

Though she was making fun of him, Dominique laughed and popped more food into his mouth.

"You like it?" she asked, poking her dagger tip toward the last of Dominique's meal.

Dominique nodded again. The food was delicious.

"We call it mumbino-gumbino."

Wiping his mouth with the back of his hand, Dominique said, "I call it delicious-mumbicious."

Amana pulled a face, but Dominique could tell she was pleased with the compliment. "How far is it to Carnillo now?" he asked.

Amana squinted southward. "We still have nearly a half day's journey." Suddenly serious, she added, "You'd better . . ." She tipped her head sideways and indicated some scrubby bushes close by. "Don't worry. I won't look."

Dominique bristled at the teasing glint in her grey-green eyes. No girl was going to tell him when and where to do his business!

"I'll be fine, thank you."

"Suit yourself. While I visit the bush, perhaps you could put out the fire."

She tossed her head as she turned, sending her braid flipping back over her shoulder. She stalked off toward the bushes as if she were the goddess princess Clio the Invincible herself.

"I'll thank you to turn away!"

Dominique blushed as he turned back to the fire, pulled the burning logs apart, and rolled them in the dirt. This was not the work a man was supposed to do. Back at home with his tribe he had always joined the men for storytelling lessons while the women took care of such matters. Now, everything was different. Everything.

CHAPTER

5

NECESSARY PRECAUTIONS

*"No, my dears. Some stories shall not be told until men are
ready to hear them."*

—Estorian Tara story

"Where's your bird?" Amana checked the straps holding
the saddles and gear on the horses.

The embers hissed as Dominique poured a pan of
water over the smoking logs. "Navina!" he called. He
heard her high-pitched whistle before he saw the
kasyapa bird, the pale undersides of her tummy so subtle
compared to the shimmering blues of her wings, the
flaming scarlet of her breast feathers and the crest atop
her head.

No matter how many times he watched the won-
drous bird in full flight, he still felt a thrill, a delight and
disbelief that this creature had chosen *him* to be her
companion. Even though he had found her as a nestling,
he knew that she was a wild creature: he never allowed
himself to assume she would stay with him forever.

"Navina," Amana said thoughtfully. "Isn't that some
sort of Estorian goddess who brings fire?"

Navina landed on Dominique's outstretched arm and then nimbly hopped from there to his shoulder. "The Goddess of Clarity," he said, stroking Navina's head.

"Do you have a lot of stories about the kasyapa?" Amana asked.

Dominique shook his head. "Not really. Mostly the men mention kasyapas as the birds nobody ever gets to see." He thought for a moment. "When kasyapas are mentioned, they're always a small part of other stories."

Amana looked at him intently, her head tipped to the side, her eyes narrowed. "So you don't have a story about . . ." Seeming to change her mind, she pressed her lips together and turned back to the horses. "It must be a special Campriano tale. I've only heard the kasyapa story once—when I was really small. Maybe I've remembered it wrong."

Dominique doubted Amana had misremembered the story. She seemed to have an incredible memory for even the smallest details. He was curious. "You have a story about a kasyapa bird?" It was strange, now that he thought about it, that his people didn't have any stories about the mysterious birds that changed colours when they died. They were the only birds whose plumage, in death, faded away to white. He thought of the closeness he shared with Navina. Kasyapas were different, special. It was very odd that the Estorians had no kasyapa tales.

"It was a long time ago. And it doesn't seem right . . ." She stared at him hard, her look a curious mixture of disbelief and wonder. Finally, she shook her head. "Never mind. We have to go. We still have a long journey ahead of us." She patted the saddle of Dominique's horse. "Come on. Dust Storm's loaded and ready."

Stiffly, Dominique climbed back on the horse. Until he had met Amana, he had never ridden a horse. He groaned as he settled into the saddle. Amana shielded her eyes with her hand as she looked up at him.

"Listen." Something about the way she spoke, the intensity of her expression, made him forget his aches and pains.

"It will be difficult to get you into Carnillo because Lord Emberto has been worried about an invasion for some time . . . spies . . . war."

Dominique didn't say anything, but he felt uneasy. Amana seemed worried.

"So," she said slowly, "I think it would be best if you looked more like a prisoner and—and I looked more like a guard."

"What do you mean?"

Instead of answering, Amana pulled a length of leather cord from a pouch behind her saddle.

"Hold out your hands."

"But—"

"Just do it. It will be safer for both of us. When we get to the palace this won't be necessary. At the last palace meeting of the scouts and tellers, Lord Emberto asked to meet with as many tribal representatives as possible—"

"But I'm not a—"

"Shh." She reached up, twisted the leather cord snugly around his wrists, and secured his hands to the korval.

"You may not be an official representative, but Emberto wants to know about the movements of the Estorians—you can tell him that, can't you?"

"Why would he want to know that?"

"Lord Emberto is a warrior. He needs to know as much as possible about his potential enemies."

Dominique tugged at his tether, but his slender wrists were caught tight. Potential enemies? Would Emberto want to attack the Estorians if he knew where they were? The last thing Dominique wanted to do was put his people in danger. If there was any risk of Emberto starting some kind of trouble . . .

"I can't do that," he said tersely.

Amana checked the knot and said, "You *must* tell him. If you don't appear to be willing to cooperate, you will find yourself a *real* prisoner. Emberto—well, he doesn't think well of people he doesn't trust."

There had to be some other solution, someone else Dominique could speak with who might be less dangerous. "You told me last night that Lord Emberto's father—"

"The Elder, yes—"

"—that the Elder was the only one Emberto would listen to. What if Emberto decides he doesn't like Estorians? That no matter what I say, he doesn't trust me?"

"Don't give him a reason not to like you. Tell him what he wants to—"

"Let me speak. What if I talk to his father?"

"The Elder? That's not a good idea."

"Why not?"

"Because the Elder is very old and not well. He's been sick for a long time. I would not want to trouble him with such a minor matter."

Dominique didn't feel like a minor matter.

Amana tried again. "If you know what's good for you, you will tell Emberto where your people travel, where they make their encampments, how long they stay in one place . . ."

Dominique shook his head and tried to free his wrists. Amana had done a good job with the knots.

"Listen to me." She put her hand on his knee. "I don't believe you really want to visit Carnillo just to pay your respects to Emberto."

Dominique blushed. Another lie he had told the girl that first day—did she remember every word he had ever spoken to her?

"I don't need to know why you have travelled here," she said. "And maybe it's better you don't tell me. But you and that bird are meant to come to my city. We both know that."

Dominique met and held her gaze, trying to understand. It seemed her eyes, her whole intent expression, were trying to convey some important information she was unwilling or unable to speak aloud.

"Why do you want to help me?" Dominique asked.

For a long moment he thought she was not going to say anything.

"Because . . ." She cleared her throat, turned her head away, and gazed across the marsh toward Carnillo. "Because we shared a vision . . . and because of the bird. Beyond that, I don't know. Once we are back in the city I can meet with . . ." She faltered. "I can make some inquiries."

He waited for her to clarify, to explain. But she did not.

Dominique's gut churned. Nothing about this girl made any sense. He did not want to trust her, and yet, what choice did he have? He was tied to her horse, too far away from anything familiar to dare attempt an escape. And she was right: they had shared the vision. That had to mean something.

"I . . ." His voice shook. Despite the fact his people had cast him out, he couldn't imagine betraying them to Lord Emberto.

"You must tell him *something*." Amana leaned forward in her saddle as if willing Dominique to understand what she really meant. "And remember—even though the Elder has some influence over his son, the real ruler of Carnillo is Lord Emberto. He would be very—" She stopped, choosing her words carefully. "He would be very *angry* if he believed you thought the power lay anywhere but in his hands."

Dominique took a deep breath and started again. "Very well. I will tell Lord Emberto . . ." He hesitated again and then, squelching his revulsion at telling yet another lie, added, "I will tell him what he wants to hear." When the time came he would make something up, a story that might save him and protect his people.

Amana just nodded and then mounted her horse. Almost apologetically she turned to him and said, "To be convincing, I have to insist you behave like a proper prisoner. And that means I have to act like a proper guard."

Amana pulled Dust Storm's reins over his head and led him with one hand, guiding Brimstone with the other.

"Don't worry," she said without looking back. "There's no place to turn off this road until after we've arrived at the city gate. You don't have to steer. Even if I let go, you won't get lost."

Amana pressed her heels to Brimstone's sides and the mare trotted forward, dragging Dust Storm and his unhappy passenger along behind.

6

FIRST BLOOD

To the boy alone, the kasyapa spoke.

—Ancient Campriano tale

Slow down!

Dominique didn't bother speaking the words aloud. Astride Brimstone, Amana seemed to be taking her role as guard altogether too seriously. Since they had set off on the white road she had rarely bothered to look back to see how Dominique was faring.

For someone used to riding, the steady trot across the marshlands north of Carnillo was nothing more than a quick way to cover ground. However, to Dominique, Dust Storm's bone-jarring movement was sheer agony. How much stamina could these stout animals from Ranginoor possibly possess? It seemed unnatural to Dominique that they could be ridden on and on without needing to rest.

Riding hardly described what Dominique was doing. With his hands tied to the korval he felt more like a trussed-up hunting trophy than a rider, his teeth smashing together with every step. He couldn't seem to rise up and down as he had earlier—doing so yanked at the wrist tether and caused him to tip forward. Long ago, Navina had given up on the bumpy ride and had flown off across the marshlands.

Just ahead, Amana sat deep in her fine leather saddle as if it were lined with the softest moss. She never bounced, but looked as though she could ride all day and night without ever needing a break.

"Please," Dominique whispered, "let's stop and rest." Amana, if she heard, didn't even slow down.

The sun burned down on them. Sweat trickled from the bridge of Dominique's nose and into his eyes, making them burn. He leaned forward to wipe the tears on the back of his bound wrists just as his horse took an awkward step, smashing his nose into the korval. A fresh spurt of tears flooded his eyes.

"Ow!" Dominique jerked upright, his eyes squeezed shut. When he was able to open them again, he looked down. The backs of his hands were spattered with blood.

"Amana!" His cry of alarm was out of his mouth before he could bite it back.

The girl ahead of him glanced over her shoulder. Her eyes widened: she was obviously not expecting the pathetic condition of her travelling companion.

"Whoa," she said, pulling Brimstone to a walk.

Dominique swallowed miserably and coughed as he tasted the thick, salty smear of blood at the back of his throat.

"What happened to you?" she asked, stopping and then turning her horse to face his. Both animals were breathing hard. They stretched their necks forward and touched noses in a quick greeting before putting their heads down to snatch a few mouthfuls of the thin grass growing tenaciously at the side of the track.

"I . . . I . . ." Dominique couldn't speak. How could

he admit he had bumped his own nose and made it bleed?

"Too bad you don't have any more of that stuff," Amana said.

Dominique knew that she was talking about the vial of healing potion in his deerskin sack, though she didn't know the leranons had given it to him. He had used most of his supply to heal the stab wound she'd delivered so deftly with her dagger back in the Cave of Departure. Judging by the tone of Amana's voice, Dominique wondered if she had believed him earlier when he said he'd used up the last of the potion. He could hardly change his story now and admit he really had a few drops left—she was already suspicious enough. Besides, he should probably save the precious stash in case he ever had a more serious injury.

Amana turned away from him and lifted her hand to shield her eyes against the bright sun. "It's not so far now. We could ride faster."

"No!" Dominique lifted his hands against his bindings and tentatively sniffed. "I think the bleeding is slowing down. Could we rest a minute? And maybe eat something?"

"Again? It's not my fault you threw your food on the ground. You should be more careful." Amana gestured at the narrow path where they were stopped. "Besides, there's no place here to make a fire. If another traveller came . . ."

Dominique knew she was right. Anyone else coming along would have trouble passing safely. Sliding down the steep embankment might not hurt a horse, but being sucked into the muddy bog would. The marsh devoured anything or anyone foolish enough to venture too close.

"How much longer?" he asked.

"The farms will start soon. See over there where the fields begin?"

Dominique's gaze followed her pointing finger and saw where the land outside the city walls changed colour from dark green to brown to gold. It was a welcome relief from the dull tan of the swamp grasses that rasped and clicked with every wind gust blown inland from the distant sea.

"From the first farms it takes little time at all to reach the drawbridge at the north gate."

Dominique sniffled again. The bleeding had virtually stopped.

"Let's go," he said, wishing, not for the first time, that they were riding a pair of leranons instead of horses. If he and Amana had been riding the powerful flyers, their journey would have been over by now, though their reception inside the city walls would not likely have been pleasant.

Amana turned Brimstone around on the narrow track. A loose clod of dirt bumped and turned as it rolled down to the swamp. It disappeared into the murky water and sank with a soft hiss. As Dust Storm started off, Dominique watched as a cloud of bubbles rose to the surface of the water where the clod had sunk. The bubbles fizzed and then the water returned to its regular dark smoothness, broken only by hummocks of tough swamp grass.

"Oh!"

Dominique smiled at the involuntary alarm in Amana's voice as Navina swooped past the girl on her way to landing on Dominique's head. He felt the familiar prickle and pinch of the kasyapa's claws on his scalp and his smile broadened.

At first he had been worried whenever Navina launched herself off his shoulder and soared out over the swamp. Soon, however, he realized that the swamp held no fear for her. Instead, she swooped and dove, flipping on her side and then upright again, buffeted by the ocean winds, her beak snapping as she feasted on the abundant insects hanging in clouds low over the water.

"Tummy full?" he asked. He realized he could not recall how long she had been gone on her last flight.

He did not expect an answer. As they trotted on and on, Navina perched atop his head, her wings twitching out to the sides to keep her balance. After a time, she lifted off again and soared toward the walls of the city far ahead.

Dominique watched until he could see her no more and then his thoughts returned to his aching body. He tried to imagine himself anywhere else but on the back of a bouncy horse. Images flitted through his mind: his mother washing the wooden food bowls in the river; his clan members gathering around the fire to hear the men's Stories; the day he had found Navina.

These pleasant memories helped ease him away from his discomfort. He tried to remember the most recent time when he had felt truly happy and decided that it was at the Cave of Departure when he had seen the amazing story images playing over the rough stone walls in the inner cavern. He concentrated on the memory of the cave walls and tried to recall, exactly, the stories that had rippled and danced across the rough surfaces, but instead another image began to form itself in his head.

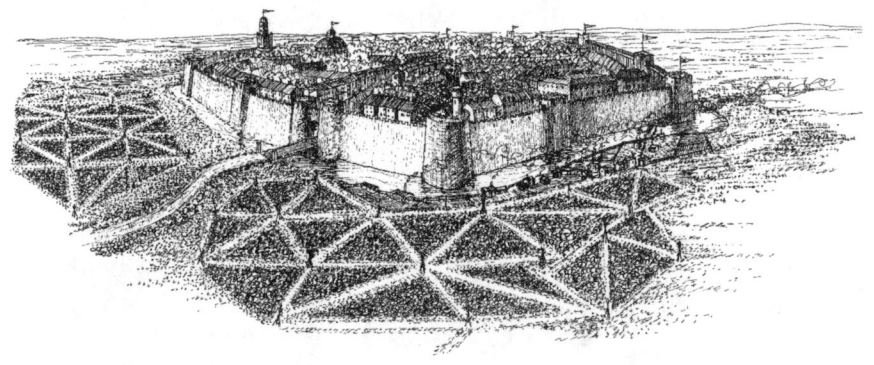

This image was different from his idle daydreams—stronger, more persistent, uncomfortable. No matter how he tried to force the image away and replace it with something familiar and comforting, it would not go. Complex and fully formed, it lay over everything he saw like a mask, or like someone else's story.

Dominique could not fight it, could not flee, could not change what he saw, and so he surrendered to it.

7

THE VISION

Flying high, the kasyapa gazed upon the landscape below.

—From the traditional Campriano
tale "Flight of the Kasyapa"

The vision itself seemed innocent enough. Six women wearing loose-fitting trousers and shapeless, long-sleeved tops bent over in a long row. The women Dominique watched were turned slightly away from him so he could not see their faces. They were outside, doing some kind of work.

The horses trotted on, but instead of fading away or changing, the way a memory or a dream might change, the picture of the women became clearer. Perhaps it was the sun making him dizzy, Dominique thought, although besides his aches and pains and general misery, he did not feel unwell. The image wavered and then became crisper, even more intense, and Dominique shuddered as if a cold hand had touched the back of his neck.

Now he saw that the strangely clad women were in a long row in a field, picking some sort of orange fruit from waist-high bushes. Each woman wore a sling over one shoulder. These slings widened into pouches that hung in front of their stomachs. The pouches bulged as the women placed each piece of fruit inside.

And then Dominique heard them singing. It was so clear that he whirled around in the saddle, as far as he could with his arms still secured in front of him, to make sure he and Amana were still alone in the marsh.

Oh-la, Emberto, Senya
Oh-la, Emberto, Canto

And this song, this lilting, haunting melody, was most disturbing of all, for it made the image as real as the horses, the marsh, the wide blue sky above. Dominique gasped, clutched at the korval, felt dizzy and terrified all at once. He wanted to cry out but stopped himself, vaguely aware that there was no way to explain to Amana what was happening. Had he gone mad, like the donkey keeper in the story of Young Tucker, who heard voices until the day he died?

Or was this some sort of warning? It was ominous, the way he could not push the picture aside. Behind the labouring women, the walls of a city loomed dark and forbidding. Dominique shook his head, but the image grew stronger, more grating, as irritating as if grinding beetles had wriggled in through his ears and were chewing at the edges of his brain. What was he supposed to make of it?

And then, just as he felt he could stand it no longer, that he would have to shriek or bash his head against the korval to rid himself of the strange, crawling pain of the vision, it began to fade as if he were drawing back, floating away. Now, perversely, he tried to hold on to it, but it was like trying to gather the pieces of a dream fleeing before the harsh light of morning.

As the women's voices faded, he felt a deep sense of loss and sadness so profound that again he almost cried out, this time to call the women back.

Looking around him, all Dominique saw was Amana

and Brimstone directly ahead on the white road, the marsh grasses stretching to either side, and in the distance, the walls of Carnillo rising up out of the fields, an impenetrable barrier between the riders and the sea.

Navina swooped toward the riders on the stiff breeze, her wings extended, the tips quivering, and Dominique longed to lift his hand toward her. She landed on Dominique's head and clutched his hair with her slender toes. He drew a deep, shuddering breath, felt his heartbeat slow, his confusion retreat. Perhaps, he tried to convince himself, he had imagined everything.

"Soon!" Amana shouted, her voice bright with excitement.

Dominique jerked in the saddle as if she'd slapped him. He had the strange sensation of having returned from an excursion, though tied in place as he was, he obviously hadn't gone anywhere.

As they approached the closest of the fields, Amana slowed the horses to a walk. Dominique was very glad of her company and urged Dust Storm forward so that his nose was practically touching Brimstone's rump. Brimstone pinned her ears and swished her tail.

"Don't get so close!" Amana scolded.

"You wouldn't want to lose your prisoner, would you?" he answered back.

"Not much chance of that. Where were you planning to go?"

Dominique felt better, more normal, bantering with Amana. He blinked. No vision. He allowed himself to relax, study his surroundings. They were no longer in the middle of a wild marsh. Now, for as far as he could see, drained and cultivated farms blanketed the land between them and the walls of the city.

Nearest the berm where they rode, weeds clung to the edges of the fields. Where the fields became level, the weeds disappeared and were replaced by rich, dark soil neatly plowed and planted into patterns. Since the plants in the first fields were low, the riders up on the berm could see over them easily. At least four different plants grew here on the first farms. Dominique could tell by the distinctive bands of colour that formed intricate patterns against the dirt background.

The richest green bands were made up of some type of cabbage—thousands of them blended together in five interlocking diamond shapes. Two other crops grew in the spaces between these angular rows—a low, bushy shrub with deep purplish leaves that Dominique didn't recognize, and the distinctive slender leaves that marked the underground treasure of peska root. Though most of what grew in the fields was unfamiliar, this was a plant Dominique knew well. His mother and the other women spent hours hunting for wild peska. They dug the firm, bulbous roots and ground them up to make all sorts of tasty dishes. Here on the approach to Carnillo, the leaves of the peska plants were such a pale green they seemed almost white against the deeper purple and green of the plants around them.

How envious his mother would be to see peska plants so easy to find here in these fields! The Estorian women wouldn't have to spend nearly as much time hunting for wild peska if they lived close to a town like Carnillo and could grow their own. Dominique shook his head slightly. This wasn't the place for his mother, no matter how easy it might be to find peska root. She would miss the travelling, the way the tribe followed the seasons, moving north and south in search of sun during the winter and milder weather during the hottest part of summer. Dominique pushed the memory of his mother away.

At certain places among the crops, conical stick structures supported tangled vines covered with pendulous white buds ready to burst into blossom. He supposed these fields belonged to farmers who supplied those in the city with fresh fruit and vegetables. He wondered where they all lived—within the city walls? Then he noticed clusters of small houses and animal sheds and enclosures along the base of Carnillo's stone walls. Thin trails of smoke pushed out of tall, stone chimneys before being swept inland by the breeze.

It was still early in the spring, so all the plants were relatively small, but Dominique could well imagine that at the height of summer the growth would be so lush that no dirt would be visible between the different kinds of plants. All a traveller would see then would be a vast patterned landscape of green, white, orange, and the lovely deep purplish brown of the low shrubs. He concentrated on these details so he would not think of the women in the vision, as if by filling every part of his mind with what lay before him, he could prevent the return of the strange image.

Up ahead, the walls of Carnillo ran in a straight line east and west, blocking Dominique's view of the sea beyond. Off to the right he saw the bright glint of sunlight catching on water, and he realized he was seeing the place where the mighty River Epilobium joined the sea.

At regular intervals, stone towers with gold and blue banners fluttering atop their crenellations broke the smooth facade of the massive city walls. The road on which they travelled headed due south, straight toward a gate flanked by two of these towers. A larger, round tower, a great hulking monstrosity at least four times larger than any of the others, was set into the wall not far from the gate at the end of the road.

Dominique swallowed hard and tugged at the leather strap binding his hands. Carnillo. All his life he had heard stories of the barbaric Carnillians who dominated the eastern peninsula of the island of Tanga. He couldn't even count how many stories he had heard about the

Campriano storytellers, the liars and scoundrels who were the Carnillians' closest allies. More than that, according to Amana, the citizens of Carnillo and the Camprianos had intermarried so often they had virtually become one people.

The quiver of arrows bounced against Amana's back as she urged her horse into a trot. A savage people, Dominique thought, to force even their women to carry weapons.

Dominique sighed. Perhaps it would have been useful to have learned more about battle. His training as a storyteller had taught him much about the theory of warfare—many of the best stories related bloody battles and invasions. But in reality, Estorians frowned upon fighting, even the minor tussles that sometimes occurred among young boys, and Dominique knew he would not stand a chance in a real fight.

His cheeks burned as he remembered how easily Amana had wounded him when they first met. If she had wanted to kill him, she could have done so. She hadn't exactly struggled to tie his wrists, either. No, she was quick and strong and skilled in the fighting arts.

Dominique relaxed against his bonds and squinted toward the east. The wind blew steadily from this direction now that they were so close to the sea. It was relentless in its passage across the fields of crops laid out in such careful patterns.

"Navina," he whispered as the bird lifted off his head and rose on a current of air. The horses trotted on and the riders drew even with another field, this one planted with long, straight rows of waist-high bushes. His scalp prickled as he heard voices raised in song.

Oh-la, Emberto, Senya
Oh-la, Emberto, Canto

He turned to look along one of the rows and saw women picking orange fruit, placing one after the other

53

into bulging slings held close to their bodies.

One woman approached the side of the road and called out, "Olio melons! Fresh olio melons for sale!" The scent of sun-warmed melons rose so thick and sweet that Dominique gagged.

He wanted to shout at Amana, to make her stop. These were the women of his vision! But Amana kept the horses moving along at a brisk trot. Dominique's head swivelled as he tried to keep the women in view. How could it be? The slings, the strange outfits, the fruit—it was all exactly as he had seen it! He twisted so far around on his horse he thought he would fall off. The women, oblivious, continued to pick and to sing.

Oh-la, Emberto, Senya
Oh-la, Emberto, Canto

Seeing them so close, so real, made him shudder. He snapped his head around, fixed his gaze on the horse's tail ahead of him, and tried to still his thudding heart.

Though he closed his eyes, Dominique could not clear his mind of what he had seen. The real women picking fruit in the field merged with the memory of the vision. He felt a wave of nausea rise and threaten to overwhelm him, the movement of the horse terrifying now that he couldn't see.

"Put your head down and hold on! Someone's coming!" Amana's shout chased away the last feelings of unreality, and Dominique grabbed the korval as if it might save him from whatever lay ahead.

8

OUTSIDERS WITHIN

The small army approached the city walls. To expect defeat would have meant a certain loss, but to expect a win was simply foolish. Instead, the warriors thought of home.

—Estorian story

Dominique bent forward and pressed his forehead against the backs of his hands—but not before he caught sight of three riders approaching them. The narrow berm forced them to ride in single file. The leader, a tall man whose face was bare except for a pointy black beard at his chin, wore a heavy leather doublet and a scarlet-and-blue sash, and carried a sword at his side.

"Halt!"

Amana did not answer. Dominique kept his head down as all the horses stopped.

"My prisoner is ill," Amana said, her voice loud and confident. "He wears the name ring I gave him. You may see it as we pass."

Dominique was impressed. Amana's voice didn't waver at all as she lied to the soldier.

"What business have you here?"

"I return to Lord Emberto with news of the Estorians.

This one *is* an Estorian. I captured him in the Misty Mountains."

Dominique wished he dared raise his head so he could see the men, see what Amana was doing. Were these men Camprianos? Why did they sound so hostile, as if they might arrest Amana? How could she possibly defend both of them against the soldiers if they decided to attack? Dominique squeezed the korval and held as still as he could.

"How long have you been travelling?"

"I left the city ten days ago."

The men exchanged a few words so quietly that Dominique could not hear what they said.

"Your name ring?"

"Here."

The horses shifted slightly and Dominique guessed that Amana was showing the wooden ring clasped around her ankle.

"A member of the court," the bearded man said slowly, as if he had trouble deciphering the Campriano symbols.

"I have full access to the court, yes," Amana said, "through my association with the Tellers Guild. My name is Amana Elnedo."

"Amana Elnedo of the Tellers Guild?" The man's tone changed from one of suspicion to one of respect. "Are you not the First Teller Born?"

"Indeed," Amana answered.

"Forgive me. We have not met. Antorio Pembina at your service. With Lord Andalon of Crestio. What is wrong with your prisoner?"

"Shoulder wound," Amana said. "He is much weakened from loss of blood, but I had no choice when he resisted arrest."

Much as it rankled to do so, Dominique emitted a low groan. There was something about the arrogance of the men that frightened him.

Antorio Pembina snorted. "Typical Estorian—weak. I'm surprised he fought back at all."

Dominique stiffened. How dare the man speak of Estorians like that!

The soldier continued. "Are you certain Emberto wants this one alive?"

Dominique tried to swallow, but his mouth was suddenly dry, as if someone had poured sand down his throat. He fought the urge to choke, cry out. Instead, he slumped sideways as if his shoulder caused him great pain.

"You must forgive me if I do not divulge Lord Emberto's reasons." Amana's clear voice rose and Dominique could tell by the hard edge to her speech that it was an effort for her to remain civil. "However, I can assure you that he wants this one alive."

Dominique groaned, determined to do his part to convince the men he was supposed to reach Emberto in one piece and that he was too ill to be a threat to anyone. It would not be difficult for the soldiers to believe: Dominique found it easy to sound miserable.

"You have been gone how long?" the soldier asked again.

"As I said, ten days."

"You will not have heard the news, then. Things have changed since you left the city."

"Changed? How so?"

"Lord Emberto's father, the Elder, has died."

Amana gasped and then drew a deep breath. When she spoke again, her voice was measured, calm. "A great loss to us all."

"Indeed," the soldier said. "The people are deeply saddened."

"So I would imagine."

"Since his death a week ago there has been much

trouble in Carnillo. Many have been arrested."

"Arrested," Amana said. "Yes. This does not surprise me."

Dominique held his breath. It was impossible to know what Amana was really thinking.

"Lord Emberto is expecting my imminent return. My prisoner has information that will be useful to him, now more so than before. Lord Emberto will not be pleased should I be detained."

There was a pause, and Dominique thought he heard the men backing their horses up and conferring quietly before approaching Amana again.

"We merely wish to help Lord Emberto hold his lands secure," Antorio Pembina said.

"Know that I have been at Lord Emberto's side since the beginning of his rule here and I shall still be at his side long after you and your men have returned to Crestio."

Antorio Pembina cleared his throat and said, "Emberto's allies are, to a man, and to a woman, loyal indeed. May I add only that you should use caution in your dealings in the city."

"As always, I shall be careful. Travel safely, sir."

As his horse shifted beneath him and then moved forward, Dominique braced himself, scarcely believing they would be able to proceed. Instead of advancing slowly and carefully along the narrow path, Amana urged the horses forward. Tipping his head a little to the side, Dominique could see the men on horseback close by as they passed. He held his leg out so they could see the name ring fastened around his ankle, but Amana was moving so quickly it was all any of them could do to keep their horses from slithering sideways off the road.

"Clear!" Pembina said. Dominique pulled his foot back in close to his horse's side.

He had to admit that Amana was smart. She had said they were in a hurry. Pembina had caught sight of

Dominique's name ring, though he couldn't possibly have deciphered it so quickly. And that, apparently, had been enough.

When they were out of earshot of the men, Amana said, "Pompous swine. He had no right to stop our approach. Carnillo is my city, not his. I should have put an arrow through his neck."

"Can I lift my head up?" Dominique asked.

"Yes." But Amana hardly seemed to care what Dominique did. "He was right about one thing: everything will have changed with the Elder dead." Amana's face was pale.

"What do you mean? Changed how?"

Dominique saw by the shuddery way Amana drew a deep breath that she was close to tears.

"Emberto's father is—was—a wise and gentle man." She caught Dominique watching her and quickly added, "He was a good solider, too, in his day. Before the seizing."

"The seizing?"

"Shortly before I was born, the Elder was stricken with a terrible illness that paralyzed his right side and made it hard for him to speak."

Dominique nodded. He had seen this sort of thing happen to some of the old members of his clan. They usually did not live long after.

"The Elder was unable to lead his army into war, but his mind was clear and he understood how to lead so his people would follow."

"But I thought Lord Emberto was the ruler of Carnillo."

"He is. When the Elder became seized, his son, Lord Emberto, became the Carnillian leader. I was born soon after that, which is why I became the First Teller Born, even though the Elder had been ruling for a very long time. But as long as Lord Emberto's father lived, Emberto was—he had to be . . ." Amana faltered. "He was forced to be reasonable. There would have been a bloody revolution long ago had he ignored his father's advice."

"And now the Elder is dead," Dominique said. Though he knew very little about the old man, Dominique felt a keen sense of loss—not grief, exactly, but an uneasiness, a sense of foreboding.

"Yes. And already Emberto has brought in foreign soldiers to help him." This comment seemed to remind Amana of how much she resented the audacity of the outsider.

"How could that Pembina dare challenge my right to travel with *my* prisoner to Emberto!"

Dominique straightened up. "I'm not *really* your—"

"But *he* doesn't know that," she said, fuming again. "When I tell you, put your head back down if you would like to arrive at Lord Emberto's palace with your skull still attached to your neck." Amana nodded toward the two rounded guard towers flanking the opening in the wall at the north gate.

Dominique licked his dry lips. His destination was so close now—and suddenly, he was terrified. Had it been a terrible mistake to let Amana bring him to this place, its high, dark walls so formidable before them? Maybe he should try to get away. Would Amana give chase if he turned and galloped back along the white road?

The minute he formed the thought he dismissed it. It was hopeless. Even if Amana did not chase him, and even supposing he were a good rider and did not have his hands tied to the saddle, there was only one road leading away from Carnillo. Dominique knew there were at least three soldiers on it, and he already knew how they felt about Estorians.

Amana shifted in her saddle and then drew her dagger. "I don't know how else things may have changed in Carnillo. We may need to defend ourselves." With two quick swipes of her knife she cut Dominique's tether. He rubbed his wrists, groaning as the blood began flowing again. "It's hard to defend yourself with your hands tied together. But when we get to the gate you have to slump over again and pretend you are still tied up."

Mute with fear and indecision, Dominique nodded. If he were going to make a dash for freedom, it would have to be now.

Amana clucked to Brimstone and the mare moved off with Dust Storm close behind. Dominique felt his last chance for escape slip away.

Dominique was grateful that the girl seemed to be trying to keep him alive. Still, he would be hard pressed to defend himself since she had taken his long, curved dagger and tucked it into a bundle tied behind her saddle. He watched as she tipped her head back to better see the city walls. They were getting very close now: the great walls loomed above them.

"What about my weapon?" he asked.

Amana halted Brimstone and turned her horse to face his. "True." She studied him for a long moment, and Dominique held his hands out before him, his palms facing up.

"I would be a fool to let you ride behind me with your dagger drawn."

"But I would never—"

"Perhaps. Nor would it be wise for you to approach the gate first—you would be questioned."

Dominique nodded. The last thing he wanted to do was be arrested by a suspicious gatekeeper.

"So, if I give you back your dagger, you must ride beside me through the city gate. That way I can keep an eye on you. I'll ride on the left." She manoeuvred Brimstone alongside Dust Storm. Here, closer to the city walls, the white road was wider. "The guard is on the left. I'll talk to him."

Dominique's skin crawled. What kind of danger was Amana leading them into? Her quiver bristling with arrows and the sharpened dagger at her side hardly reassured him. She was just as likely to get them both killed with her unpredictable, hot-tempered tongue. She was clenching her jaw so tightly the muscles in her cheek rose in a tight cord. It wouldn't take much to set her off.

"We don't have far to go," she said. "Stay close to me. If something should happen to me, Dust Storm knows the way home to a snug stall and a good feed. Give him his head and he'll take you to Emberto's stables. From there, ask for Filial. I have known him my whole life—he is one of Emberto's servants at the palace. Ask Filial to take you to the Recitatorium. I think the Grand Teller would give you sanctuary."

Dominique's stomach pitched and he suddenly had a desperate desire to relieve himself.

"Pick up your reins, both in your left hand, so your right hand is free for this."

With one smooth movement, Amana handed Dominique his dagger. Fumbling with the reins, the lead rope, and the dagger, Dominique clutched at the horse's mane to keep his balance.

"As we pass through the gate, hide your dagger under the front pannier. Once we're on the other side, wait until we're well clear of the gate before you pull it out. And remember to keep your head down." She had dropped all pretense of calm. Her breath came in short puffs as if she had been running.

Dust Storm and Brimstone moved forward together, and Dominique only just managed to conceal his dagger under the pannier and pick up his reins again before Amana said, "When we get to the gate let me speak for us both."

Dominique nodded. The gate was on the other side of a wide canal that ran along the base of the city walls.

A wooden bridge spanned the canal, and as Dust Storm stepped onto it, Navina flew to Dominique's shoulder and pressed close against his cheek.

"Put her away!" Amana hissed as she stopped beside him on the bridge.

The travellers stood there for a moment, the boy, the bird, and the girl. Despite the brilliant sun, Dominique shuddered as if a chill wind had blown right through him. He knew that if he were able to step back and look at the scene from behind, he would be seeing the image from the Cave of Departure. Then, the three of them standing outside the city gates had seemed exciting and full of promise. Now that he was inside the picture, what he felt was a mounting panic. Too scared to know how to protect himself, he protected his bird instead.

"Inside," he said, his voice scarcely louder than a whisper. Obediently, Navina crawled inside the deerskin travelling sack slung over his shoulder.

CHAPTER

9

THE NORTH GATE

Bearing sacks of treasure worth more than all the kinnels in the land, the prince arrived at the gates of the City by the Sea.

—Campriano cautionary tale

As soon as the kasyapa bird was out of sight, Amana said, "Give that here."

At first, Dominique thought she was going to take his dagger back again.

"The sack. It will be safer with me."

"But—Navina—"

"Give it here, now, before someone notices us out here arguing. No real prisoner would be allowed to keep his possessions. I'll give it back when we're safely inside the palace."

"But you can't—" Dominique gripped his sack so tightly his knuckles turned white.

"I must have it—now." Seeing the stricken look on his face, her voice softened. "Don't worry. I'll look after her."

"No!"

The slash of the blade was so quick Dominique did not have time to pull his hand away. Across the back of his hand a row of tiny red dots welled up out of his skin. Horrified, he looked up, not believing that Amana had cut him again.

"It's for your own good," she said. Though her voice was firm, Dominique thought he saw a look of apology flicker across her face as she reached over and snatched the bag away.

"Navina!"

The side of the soft bag rippled as Navina moved inside, but Amana had a tight grip on the top of the sack: there was no way for the bird to escape. Dominique felt a wave of misery mingle with the searing pain in the back of his hand.

"Wrap your hand in your shift and hold it tightly to stop the bleeding," Amana said. "The cut isn't deep."

Too shocked to sob, too scared to argue, Dominique pulled the bottom edge of his cotton shift free, wrapped it around his wounded hand, and pulled it close to his body.

Amana tipped her head toward the north gate. "Let's go."

Dizzy and sick with misery, Dominique folded forward over the korval, his left hand balled into a fist and jammed against his stomach.

The horses' hooves clomped loudly over the bridge. Below, the water lapped at the base of the city walls. On the far side of the bridge, the horses stopped in front of the closed portcullis. The heavy beams of the solid gate criss-crossed so it was impossible to pass through, though when Dominique turned his head sideways he could see through the first obstacle to a second, identical portcullis on the far side of a passageway between the two stone towers.

A noise above them caught his attention. A shadow

of movement flickered between the floorboards of the hoarding directly overhead. He recalled the story of Lord Penalto of Sedna, who dropped stones and boiling oil on the heads of his attackers. Dominique put his head back down and groaned. It was getting easier and easier to act like a miserable prisoner.

"I return with a prisoner for Emberto!" Amana called.

"Your name?" a man called back from somewhere inside.

Dominique squinted into the gloom beyond the portcullis but could see nobody.

"Amana Elnedo of the Tellers Guild, loyal assistant to Emberto and First Teller Born."

"Ring?"

Amana reached down, unsnapped her name ring, and held it aloft. Tipping his head sideways and peeking upwards through the tangle of his long hair, Dominique noticed a narrow slit above their heads in one of the towers. Protruding from a second slit just above the first was an arrow pointing directly at them. At such close range, it would be impossible to miss. With his good hand, Dominique clutched the handle of the dagger he held hidden under the front pannier. His palm was so sweaty that he was terrified it would slip from his grasp and clatter to the ground.

A pale hand poked out of the first slot and took Amana's ring. "I have put a prisoner name ring on this low-dog." Her voice was so filled with revulsion and disdain she might have been speaking of a filthy murderer. "Do you need to inspect it?"

A moment later the hand reappeared with Amana's name ring. "That will not be necessary, Miss Amana. Good to see you back safe and sound."

"With thanks, and power be to Emberto," she replied. "And may I express my deep regret at our loss of the Elder."

"A terrible loss for all of us, yes."

As the guard spoke, the sound of grinding gears and clattering chains made the horses flare their nostrils and toss their heads.

The first portcullis rose to allow them entry into the space between the two guard towers, and Amana leaned forward to refasten her name ring around her ankle. When the heavy gate had risen high enough that they could ride on, their horses moved forward until they were stopped behind the second portcullis. The first of the two heavy gates rumbled closed behind them.

"Steady," Amana said to the fidgeting animals. "Steady."

Dust Storm's ears flicked back and forth and Dominique felt the horse tense beneath him.

The second portcullis began to rise with an ominous clatter and groan. Stepping out into the teeming streets on the other side of the wall, Dominique felt as if he had been transported into another world. After days of travelling alone or trailing along behind Amana, he had nearly forgotten what it was like to be surrounded by the noises of human activity.

"We have been very lucky," Amana said, her face bright and giddy with relief. "If that guard did not know me for the loyal servant that I am, our entry into the city might not have been so easy."

From his hunched position Dominique asked, "Is it safe to sit up?"

"Yes. But stay beside me," Amana said as she rode forward into a plaza filled with vendors and their hand-carts, makeshift stalls, and dozens of children. "Leave me alone," she said, pushing a child aside with her boot. "Beggars," she explained. "Best not to give them anything. They only ask for more."

Dominique's mouth dropped open at the sight of a girl not much older than he was, nursing a baby.

"Hurry," Amana said and urged Brimstone forward as quickly as she could through the milling crowds.

Dominique wondered where the street children lived. They crowded against the horses, pushing each other out of the way, their wide eyes and upturned hands pleading for food, coins, anything. He thought of the Cave, the abundance of rice, beans, and dried food. If he'd known, he could have taken much more. He still had a handful of rice left, though Amana carried his sack. But even if he had been able to give away every last grain of rice, there were too many children to feed. A single grain of rice wouldn't ease the ache in a child's belly.

Amana didn't even look down. She rode her horse straight ahead, making the children leap out of the way so they weren't trampled beneath Brimstone's hooves. *Indio-bag.* He bit back the swear word before he could say it aloud. How could she be so uncaring? Amana seemed more concerned with a persistent itch inside the top of her boot than with the hungry faces.

Then Dominique smiled. She wasn't really scratching. Each time she bent forward, her hand dipped into the pannier and she surreptitiously passed out handfuls of food to the children.

They seemed to understand the rules of this peculiar game for they did not acknowledge these gifts. The morsels disappeared into pockets and pouches, and the children who had received something backed away into the crowd to be replaced immediately by others who pressed in to take, in silence, Amana's offerings.

Loudly, Amana scolded, "Get away! Filthy beggars!" She waved them off with one hand even as she fed them with the other, and Dominique had to look away so he did not laugh aloud at her deception.

They rode deeper into the teeming streets of the city and Dominique glanced behind him. The massive round tower at the northwest corner of Carnillo dwarfed the gate through which they had passed. The ugly structure loomed over everything. From somewhere inside the tower, Dominique thought he heard a sharp crack and then a cry of anguish.

On the far side of the plaza, Amana and Dominique entered a narrow road. Her supply of handouts extinguished, Amana was no longer pestered by the street children. Tall houses jumbled up toward the sky, crowded against each other like a mouth filled with too many teeth. There were people everywhere, moving quickly, speaking with such urgency that Dominique swivelled in his saddle as if someone or something was about to jump out from an alley and pull him from his horse.

Amana raised her dagger in front of her. "Hurry."

Somewhere off to the left, loud shouts and then the sounds of running were followed by a scream and more shouting.

"Quick!" Amana clapped her boots to her horse's sides and Brimstone trotted forward, her hooves clop-clopping over the rough paving stones. Without urging from Dominique, Dust Storm also picked up speed. They passed the blackened shell of a burnt-out building. "That was a tavern," Amana told Dominique. "I wonder what happened." Directly ahead, the road widened into another square, crowded with people.

"This way," Amana said. She ducked into a road running off to the left just beyond the tavern. They rode over a wooden bridge that traversed a narrow canal. Almost immediately, Amana turned right into another street flanking the square, but halted when she saw half a dozen armed men on horseback in her path. They stood with weapons drawn, watching the gathered crowd.

She wheeled around and caught Dust Storm's bridle. "Come on."

Instinctively, Dominique grabbed for the korval, the red slash across the back of his hand an ugly reminder that he could not afford to completely trust this girl who was also his guide and protector in the troubled city. He held on tightly as she pulled his horse's head around and kept them moving quickly.

Back over the little bridge they went and turned another corner. On their right a pale yellow wall was so close that Dominique's foot would have scraped along it if he hadn't snugged his leg close against Dust Storm's side. The wall was decorated with an intricate mosaic design. The tiled picture depicted the many guard towers and gates of the city. Even astride his horse, Dominique was not tall enough to see over the yellow wall. What, he wondered, was behind it?

The path they now travelled parallelled the canal on one side, the wall on the other. Though the path was not wide enough for a cart, the horses trotted along easily, one behind the other. Several times, men and women on foot flattened themselves against the yellow wall to allow Amana and Dominique to go by.

At the end of the wall they came to another road leading off to the right. The canal continued straight, but they turned away from it and followed the wall's mosaic designs down another street, this one very narrow but dead straight. Just before they came to another cross street and the end of the high wall, Amana stopped in front of two tall wooden doors. The doors were reinforced with wide bands of steel, and great spikes protruded toward the street.

A rope dangled off to one side and Amana reached out and gave it a good yank. Dominique jumped when a big brass bell clanged, announcing their arrival. The horses shifted uneasily.

"Come on!" Amana said. "Where are you, Filial?"

There was no sound from the other side of the doors.

Amana reached up and rang the bell again, even more loudly than the first time.

Six or seven men on horseback trotted around the end of the wall and passed Amana and Dominique.

"More of Lord Andalon's men," Amana said after they had disappeared toward the canal. "I wonder how many are here in Carnillo." She reached over, poked at the door with the tip of her dagger, and sighed with exasperation. "Where is Filial?"

Once more she rang the bell, this time so vigorously Dominique felt sure she would pull the whole thing down on her head.

A small door no more than a hand's width across opened at head height in one of the larger doors. "Hush!" a raspy voice said from the other side. Two eyes and a pair of bushy eyebrows glared out at them. "Lord Emberto is not—"

"Filial—it's me, Amana."

"Amana! Name ring . . ."

Amana had taken off her name ring to hold it up in front of the little slot, but Filial started to slam the peephole shut before he even looked at it. Dominique heard the rattle of keys on the other side and then the sound of bolts being turned back. When they heard what sounded like heavy timbers being shifted, Amana said, "Things must be very bad. It is not usual to use the door timbers during the day."

To Dominique's surprise, the doors did not swing open to admit them. Instead, the little peep-hole opened and again Filial peered out. "Anyone else out there?"

Amana scanned the street. "Just the old woman across the way with her babies . . . the ragman with his cart down near the canal . . ." Amana rode Brimstone to the corner and peeked around the end of the wall. She rode back and added, "And a few soldiers down along at the end of the next street. And my prisoner, of course."

Dominique blushed. When and how was she going to explain that he wasn't really a prisoner? What if she couldn't persuade these barbarians not to arrest him?

On the other side of the door, Filial shifted his gaze to Dominique's face. His eyes widened, almost as if he recognized Dominique. "Come in. Be quick."

The small door snapped shut and the two huge, heavy doors swung inward.

"Hurry," Amana said, urging Brimstone forward.

The last thing Dominique saw before he followed Amana inside was the ragman pulling a bright red cloth from his pushcart. Then the great doors swung closed behind them.

10

A PALACE WELCOME

And Tara said, "Remember, men. No matter how far you may journey, keep your Stories close to your hearts and no harm shall come to you."

—Estorian Tara story

Dust Storm stepped forward into the courtyard and let out a high-pitched whinny. From stables to the left and directly in front of them on the far side of the area protected by the yellow walls, a chorus of whinnies answered back as horses' heads emerged over the top of their stall doors.

Behind the riders, the great doors banged shut and Filial, with the help of two younger men, slid home the bolts and replaced several large beams in brackets so the beams spanned the entire width of both doors. His face glistening with sweat, Filial shuffled around to the head of Amana's horse and held her reins as Amana dismounted. He was so old and hunched over, he had to twist his neck to see Amana properly.

"Chud!" he called across the courtyard. "Chud!!"

A stout woman trotted out from behind the farther

row of stalls. When she spotted Brimstone and Dust Storm her round face broke into a huge grin. "Amana! You have returned, my girl!"

"Chud. Good to see you."

"And you. Will you stay here tonight? Or must you return to the Recitatorium immediately?"

"I suppose I shall have to wait to speak with Lord Emberto about Dom—about this prisoner. And Lord Emberto may wish a performance this evening."

Chud and Filial exchanged awkward glances, and Chud said quickly, "The horses are well?" She touched the sweat-soaked animals on their necks and shoulders, ran her hand lightly down their legs, peered at them, and, when her inspection was over, said to Dominique, "They need to rest. Get down."

"I'll take your weapon back now," Amana said as Dominique tried to manoeuvre his right leg past his dagger and over the saddle.

"What about my sack?" he asked, sensing it might not be a good idea to mention the bag contained a kasyapa bird.

"Your sack and meagre possessions are safe with me," she replied coolly.

Dominique wished the others would go away and leave them alone so he could talk to Amana, find out what he had to do to get Navina back. "Now," Amana said firmly. "Please pass me your dagger."

Given the opposition and the huge barricaded doors standing between himself and freedom, Dominique saw no advantage to arguing. He passed his dagger down to Amana. Then he, too, dismounted. Unlike Amana, however, who stood tall, clapping Filial and Chud fondly on their backs, Dominique fell in a crumpled heap on the paving stones as his legs collapsed beneath him.

"An Estorian," Amana said with a sniff, though Dominique thought he detected a hint of guilt in her glance. "What else would you expect?"

Chud chuckled. "They prefer donkeys, don't they?"

"Or walking," Amana said.

Dominique groaned. His legs felt as if they would never again find their usual shape or strength.

"Get up." Amana turned to Filial and asked, "Where is Lord Emberto?"

Filial shook his head. "Much has happened," he whispered. "Chud. Take the horses, would you?"

Chud nodded and led the two horses away. Dominique managed to push himself up so he was sitting on the ground. He stretched his legs, bending and unbending them at the knees.

"I must speak to Emberto. He still wants to see members of other archipelago tribes, does he not? That hasn't changed since—"

Filial reached out and touched Amana's shoulder. "You have heard, then?"

Amana nodded. "From one of Lord Andalon's men."

"The death of the Elder is . . ." Filial hesitated and tipped his head toward Dominique.

"Filial, it's all right." Amana dropped her voice and glanced around. "I had a vision. I believe Dominique was meant to come here."

Filial raised his hand. It shook slightly and he waved it slowly from side to side. "Amana, if he is not a Campriano, he is not safe here."

"But Emberto said—"

"That he wanted to meet tribal representatives, yes."

"So, I have brought Emberto this—"

Again, Filial raised his hand to quiet her. He squinted and deep lines folded around his watery blue eyes.

"While you were away, soldiers brought in others—two from Alesto and several from Fermi."

"And?"

"The two from Alesto went straight to the Dark Tower."

"The others?"

"Dead."

Amana turned back toward the barricaded door.

"You cannot let him go, if that's what you're thinking," the old man said. "He will not survive a day on the streets."

"But what should I do?"

"Why would you even want to save this . . ."

"Estorian. He is an Estorian. Dominique Bertolescu. I thought Lord Emberto would be pleased."

Filial's eyes narrowed again and he stared hard at Dominique as if trying to remember where they might have met before. Dominique had never in his life felt so vulnerable.

"Bertolescu? Oh, yes—Emberto should be pleased you have brought him this Estorian. His detention, or death, will send a powerful message to forces determined to oppose his rule."

Dominique could no longer stay quiet. "The Estorians are peaceful! We have no interest—"

"Quiet!" Amana and Filial said in unison.

"No! I won't be quiet!" Furious, Dominique's voice rose. "I have done nothing wrong! I agreed to come with you! I had a vision, too!"

"Dominique." Amana spoke only his name, but her hand had moved to the hilt of her dagger and her eyes blazed a warning.

"The fact is, Amana," Filial said softly, "he is an enemy of the state. Anyone who is not a Campriano or an ally is in danger without the Elder to speak a word of reason. Emberto will dispose of this Estorian as he sees fit."

"But he can't!" Amana said. Dominique edged out of dagger range.

"Amana! I can't think of a single reason why you should care what happens to this—this swine-kissing master of deceit—"

"Don't call him that!"

Dominique nearly smiled to hear the hot-headed girl defend him, though he took another step backwards. Could he make it to the big doors and out? Was there another way to leave this place?

Filial took Amana's arm. "Amana. What is wrong with you? Does this boy have some sort of power over you?"

Amana laughed. "This boy does not have power over much!"

Filial held his hands out, palms up in front of him. "Then I do not understand—"

"Filial. Somehow we must save him."

"Oh, no. You know how I feel about you, Miss Amana, but I cannot be party to assisting this enemy of the state in any way."

"But Filial," Amana took the old man's hands in hers, "he has a kasyapa bird."

Dominique had never before seen a look of such astonishment as the one that now passed across Filial's face. His lips worked as if he wanted to speak but was unable to form any words. Finally he managed to say, "A kasyapa?"

"Yes!"

"Well, then . . . that's different, isn't it?" Twin furrows carved Filial's forehead into sections. "Are you going to tell Lord Emberto?"

"I—I don't know what to do. The Elder might have understood, but Emberto, now . . ."

"You have known Emberto all your life. What do you think he will do to you, to the boy, the bird, if you tell him the old story?"

Amana's lower lip quivered. She looked small, lost. "By law, for the sake of tradition, he must listen to my stories, but he does not have to hear what I say."

"Precisely."

"Oh, Filial, what am I going to do? Why did the Elder

have to die now?"

"Just let me go," Dominique said. The more he heard, the less he wanted to have anything to do with the great Lord Emberto.

"Too dangerous," Amana said, and Dominique was shocked to see how close she was to tears. She drew in a deep breath, straightened her back, and said, "I shall consult with the Grand Teller."

Filial nodded his agreement.

"What about me? You can't leave me here." Dominique could hear the panic in his own voice, but he couldn't stop the words from tumbling out. "Take me to the Grand Teller. You said she might give me sanctuary. Why didn't you take me there instead?"

Filial ignored Dominique's outburst completely. "If you want to protect him, why don't you put him in the palace prison?"

"What do you mean? Would he be safe in prison?"

"He would be safe enough for now, at least until you are able to speak with the Grand Teller. If you wish to hide a walking stick, poke it into the woodpile."

Dominique's skin crawled. "You can't lock me up!"

"You can't take him directly to the tower—only Emberto can authorize that. But there should be space here at the palace in the holding cells. He would be safe enough here until sentencing."

"And then?"

"By morning you will have spoken with the Grand Teller. Emberto oversees new trials every morning. Since you captured the boy, and because of your position here at the court, Emberto will let you speak on the prisoner's behalf. Say what you want about him, but Emberto puts on a good show. He's working hard to keep the trust of the people now that the Elder is gone. If you are careful, you may be able to sway him, spare the life of this—" Filial narrowed his eyes again. "Of this boy."

"But, Filial, I don't think that Emberto will be swayed by an old tale of the kasyapa."

"Amana. Think about the story. If you tell Emberto in a private performance that a kasyapa has come here to Carnillo—do you honestly think he would ever release the bird? Do you think for a moment he would spare the life of the boy who brought the bird here?"

"No, of course not."

"But if you speak in public, in front of hundreds of citizens in the square, he would be forced to let the boy live. Even if Emberto does not believe all the old stories, he is no fool. He knows that most of his people do."

Amana nodded slowly. "You are right. Even Emberto and all his visiting soldiers could not hold back a full-scale rebellion of all his people."

"He's not likely to let the boy go, but as long as—"

"His name is Dominique."

"As long as Dominique is alive, then you have bought some time."

"Filial, thank you." Amana gave the bent old man an awkward hug.

"No time for that, Miss Amana. You have much to do, and the boy is far from being out of danger. Miss Amana?"

"Yes?"

"Where is this bird?"

Amana did not hesitate. "She is a bird, Filial. She flies, comes and goes as she pleases."

The old man scanned the sky, the tops of the court-yard walls.

Dominique nearly fainted with relief. For the first time since Amana had seized the bag, Dominique felt she might actually look after Navina until he could get out of this awful mess. The thought gave him the merest glimmer of hope, and he stood a little straighter despite the ache in his back and shoulders.

"Very good," Filial said. "As far as I know, you captured an Estorian and brought him here to lock him in the palace holding cells until Emberto can deal with him."

"Yes," Amana said. "You know this is true because that is exactly what happened." They both turned to Dominique and Amana said to him, "Isn't that right, prisoner?"

The expression on her face showed only concern, a silent pleading that he would understand she was trying to help in the best way she knew how.

Torn, he wanted to run, to take his chances on the streets. But that would mean leaving Navina and fighting off arrest without a weapon. As well, he had no idea where he would go in the confusing maze of streets. Even if he managed to find the place they called the Recitatorium, there was no guarantee that the Grand Teller would let him in and protect him, certainly not if Amana arrived there first and spoke of this new plan.

Dominique shrugged his shoulders. He could not see an alternative. He nodded his assent and did not resist when Amana and Filial each reached down, grabbed him under his arms, and lifted him to his feet.

11

A PRISONER IN FACT

When Chino reached the top of the mountain he saw
before him a thousand other mountains.

—From the Estorian story "The Boy Who Never Arrived"

Dominique didn't struggle as they crossed the courtyard toward the massive building to their right. The part of the palace that Dominique could see was three storeys tall. On the top two floors, green shutters flanked the rows of large windows, evenly spaced and lined up one above the other. Each window was made up of many smaller panes of glass that glittered and winked in the sun. Atop the roof, stone figures wielded swords and pointed arrows down into the courtyard below.

At first Dominique thought they were going to enter the palace by way of the huge front doors, guarded on either side by two statues of snarling lions. But instead of mounting the ornate staircase with its carved balusters, Filial and Amana turned to the left and headed toward a small door at the end of the building, partly hidden by an urn on a stone pedestal.

"Filial, you must tell me what has been happening

since the Elder died."

Filial sighed and shook his head. "It didn't take long at all before Lord Emberto started arresting people. He has been in court nearly every day since."

"Just how many arrests have there been?"

Filial grunted. "Many. Some Camprianos turned traitor were caught meeting in a false fish stall at the market."

"Who else?"

"Spies. They wore no name rings, of course. But I have heard they had maps of Ranginoor and that some of those arrested spoke with the dialect of High Chem."

"Ranginoor?"

"Yes, and a ship was found anchored in the Epilobium Delta with papers from the Port of Santorio."

"So this is not just a local problem? Emberto has good reason to be worried?" Amana sounded almost hopeful.

Filial shook his head as they approached the smaller door. "I don't know what to make of it. But you know there have been rumours of rebellion for a very long time."

Amana nodded. "I've lived my whole life with threats of invasion. Carnillo is the gateway to the archipelago." She glanced at Dominique and gave him a quick smile. It did little to reassure him: the talk of invasions, rebellions, attacks, and spies made his knees weak.

He concentrated on keeping his legs moving so that he didn't stumble and pull the others down with him.

"When do you think Lord Emberto will hold a trial for Dom—" She caught herself and said, loudly, "For my prisoner?"

"Emberto has been at the courts and then meeting with advisors until late each evening." Filial nodded at Dominique and said, "When he hears you have brought *this* Estorian, Bertolescu, my guess is that Emberto will want to try him as quickly as possible. You won't have much time."

Once again Dominique had the strange feeling that the man looked at him for longer than was necessary.

"Where will the trial take place?"

"Most likely in open court."

"Open court?"

Filial nodded. "To expedite the trials, Lord Emberto holds them in the main square. You'll see. They continue every day, all day."

They passed through the hidden door into a second, smaller courtyard within the palace complex. Amana and Filial led Dominique to another gate, this one guarded by two men in light armour. Their shields and swords were at the ready and they stepped forward to bar the way.

"Amana. Filial." The older soldier nodded at each of them as he said their names.

"Good day, Turannia. I come with my prisoner," Amana said. "Let us pass. We wish to escort him to the holding cells."

Turannia still blocked their way while the second soldier circled them, his sword drawn.

"Check his name ring, Roburo," Turannia commanded, and the younger man tapped the wooden ring around Dominique's ankle with the tip of his sword.

"For goodness' sake, let us pass. You know who we are." The pitch of Amana's voice rose and Dominique braced himself for the worst. Surely the guards would know something was wrong, that he was not an ordinary prisoner.

"I beg your forgiveness, Miss Amana," Turannia said as Roburo unsnapped Dominique's name ring and handed it over. "Orders from Lord Emberto are that no unauthorized persons are to be admitted to the inner palace. Who is this? What is this ring?"

"We used it for security," Amana said more matter-of-factly. "So we would not be troubled as we travelled through Carnillo County."

"Bernio Denga, I think. Explorer Guild. What do you think?"

Roburo took the ring back and squinted at the markings carved into the wood. "I think you are right. Denga—wasn't he part of the Epilobium Expedition?"

"Yes. That's right." Turannia's hand moved to the hilt of his sword. "It is a crime to wear another man's name ring."

Dominique would have moved back, but Amana and Filial held him firmly.

"I told you, it was just to get him here. It's not as if Bernio Denga was an important—"

"And how did you come by it? Did you not know it was Denga's?"

The younger guard circled Dominique again as Turannia continued the interrogation.

"Please," Filial said. "You know Miss Amana has not been schooled in the way of name symbols."

"Of course not," Turannia agreed. "She is a teller—the First Teller Born. But my question is a fair one—how did he come by the name ring?"

"He already had it when I found him . . . met him . . . arrested him . . ." The guards moved closer as Amana faltered. "I thought that letting him wear a name ring seemed like a good—"

Turannia put up his hand and Amana fell quiet. "Take him to see Prensio."

"But I wanted to deliver him myself."

"With respect, Miss Amana, it is not your responsibility to incarcerate prisoners. Until I hear otherwise, you still have palace access and so you may express your concerns to Lord Emberto when you next see him. In the meantime, he will deal with the prisoner. This Estorian is not the first foreigner to have infiltrated the city walls by wearing a false name ring. He may have hidden weapons on his person."

Roburo patted Dominique's back, under his arms, and up and down his legs.

"Do you think I know nothing? I confiscated his dagger. Here it is!"

"Miss Amana, First Teller Born or not, if you don't put that away, I'll have you arrested, too!"

Amana's mouth opened and then shut, but to Dominique's relief, she did lower her dagger, if slowly.

His search for weapons complete, Roburo yanked Dominique's arms behind him and bound them together tightly at the wrists. Without further discussion he pushed Dominique forward so he stumbled and nearly fell. "Stand up!"

"You can't arrest my prisoner!" Amana protested.

"You have taken care of the arrest for me," Turannia said, somewhat smugly. "We are merely escorting him to his new quarters."

"No! You can't do this! Lord Emberto will be furious when he hears! I am a member of the Inner Circle! I have a certain authority—"

"Miss Amana, I am well aware of your position in the court," Turannia said, his lips pulled back in a smile that was distinctly threatening. "But the fact remains, I have my duties to perform. If Lord Emberto felt I was not adequately protecting him . . ." He slashed his hand across the front of his throat.

Dominique glanced back at Amana as he was pushed again. He wanted her to save herself, to stop arguing, but he knew he could say nothing without further raising the guards' suspicions.

"Amana," Filial said firmly. "Amana, it's best you let him go."

When the old man spoke, Dominique felt a huge sense of relief, even as he was being propelled away by Roburo. Filial would look after her.

Dominique heard no more after he was shoved

ahead of his new captor through a wooden door, much lower than the one they had passed through to get into the palace complex with their horses.

The door led to a narrow foot passage scarcely high enough to stand up in. Stone walls closed in on all sides. Dominique and the guard seemed to be moving along inside the palace's outer walls in a space just wide enough for two men to pass. Every so often they passed alcoves in the thick walls. Each was large enough for two soldiers and their weapons to be stationed inside. At regular intervals toward the tops of the walls, smoky lanterns spilled warm pools of yellow light. Dominique and his escort dipped in and out of shadow as they moved along the passage.

Dominique was shocked to see that several of the soldiers positioned in the alcoves were women. They stood as straight and vigilant as the men. Men and women alike glared at him as he passed, as if he were some filthy animal. Several times Roburo gave him a hard kick from behind that nearly sent him sprawling across the stone floor of the passageway.

When they reached the end of the long tunnel they came to a junction where they could either turn to the right and ascend a narrow, stone, spiral staircase or turn left down another passageway. They mounted the stairs. Dominique leaned against the inner wall of the stairway as he tramped up.

At the first landing, Roburo told him to stop. A heavy door to the left had smaller metal spikes similar to those on the outside of the great doors leading into the palace courtyard. The guard rapped sharply at a grille set into the door at head height. A moment later a peephole opened behind the grille and a wizened face looked out.

"Aye?"

"Prensio. I have another one for you."

"Traitor? Thief? Murderer?"

"All three, perhaps. He wears the name ring of a man missing for weeks. Bernio Denga."

The door swung inward, groaning on its massive hinges.

"Ah, Bernio. I knew him. He was a friend of my son. Part of the Epilobium Expedition and then never seen again," Prensio said.

"Take him," Roburo said and spat on the ground at Dominique's feet. "Lord Emberto will sentence him when it pleases him."

"But—" Dominique started to protest.

"Quiet." Prensio's voice was soft, but Dominique felt chilled as the man spoke. "I will deal with our newest *guest* in the meanwhile."

CHAPTER

12

REUNION

"Listen," Prince Ullulato said. "If you wish to remain my guest, you must bring me three gifts—and one of them must be a story I have never heard before."

—Campriano tale

Prensio looked to be nearly the age of Granny Poona before she died of the cough, but as the old man locked the door behind the retreating guard, Dominique saw the sinewy muscles of his forearms ripple. Though he was slightly stooped, his walk was both powerful and purposeful, and Dominique had no doubt who would come out the winner in a struggle.

Dominique could not think. It was as if his mind was as dim as the passageways in which he now found himself. The prison was not large—only four cells—and only one of these had an occupant.

"The Lord Emberto is at the open court with the other prisoners. You will wait here until new trials begin."

Dominique wanted to ask how long that would take, but he knew questions would be useless here. He wanted to know whether Amana would have enough time to speak with the Grand Teller and wondered how that conversation could possibly help him. He had no idea what would happen at a trial or how serious a crime it was to wear someone else's name ring.

Amana's plan to tell everyone at the trial about Navina seemed foolhardy and dangerous. Surely talking about Navina would not help him.

"In there." Prensio undid the leather ties binding Dominique's wrists behind him. The guard pushed his prisoner into a cell and the heavy door clanged shut, leaving Dominique in near darkness. The only light spilled in through a small barred window set high up in the door and through a crack beneath the door. A narrow slit in the wall far above his head seemed to lead to the outside: a shaft of sunlight filtered in from above whenever the breeze lifted a flap of animal skin fastened over the small opening. He stood on tiptoes and reached up, but the ledge and the tiny window were still well beyond his fingertips.

It took a few minutes for his eyes to adjust to the gloom, and when they did he saw there was nothing in the room but a heap of straw piled against the wall opposite the door. The walls and floor were solid stone and the space was so small he could touch both walls when he spread his arms out on each side.

Dominique looked down at his bare feet on the stone floor and caught sight of his ankle, now free of the troublesome name ring. He tried to remember whether he had seen any evidence of a Campriano called Bernio Denga, a dropped dagger, bones. He cursed himself for having picked up the ring in the first place. He should have left it lying on the ground near the stinking yagabono pit where he'd found it.

Dominique kneeled on the stone floor beside the heap of straw. The straw was damp, and when

Dominique nudged it, a mouldy smell rose. He wrinkled his nose and moved back. Already the cold seeped into his knees and so, unpleasant though it was, he spread the straw along the back wall, tucking the dirtiest underneath. As he scuffled about in the straw he tried to ignore the growing pressure in his bladder. Moving seemed to make it worse, so Dominique lay flat on his back on the matted straw and stared at the rough-hewn stone ceiling overhead.

A lump formed in his throat and Dominique had to press the heels of his hands against his eyes to stop the tears from coming. He drew a deep breath and tried to think of anything but his predicament. There was nowhere he could relieve himself in the cell—no hole in the floor, no bucket, nothing.

It was quiet in the cell except for the soft noise of the window cover tapping against the flat of the wall high above. Lying still was worse than moving around. Though he knew there was nothing, Dominique searched the cell again, looking for something that he could use to climb or pull himself up to the window ledge. If he could at least look out, maybe he could— what?

He slumped back against the wall, drew his knees up to his chest, alarmed at the ache in his kidneys. Finally, when he could stand it no longer, he crawled to the door and shouted, "Help!" But there was no answer and Dominique crawled back across the cell.

Far above, the flap of hide lifted and fell, lifted and fell, and Dominique's breath caught in his chest with each movement of the flap. Desperate to distract himself, he kept his gaze fixed on the wedge of light that widened and narrowed in time with the city's exhalations. The undulating light reminded him of lapping waves and he nearly cried out with the agony of holding on.

Dominique sat back down in the pile of straw, his back to the wall, his knees drawn up to his chest, his chin resting on his folded arms. His gaze wandered across the little room, following the cracks between the stones to the door, noting each wisp of straw, each clod of dirt that lay between him and the heavy door.

A small movement at the bottom of the door caught his attention. At first he thought it was the shadow of the guard, perhaps coming to free him, take him to a place where he could relieve himself. Dominique's stomach rumbled. Maybe it was time for some food. He shifted slightly in the straw, trying to ease the ache in his back-side and the discomfort in his belly. The movement beyond the door stopped and Dominique sat still. A few minutes later the movement at the door resumed—back and forth it travelled until, after several more passes, a sharp black nose and a set of long whiskers poked under the door.

Squeezing itself nearly flat, a black rat wriggled into the cell. Dominique held his breath and his heart hammered in his ears.

In the black time the rats came
Calling out the dead man's name.

The rhyme from his childhood came unbidden to his mind and repeated itself over and over. Frozen in place, Dominique could not move as he watched the rat explore the perimeter of the room. The creature sniffed its way along the bottom of the wall, its whiskers quivering as its pointy nose wiggled.

"Go away," he whispered. The rat must have been aware of the cell's occupant, but it paid him no attention.

Dominique tried to think what he would do if the rat continued all the way around the small cell until it reached him. He had no weapon, and the idea of trying to kill the creature was too horrifying to consider seriously. On the other hand, black rats carried the Sickness, the same disease that the Stories spoke of with such dread.

A person didn't even have to be bitten by a sick rat in order to contract the disease. And the Sickness was hideous. Great sores opened over the person's body and a fever and deep cough soon took hold. It did not take long to succumb. All those who handled the body were at risk. Many of the Stories spoke of bodies left to rot where they fell, of children loosely covered with dirt tossed over them from a distance.

The rat continued its exploration of the cell and Dominique shuddered. He reached beside him for a handful of straw. His fingers closed on the wisps, and with one quick motion he threw the straw at the rat. It fluttered to the ground, but the sudden movement startled the rat and it leaped forward and disappeared into a crack at the base of the wall close to where Dominique sat.

Dominique closed his eyes and licked his lips. What he wouldn't give for a sip of cold water. Water. No, the last thing he needed now was water. With a desperate moan, Dominique knew he could last no longer. He scooped up several handfuls of straw and moved them to another corner, away from his bed. As he hopped from foot to foot in front of the pile, tears started streaming over his cheeks. He tugged down his leggings and sobbed as he relieved himself, his face burning with misery and humiliation.

Small though the cell was, Dominique, his knees once again drawn up close to his chest, felt smaller. He closed his eyes and concentrated on slowing his breathing. The rat could come back at any time, the guards might forget to feed him, Amana might not have any luck with the Grand Teller and he'd be stuck in the holding cell forever—or worse.

He needed to think clearly, to make some sort of

plan. If only he and Amana had been able to speak privately. Now he had to guess what to say to keep himself alive at Emberto's trial. Amana had said Lord Emberto wanted to know about Estorian movements and camp locations. He could make something up—it would take a little time for Emberto to find out the information was useless. But what did Amana have in mind? Was it really such a good idea to mention Navina? His heart constricted in his chest as if a great hand had taken hold and was giving it a good squeeze.

Dominique gazed longingly up at the tiny window so far above. Maybe he could escape. If there were rebels in the city, perhaps they might shelter him, or at least tell him the best way to leave. Maybe he was not the only Estorian in Carnillo. His thoughts seemed ridiculous, like the kind of foolish stories a mother would tell to a restless child. Unbelievable. Full of hope.

From outside the window he heard the rumble of carts along the stone streets, and then shouts and a loud clatter followed by the crack of whips. What was going on out there?

Dominique's gaze shifted to the stone wall. Strangely, as his eyes travelled the wall they were no longer seeing the stone but an odd space. Dominique felt lightheaded and blinked. It was hard to focus. It seemed he wasn't looking at a wall any more but at some kind of street. A city street. Guards stood at one end of the street, blocking the entrance to the square, the same square he and Amana had skirted around earlier that afternoon.

Dominique squinted harder, but rather than going away, the image grew clearer, brighter. Dominique squeezed his eyes shut completely and the town square became even more vivid. The same pain he had felt earlier when he first saw the olio pickers now returned, and he put his hands to his head as if he could push the ache away. The vision grew stronger.

All around the well at the centre of the plaza, hundreds of people had gathered. Soldiers on horseback, dressed like Andalon's men in scarlet and blue, stood watch over all the entrances to the square. A platform had been built behind the well and several prisoners stood chained together, their heads bowed, their wrists bound behind them.

A tall man wearing a long tunic with a large eagle embroidered in gold across the back and shoulders stood facing the crowd. He stood straight as an ancient centrinel tree. Dominique gasped as he realized he could see the man first from the front and then from the back, as if he were somehow circling around and above him. The sensation of movement was so real that Dominique swayed from side to side and had to put his arm out to hold the wall and steady himself. Though he opened his eyes, the vision was so strong he could see nothing else and so he shut his eyes again, trying to make sense of what was happening.

The people in the square, hundreds and hundreds of them, chanted and punched their fists into the air. The man on the platform shouted and waved his arms, his fingers rigid, extended as if he were trying to gouge the sky. Occasionally he turned and brandished his sword in the general direction of the prisoners lined up on the platform behind him.

Several large carts pulled by heavy workhorses clanked and groaned into the square, and Dominique recognized the sounds as those that had drifted into his cell from somewhere outside a short time earlier.

In the back of each cart a huge iron vat swung from chains attached to a tripod of iron stakes. This seemed to be the source of the loud clanging. When the prisoners saw these vehicles arriving, several screamed and tried to run away. Immediately, two guards stepped forward and struck their shoulders with such brutal force that the prisoners were forced to their knees. Dominique wanted to turn away, to stop watching, but he was unable to make the vision disappear.

A great roar went up from the crowd and Dominique felt himself reeling, spinning sideways. He flung his arms out and gripped the cold stones to either side of his head. As two soldiers led one of the prisoners, screaming and crying, toward one of the strange carts, the crowd began to chant "Campriano victorioso!" over and over, each time more loudly, until the sound drifted in through the window and echoed both inside and outside Dominique's head.

"No!" he cried out and released his grip on the walls, slapping his hands over his ears and burying his face in the straw, oblivious now to the smell and to the bugs crawling from the straw into his hair.

The crowd below him tilted and then he saw a solid stone wall looming directly in front of him. It seemed he was heading straight for the wall, that he would surely hit it and fall to his death below.

Dominique was too terrified to scream. His mouth opened and shut as a narrow slit appeared in the wall and he slipped inside, landing on a narrow ledge.

At the sound of the flutter of feathers above his head he opened his eyes and rolled over to see Navina perched by the narrow opening to the outside. Her breast heaved and she tilted her head from side to side.

"Navina! Oh, Navina! Come here."

He extended his hand and the kasyapa bird lifted from the ledge and glided down to land on his wrist. Dominique lifted her close to him and inspected the bird. Her scarlet crest stood up in a familiar greeting and she tipped her head forward, asking to be scratched on the back of her neck. Though her curved beak was sharp, Dominique was not worried she would bite him. She seemed as glad to see him as he was to see her.

"Yes," he whispered. "Yes, I saw what you saw. How did you do that?" he asked. "How did you make me see what was happening outside?"

A chill raised bumps along his arms as he remembered the other vision he had had earlier that day.

"Those women in the field," he said slowly. "Were they . . . did you?"

Navina said nothing, and no new pictures came into Dominique's head.

"It was you, wasn't it? Can you make me see things from far away?"

But the bird did not answer. She didn't have to. There was no doubt in Dominique's mind that somehow Navina had shared what she could see even though they were far apart. He wondered if she understood what she had done, how far away she needed to be to make it work, how she controlled what images she decided to share.

As he ran his forefinger over and around the back of her head until he felt her relax and lean into his touch, he shook his own head back and forth in wonder. "And she let you go, didn't she?" A surge of conflicting feelings made him want to laugh and cry and bury his head back in the straw, all at the same time. Amana had released Navina. It was a message. She really was trying to help. And Navina . . . He gazed at the bird with awe. Somehow he could see the things the bird could see.

Navina seemed oblivious to it all. When he brought her close to his face to inspect her more closely, she ruffled her feathers and then scratched her beak with her foot. Surprising himself, Dominique smiled.

CHAPTER
13

A FAMILIAR FACE

Of the seven boys who climbed to the summit of Aerendale Mountain, only one returned. But the scars he bore sometimes made him wish that he, too, had perished.

—Estorian cautionary tale

Bang! Bang! Bang!

Dominique's head jerked up. In the total darkness, his arms flew out sideways. He yelped as the back of one hand smacked into the cell wall.

He moved away as far as he could as the door swung open. A smoky torch flickered, lighting a new guard's face and casting an uneven light across the rough floor. This guard was younger and much taller than Prensio. His black hair glistened as if it were wet. He wore heavy leather body armour and thick black gloves that flared at the wrist and reached nearly to his elbows. In one hand he held a staff, which he pounded on the floor.

Bang! Bang! Bang!

The man did not speak but covered the small space between them in two strides. The guard's boot jammed into Dominique's side and the boy gasped. When he didn't get up, the guard kicked him again. Clutching his ribs, Dominique pushed himself to his feet, leaning against the wall as he rose.

The guard grabbed his shoulder, spun him around, and then shoved him toward the door. Gasping with pain and terror, Dominique staggered out into the passageway running between the cells.

"Where are we going?" he asked.

The guard did not answer, but a disembodied voice from the second cell said, "You'll miss this place, you will."

No, he wouldn't! No matter where he was being taken it could not be worse than this cold, rat-infested cell. The guard clanged his staff against the bars of the other prisoner's cage and the stranger fell silent.

"Where are we—" Dominique tried again, but the guard just gave him another hard shove and Dominique decided to keep his questions to himself. He ran his tongue over his parched lips, desperately thirsty.

Once again Dominique found himself being propelled through dimly lit passageways. At one point the guard pushed him out into a tiny courtyard and Dominique could see the sky was beginning to lighten. Dawn was not far off. He had slept longer than he would have believed possible.

He sucked in a deep breath of fresh air. What a joy it was to be outside! If only he were free. He glanced at the walls surrounding the courtyard. Even if he could somehow sprint away from the guard, the walls were too high to scale, and he could not tell what lay beyond them. The pair ducked under a low archway and passed into a long hallway running between two sections of the building. A row of tall windows overlooked a sunken courtyard to the right. A circular fountain in the middle of the courtyard squirted a tantalizing cacophony of gurgles and splashes. Dominique tore his eyes away and noticed a series of doors opening off to the left.

Dominique was completely disoriented. Where in Tara's name was he? The guard whacked him across the shoulders with his staff to indicate that he should stop. When the guard fumbled for an iron key to unlock yet another door, Dominique fully expected to be led into another passageway, but instead, when he stepped into the space beyond the door he was amazed to see he was actually outside the palace wall and standing on one of the streets along which he and Amana had passed after entering the city.

He was not surprised, therefore, when the guard locked the door behind them. They hurried along to the square that Dominique had glimpsed shortly after his arrival and had studied more closely when Navina sent the pictures into his head.

Navina. Where was she now? Still in the cell? Or had she escaped? He hoped the bird had flown away before the guard came, but he dared not look around in case he happened to spot her and give away her whereabouts. Dominique bit the inside of his cheek and wondered if he could stand the heartbreak if he looked up and found himself alone. He waited for an image to come into his head that might show him where she was, but there was nothing.

Though it was very early, the square was far from empty. Vendors pushed their carts through the area, perhaps heading to other markets within the city walls. Others seemed to have spent the night huddled in doorways. As Dominique and the guard approached the platform in the middle of the square, several more people, bundled in shawls and loose cloaks, crawled from beneath it and scuttled off into the still-gloomy streets.

Dominique was not the first to arrive at the platform. Another prisoner stood there already, a round, older man with a shiny bald head. He looked up as Dominique approached and dipped his head in a virtually imperceptible nod. Dominique's heart leapt with delight.

Don't nod back, Dominique told himself firmly, though he wanted to shout out and run to the other prisoner. The man tethered by chains to a stake on the platform was no stranger. It was Sir Riley, the rotund knight Dominique had met what seemed like years earlier on the banks of the River Epilobium.

"That one's just a wee boy," Riley said. "Surely you can't be threatened by a mite like him."

The guard gave Riley a whack across the back of the knees with his stick. "Enough from you." He shoved Dominique along.

Dominique cried out as his arms were wrenched behind him so that a second guard could chain his bound wrists to another stake one stride away from Riley.

Once fastened to the stake, Dominique risked a sideways glance at Riley. There was no doubt about it: the man beside him was the same knight who had once pretended to help him and who had then stolen his knife and other possessions. Despite the fact Riley's inexplicable actions could have cost him his life, Dominique was so delighted to see a familiar face that he could muster only a fleeting moment of irritation.

Careful not to attract attention, Dominique gave the slightest nod so Riley would know he had been recognized. Then, glancing around the square, Dominique saw that the heavy carts with their large cauldrons had disappeared. He listened carefully but could not hear their distinctive rumble. Perhaps that was a good thing. The prisoners had seemed terrified of the carts. He could only imagine what would happen after a prisoner was lowered into one of those cauldrons filled with—what? Venomous snakes? Boiling oil? Dominique shuddered and concentrated on the planks beneath his feet.

Only a few minutes later, four more prisoners, all men, were led up to the platform. They, too, were chained to stakes. One of the men was weeping and pleading to be freed. Another had long, tangled hair and a deep cut across one cheek. The third stood straight and tall and spat defiantly at one of the guards. He was thanked for this gesture with a smashing blow across his back. Dominique closed his eyes and tried to ignore the sticky feeling in his mouth. He was so incredibly thirsty he found it hard to think of anything else. He forced himself to imagine being back in one of the peaceful encampments of his childhood.

Holding on to a vision of his mother baking crisp pikka bread was nearly impossible, though, given the grunts and curses of the men all around him. Besides, pikka bread was best consumed with a steaming mug of dragonberry tea.

Tethered to his stake, Dominique swayed, weak and lightheaded from lack of food and water and from the malignant fear spreading throughout his entire body.

The sun crept higher, and though it had not yet cleared the eastern wall of the city, the streets were awakening. All sorts of people were crowding into the square. Many were drawn to the platform, where they pushed close to get a good look at Dominique and the five other men chained around him. Soldiers began to appear on horseback and on foot, wearing both Emberto's colours and those of Lord Andalon of Crestio. They did not directly threaten the people, but Dominique noticed that the residents gave the soldiers a wide berth and kept their eyes down, as if hoping they would not be noticed.

As the sun rose higher, Dominique licked his parched lips. He sighed and closed his eyes. Immediately, an image filled his mind. A tall man on horseback rode through one of the narrow streets of Carnillo. He was flanked by a number of soldiers dressed in red and black. This time the sensation was not quite as painful, more like a firm squeeze inside his skull, and he didn't feel nearly so panicky. Instead, he tried to relax and concentrate on what Navina was showing him. A large group of civilians followed the entourage on foot. A man with a hand drum beat out a steady rhythm as they moved along the street.

The vision changed as, Dominique assumed, Navina rose higher. He saw rooftops and courtyards and caught a glimpse of the edge of the square. Then, as abruptly as the vision had started, it went away again.

Dominique glanced up into the sky but could see no sign of Navina. He hoped she had the good sense to keep out of sight. He dared not let himself imagine what would happen if one of the soldiers caught sight of her. Each of them wore a quiver bristling with arrows, and he had no doubt they were accurate shooters.

CHAPTER

14

OPEN COURT

The king raised his hand and the music stopped.

—Campriano palace story

The sound of a drum thumped around the square and soldiers, civilians, and prisoners alike turned to locate its source. The soldiers saluted toward a narrow street that opened into the square. Craning his neck, Dominique watched the drummer enter the square first, his hand rising and falling in a blur, thumping and pounding on the taut hide. Behind him, the tall man on horseback halted. Dominique recognized him from the vision he'd had in the holding cell. He was the man who had addressed the crowd the afternoon before. Now, two of his guards moved past him into the square. They looked out over the crowd and then toward the prisoners waiting on the platform. Dominique's knees weakened and he fought to stay upright, leaning against the stake behind him for support.

When the escorts deemed it was safe for their leader to proceed, the tall man rode forward. He did not look at the people surrounding him, nor at the prisoners.

Rather, he fixed his gaze so intently on a point across the square that Dominique, too, turned to see what the man was looking at. The wall of the building facing him was ancient. Deep cracks wiggled up across the front. Little windows tucked under the eaves were covered with faded black shutters. Dominique looked back at the man astride the horse. Was this the great Lord Emberto?

When he was level with the platform, the rider halted.

The other soldiers and the drummer stopped, too. Still the man did not turn his head. He continued to stare straight ahead at the old building across the square as two of his men dismounted and climbed up onto the platform alongside the guards and the prisoners.

It was only then that the man turned slowly to face them.

Dominique could not help but gawk. The man's eyes were the strangest he had ever seen. One was amber, nearly the rich yellow-gold colour of a tonneck, and the other was green, as green as the eye of an emerald hawk. The colour of the eyes was strange enough, but even more peculiar was the way they did not seem to line up properly. The green eye would focus on whatever was directly ahead, while the other veered off to one side, looking somewhere completely different.

The drummer whacked his drum once, twice, and then a third time with the flat of his hand before announcing, "Good people of Carnillo, the great Lord Emberto, ruler of Carnillo, guardian of the lands of South Epilobia, stands before you."

The crowd shouted and cheered.

Automatically, Dominique ducked his head, trying to show respect for the strange-looking leader.

"Speak of the crimes committed by those before me."

One of the guards on the platform stepped forward.

"We have here before us two men, allies of King Sim, arrested in the fish market after arriving in the hold of a fishing boat."

"Step forward for sentencing," Emberto demanded.

Chains rattled as two of the men were allowed to move toward the front edge of the platform where Emberto waited.

"Speak in your own defence."

One of the men said, "Sir, we are fishermen from Crestio."

"Their boat bore the markings of a Crestian ship, that is true," the guard on the platform said, "but the holds were empty and the men were heard to speak words in Ranginese."

Lord Emberto's green eye narrowed as he studied the two accused. The second man spoke up.

"It is true we had no fish. We had troubles at sea— the boat needed repairs, and the captain became ill."

"And where is this captain now?" Emberto demanded.

The two men glanced at one another.

The guard answered the question. "Dead, sir."

Emberto's second eye bounced crazily off to the side. "Dead?"

"He had a fever, sir," one of the fishermen said. "We wanted to get him to the herbalist here in Carnillo. To get help for him so we could continue fishing."

"His body was bruised, sir," the guard added.

"Bruised?"

"He had fallen, sir—two days out of Crestio," the shorter of the two fishermen said. "I believe his injuries weakened him, and when the fever struck—"

"Enough," Lord Emberto said, raising his palm toward the man. "Take them to the Dark Tower."

One of the men cried out, "But why? On what charges?"

"Conspiracy to challenge my authority in Carnillo—"

"But that's not what—"

"And murder."

"He was ill! We came here to help him!"

"Remove them to the tower now. Next?"

The jailer who had guarded Sir Riley stepped forward.

"Sir Riley—in the employ of Lord Ronwyn. Spy. Captured in the marketplace attempting to purchase a vial of poison from one of our agents."

"Speak in your defence."

"Thank you, sir. Might I first offer you my deepest condolences on the death of your father."

Lord Emberto did not acknowledge this, but said, "Will you, or will you not, speak in your own defence?"

Riley bobbed his head, the closest he could come to bowing with his arms bound tightly behind his back. "As a man of honour, you conduct your trial with due diligence. Of that I am most grateful."

Dominique could not believe how calm Riley sounded, as if the plump knight were having dinner with Lord Emberto rather than standing trial before him.

"I did, indeed, purchase poison," Riley said, and a murmur of disgust ran through the crowd. "And, perhaps, a man less sure of his position here might have been afraid of the purposes intended for that toxic elixir."

Lord Emberto's good eye never left Riley's face, and even the yellow one settled for the moment, looking down and to the side.

"I cannot even deny that I was in the employment of Lord Ronwyn." Riley sighed. "I was reluctantly pressed into service against my better judgment, but a man has to eat—some more than others . . ."

A few spectators snickered, but hid their laughter when Lord Emberto wheeled around and glared at his subjects.

"My mission," Riley continued, "was to travel here to Carnillo to learn more about the troubles in the south part of Tanga. Though Lord Ronwyn sent me here, I had not been in your great city long before I recognized an opportunity." Riley cleared his throat before he continued. "I saw my chance to ally myself with the most powerful leader in the whole archipelago. Breaking with Lord Ronwyn would be much easier if he were to . . . errr . . . become dreadfully ill."

"And this, I suppose, is why you asked my men at the market about procuring widowmaker root?"

"Precisely." Riley nodded vigorously. "Black widowmaker root would have been most excellent to cure Lord Ronwyn of his beating heart."

Lord Emberto seemed to consider this story. He looked at Riley, and for just a moment, both his eyes focused on the knight's face. "Charming as you consider yourself to be, I have no doubt you would just as soon run me through with your sword as shake my hand. The charges are spying and intention to murder the ruler of Carnillo. Take him to the Dark Tower and hold him until I have decided on his final punishment."

Several people in the crowd cheered. Apparently, Emberto was in no mood to celebrate: he turned to the crowd and slashed his hand through the air, demanding silence. When a woman toward the back was slow to comply, one of the soldiers delivered a sharp blow to her back with the handle of his sword. The woman fell to her knees and then crumpled sideways. The soldier's shiny buttons glinted and winked in the sunshine as he straightened up, smoothing his bright red tunic.

Riley bowed his head and Dominique looked away so he didn't have to watch several of the spectators trying to revive the woman.

"Take the prisoner away!" Lord Emberto said.

Riley shuffled across the front of the platform between two guards. As they passed in front of Dominique, the older knight caught the boy's gaze for a moment and gave him the merest hint of a wink. Dominique had no time to respond. Before Riley had even left the platform, Emberto bellowed, "Next!"

15

THE TRIAL

King Penderano treated his prisoners well, but not too well.
He never knew when he might find a use for them. As his
father had once told him, "Men with broken feet cannot
carry heavy loads."

—Campriano palace story

Dominique's jailer stepped forward. "Arrested in the Misty Mountains wearing the name ring of Bernio Denga, member of the lost Epilobium Expedition."

"How did you come by this ring?"

Dominique opened his mouth to speak but nothing happened. His lips were parched and his tongue felt huge and ungainly. "I . . ." Only a whisper of breath came out.

"Speak!"

Dominique felt his knees begin to collapse and then the rough grip of the guard's hand holding him up.

"I—"

"He claims to have found the ring lying on the ground," a voice interrupted from the crowd.

Lord Emberto turned to see who had spoken, and Dominique saw Amana step forward, meeting the man's uneven gaze with a steady stare. "He claims he saw it initially in the collecting pouch of a yagabono. I have no reason to doubt him."

Dominique caught several comments from people in the crowd who seemed impressed he could have been close enough to the yagabono to examine its pouch. Others coughed and gagged, imitating the sounds one made when too close to a yagabono's overpowering stench.

"Speak."

Dominique coughed and muttered, "Yes. Yes, that's true. I found the ring."

"And why were you in the Misty Mountains?"

"I—I was travelling to the Cave of Departure . . . because . . . I can't . . . I couldn't . . ."

What began as a sigh came out as a long, shuddering breath, and Dominique would have collapsed completely had it not been for the guard's iron grip on his arm.

"I took him prisoner," Amana said, "to bring back to you. He surrendered without a fight and agreed to tell you whatever you would like to know about Estorian tribal movements."

"Your intentions may have been honourable, Miss Amana, but those of us with more experience know that even a small boy can be dangerous. Your innocence is refreshing—and, might I add, it is good to see you back—but I believe this young spy has used you to infiltrate my city. The charges are murdering a member of the Epilobium Expedition and impersonating a citizen of Carnillo."

"With all due respect," Amana replied, her voice as unhurried as if she were relating a simple sleeping story to a young child, "after spending some time with this Estorian, I do not believe he murdered Denga. This boy was unarmed when I found him and besides, look at the size of him, he could hardly kill a fully armed soldier. I

believe he has information of use to us—to you—
regarding the Estorian peoples."

Lord Emberto held his hand out over the crowd and
everyone, including Amana, fell quiet.

"What you believe, Amana Elnedo, may have been
relevant even a few short weeks ago. But events have
transpired here within the city walls that have changed
the way we must think about all outsiders—"

"What about Andalon's men? The city is crawling
with them and they—"

Emberto leaned forward, out over the crowd, and
beckoned to Amana to approach the platform. When she
was close enough to touch, he reached down to gently
brush a wisp of blond hair away from her face. "As many
of you know, Amana Elnedo has served the palace well.
She is the First Teller Born and, as such, occupies a special place in my court. She knows that I do not imprison
the innocent. It is my duty to uphold the laws and traditions of my people. If I did not believe in the importance
of tradition and fairness, would I have housed and nur-
tured the First Teller Born as tradition decrees?"

He smiled at Amana and touched her hair again.
"While I trust and value Amana Elnedo's opinion, she is
still very young and unable to see the dangers that sometimes hide behind the sweetest of faces."

Emberto's gloved hand came to rest on Amana's
shoulder. Only Dominique and the guards on the platform
beside him were close enough to see the way Emberto's
casual caress ended with a squeeze hard enough to bring
tears to Amana's eyes.

From where he stood, Dominique could see something else. Amana straightened her back and, without
blinking, turned to face the crowd.

"There is one more thing I would like to say," she
said, chin held high. "When I found Dominique, he was
not alone. He travelled with a kasyapa bird, a bird of

great power that—" As she spoke, gasps and cheers rose from the audience.

"Thank you, Miss Amana. I believe we know the quaint old story well enough. You do not need to repeat it here."

"Let her speak!" a man shouted from the back of the crowd. Emberto ignored him and regarded Amana solemnly, his hands folded behind his back, his uneven eyes taking in the crowd, his soldiers, Dominique.

"Miss Amana. If this traitorous murderer is travelling with such a bird, where is it?"

Dominique's stomach pitched. Involuntarily, his gaze darted from the top of the tower opposite to chimney, to rooftop. Where was Navina? *Stay away*, he pleaded silently.

Amana said nothing.

"As I thought. There is no such bird. Your skills as a storyteller have always impressed me, but such preposterous tales of the imagination have no place here in this court. Kindly save them for the taverns and festivals where harmless entertainment is more appropriate."

Dominique thought Amana was going to argue or try to tell more of the kasyapa story, but then her shoulders dropped and she said, "I am but young and foolish, sir. I thank you for your words of great wisdom, Lord Emberto." Her words were met with scattered applause, and Dominique felt the pit in his stomach deepen. This was going terribly wrong.

Emberto turned to one of his men. "Take the prisoner to the Dark Tower. The charges are illegally wearing a Carnillian name ring with the intention to spy within the walls of Carnillo. We will further investigate the murder charges. The prisoner will return here after fourteen days in custody for additional sentencing. Miss Amana?"

"Yes, Lord Emberto?"

"Your presence will not be required at that hearing—do you understand?"

"Yes, sir. I understand. My work is to tell stories and I shall be happy to continue to hone my craft."

The corners of Emberto's mouth twitched as he said, "Very good, Miss Amana. I am very pleased we understand each other."

Dominique wondered if Lord Emberto would address him directly, but Emberto's good eye had already found the next prisoner chained up before him. When Dominique looked back down into the crowd, Amana had disappeared.

CHAPTER

16

THE DARK TOWER OF CARNILLO

"Surely you don't want to be alone?" the witch asked as she pushed the boy into the pit writhing with mud vipers.
—Traditional Estorian tale

Dominique scarcely noticed the trip from the square to the Dark Tower of Carnillo. The guard propelled him along so fast it seemed his feet hardly touched the ground. Once, when Dominique twisted around to try again to find Amana, the guard wrenched his arm so hard he cried out.

Dominique gasped as the guard's fingers pinched his ear. His feet, scrambling somewhere beneath him, felt as if they belonged to someone else as they hurried toward the narrow street at the end of the main square. People jostled all around him, some with bundles balanced on their heads or strapped to their backs. Some pushed handcarts and others prodded donkeys laden with panniers.

"Move aside! Move aside!" A boy half Dominique's

age didn't get out of their way quickly enough. The guard's swift kick sent the boy tumbling backwards into the wheel of a wooden cart piled high with the same plump orange fruit the women had been tending outside the city walls. The olio melons spilled and tumbled every which way.

"Watch where you're going!" A large woman with her hair tied up in a twist of dirty yellow cloth swatted the boy. He clapped his hand over his ear and scuttled backwards out of the way, his dark eyes wide as she turned back to her fruit.

All around Dominique were houses and shops jumbled so tightly together he could scarcely see the sky above. On either side of the street, women leaned out of second-storey windows, fastening wet laundry to lines strung from one side of the street to the other.

"Esta Emberto!" they called to each other in greeting.

In the time it took to walk from the square to the end of the street, the wash, flapping slowly in the breeze, filled what little space there was above them, and Dominique fought the desire to protect his head as if from great birds of prey.

In the mountains, black praedavis birds made their nests high atop the cliffs. It was there they picked the bones of children clean.

With his own people, the women washed clothes in the rivers and then spread them on flat rocks to dry. He ached with a sudden longing for open places where he could run and run until he collapsed into the grass or dove into a cool, clear stream. Here, even the street seemed oppressive, tight, suffocating.

They soon reached a massive door set into the base of the city wall some distance along from the Dark Tower. Two soldiers stood at attention. Both saluted when Dominique and the guard appeared before them.

"Have you something to tell us?" one asked.

"I have heard the story of a man to hang," Dominique's guard said.

"And who might this man be?" replied one of the soldiers, taking a smart step sideways so he stood between Dominique and the door.

"A man who steals, spies, and conspires."

The soldiers continued to stare straight ahead, but in unison said, "The man's story shall end here."

All three men simultaneously raised their left arms straight up, punching the air with gloved fists.

Dominique looked from one to the other, but their faces were blank, smooth as puddles at dawn.

"So be it told," the three said together, and one of the door guards turned and unlocked the entrance to the passage that led to the Dark Tower of Carnillo.

Once inside the narrow passage within the city wall, Dominique's guard showed no mercy. He seemed to enjoy shoving his prisoner before him and didn't slow at all when Dominique stumbled and fell to his knees. The guard strode forward, grabbed the back of Dominique's loose cotton shift in his huge fist, and lifted him nearly off his feet.

"Ow!" It felt as if Dominique's arms would be sawn off where they met his body.

The guard's response was to let go of the back of the shift. Dominique's knees smashed against the stone floor and he found himself on his hands and knees in the tunnel, blinking back tears. It didn't even surprise him when a blow landed on his back.

"Get up!" the guard said between clenched teeth as Dominique's elbows gave out and he sprawled face down on the cold stone floor.

"Emmon? Are you coming with another prisoner?"

Again, Dominique felt his arm being yanked up as Emmon pulled him to his feet.

"Aye. This one's slow as feckle syrup."

Dominique shuffled forward. The voice, along with a steady *risp-rasp* sound, came from around a bend just ahead. When they turned the corner and moved into a small antechamber before yet another huge wooden door, Dominique saw what was making the noise. A squat man, much older than any of the guards, sat on a wooden stool behind a stone wheel. His foot pumped a pedal, making the wheel spin so fast its surface was a blur.

"Morning, Blaedusco," Emmon said with a slight bow.

The man at the wheel did not look up. He held the sharp edge of a curved knife to the whirling stone.

"We've no room, though I don't suppose Lord Emberto cares about that."

He leaned forward, putting more pressure on the knife. White sparks showered his leather boots. "Where is he to go?"

"The great room with the other spies."

"Who isn't a spy these days, hmm?" Blaedusco leaned back and the wheel slowed. He ran his thumb along the sharp edge of the knife and grunted. "That'll do."

He placed the knife on a low table covered with a thick woven cloth. At least a dozen other blades—several knives, two short swords, and an axe head—also lay in a row.

"Come here."

Dominique shuffled forward.

"Hold out your hands."

Emmon untied the leather straps around Dominique's wrists as Blaedusco pulled an iron cuff from a shelf behind him and measured it for size. "A skinny one, you are," he said, clamping the cuff on his table where he hit it several times with a heavy mallet. He slipped the adjusted cuff around Dominique's wrist and then pushed a rivet through two small holes at each end of the curved metal.

"Ow!" Dominique said as Blaedusco yanked his wrist forward and held it flat on his worktable.

Blaedusco replied by smashing the mallet against the end of the rivet, flattening it so it couldn't slip back out through the holes. He repeated the whole process with a second cuff and then fastened the two iron cuffs together with a length of heavy chain.

"There. That should do it."

"Fine work, as always," Emmon said. "I'll leave him with you."

"See you again, no doubt," Blaedusco said as he stood and pressed his hands to the small of his back. He arched backwards and groaned. "Too long in one spot." Then he looked at Dominique and grinned, poking the tip of his tongue into the gap where his two front teeth should have been. "You'll know soon enough."

The prison tower was not divided into separate cells for the prisoners. Rather, the building was constructed of two thick circular walls, one within the other. The space between the two walls was wide enough for a passageway that ran all around the tower. Every few feet, a narrow vertical slit had been left between the stones of the outer wall for archers.

The inner wall enclosed a cavernous, circular room, dimly lit by flickering torches jammed into brackets along the wall. Above the flames, the ceiling was blackened with soot.

As Dominique was shoved past the two guards flanking the entrance between the outer passage and the inner prison room, a bitter, foul smell caught in the back of his throat and he retched. Breathing through his mouth, he took in the strange scene. Most of the cavernous space was completely empty. A heavy grate in the very centre of the room covered a large hole. All around the perimeter of the room, prisoners were crowded together, some sitting, some standing, but all close to the walls. At first Dominique wondered why they didn't spread out more.

"Over here, boy," Blaedusco said, pulling Dominique to an iron ring set about waist high in the stone wall.

"Git over. Make some room here," Blaedusco snapped to the two prisoners in front of him, their hands chained to a big iron ring. No wonder the prisoners weren't moving around. The best they could do was move a little to each side to make room for the latest tenant of the tower. Looking more closely, Dominique noticed that some of the rings were higher, set into the stone wall above the men's heads, and others, like his, were set lower. This arrangement seemed to allow the greatest number of prisoners to be packed into the crowded chamber.

Blaedusco fed the loose end of Dominique's chain through the ring and then fastened the last link of the chain to another link attached to the cuff with a heavy padlock. He clicked it shut and gave it a good yank to make sure it had snapped closed. Dominique jerked back on the chain and the unyielding cuffs around his wrists ground against his flesh.

"Enjoy your stay," Blaedusco said over his shoulder as he marched back across the stone floor and out into the passage.

"Hope you won't be bringing many more up," one of the door sentries said. "Where are we supposed to put them?"

Dominique couldn't hear Blaedusco's answer because his neighbour was coughing violently. Dominique turned his face away and pressed his cheek against the wall.

"You can't hide here," said a deep voice from his other side. "Nor can you do much of anything else, either."

Slowly, Dominique turned his head the other way, only to see a man so dirty and unkempt that Dominique tried to pull away. Much of this man's face was covered with a thick, black beard. A mass of hair twisted and tumbled over his neighbour's forehead, but beneath the tangled mess, Dominique could see a partially healed wound above his eyebrows. On his other side, the second prisoner's cough finally subsided.

"Don't mind old Alsace," the hairy one said. "He sounds much better than he did when he arrived here two months ago."

"Must be the fine food they serve us here," Alsace managed to say before another bout of coughing over-took him. Dominique swivelled, still held tightly by his chains, so he could better see the man with the cough. He was skinny and his head was crowned by a tumble of thick curls that might have been quite fair had they not been so matted and filthy. As Dominique watched, a fly crawled over the man's lips, across his cheek, and to the corner of his eye. Reflexively, Dominique's hand twitched against its tether, wanting to brush the fly away, but he couldn't quite reach.

"What's your name?" Alsace asked, wheezing.

"Dominique."

"What have you done?"

"Nothing!"

Alsace's lips pulled back in a grimace. "Aye. The same story we all tell when we arrive."

"No, really! I—"

"Hush, boy," the bearded man said, and Dominique turned back to him. "You'll soon get used to his ways. Teasing all the time. My name's Shasta Greccio. From Ranginoor."

Horrified, Dominique pulled back but immediately relaxed forward again to relieve the pressure on his wrists. King Sim of Ranginoor was a vicious fighter and the people of Ranginoor were said to be savage in their dealings with islanders.

"Don't worry. What can I do to you in here?"

Dominique blushed. His reaction had been foolish. It was stupid to make an enemy of a man with whom he shared an iron ring.

"I'm sorry—I've heard . . ."

"Stories. Yes, no doubt you have. Camprianos are good at telling stories."

"None better," agreed Alsace from Dominique's other side. Both men stood, each leaning with one shoulder against the wall so they faced each other.

"No, actually, I'm . . ." Dominique wondered whether or not he should say anything. It was so hard to know what the right thing was to say—if there *was* a right thing. If these men were being held captive because they were enemies of Emberto and the other Camprianos, it could only be a good thing that Dominique was not seen to be one of them.

But would the men also dislike the Estorians? His people, too, lived on the islands of the Drasil Archipelago—though they usually stayed clear of Campriano strongholds like Carnillo. The two nations of storytellers had separate ranges and generally stayed well away from each other. It seemed safe to assume these strangers would know at least that much.

"I'm an Estorian," he said after a long pause.

"An Estorian, hmm?" Alsace said. "I just assumed—your light hair, being tried here in the city—we don't see many Estorians this far east."

Shasta's eyes narrowed. "Interesting. Your people hear the Stories from Beyond, is that right?"

Dominique nodded, surprised that this savage from the mainland knew this about his culture.

"My grandfather spoke of visits from the Estorians many years ago, when they still travelled frequently in

Ranginoor. They don't come our way so often now. Not where I come from, anyway. Travel has become difficult since King Sim came to power."

"So you are not—"

"Not one of Sim's men, no." If Shasta had planned to say more he didn't have a chance because just then there was a strange movement among the prisoners. Chains grated against the iron rings, and feet scuffled in wisps of loose straw and reeds strewn across the floor.

"What—"

"Shh."

Dominique twisted away from the wall as far as his chains would allow, straining to see what was happening. A slight shifting of position had started with the men down at the end of the circle closest to the doorway leading to the outer passageway. As Dominique watched, each man in turn leaned sideways and pressed his lips to his neighbour's ear. All motion ceased as the second man stood rigid, not even breathing. Then they broke apart and the second man turned to his neighbour and repeated the ritual.

A message was making its way around the circle.

Dominique leaned forward again and waited, excited himself to know what the men were speaking of.

The message arrived first at Alsace, who stood while he received it. Then Dominique leaned over, ready to listen.

But Alsace did not whisper the message in Dominique's ear. "Get down," he said.

"What? Why?"

On either side of him, Shasta and Alsace shifted uncomfortably until Shasta said, "We know nothing of you. Do as I say, boy. Drop down as far as you can."

As Shasta's meaning became clear, Dominique felt the prickle of tears. The men did not trust him. He lowered himself so he was squatting below the ring while the two men brought their heads together above him. He strained to hear the message, but the only word he thought he made out was *casket*.

When the message had been transferred, Shasta turned to the man on his left. Because there was a gap between rings, both men leaned sideways, but even so, Shasta had to whisper a little louder and Dominique thought he heard *casket of leaves* and *two nights left*. Was something going to happen in two nights? Or did they mean two knights left and went somewhere? Where did they go?

The scraps of message meant nothing to Dominique. If they were speaking in some kind of code, it would hardly have mattered if he'd been included.

Shasta nudged Dominique's ankle with a bare foot. "You can stand again," he whispered. "Do not feel hurt. We must be careful—you understand."

Dominique understood well enough. Even here among these captives, these outcasts, he did not belong. They did not trust him.

Eventually the message was passed along from prisoner to prisoner until it reached the door once again. Then a weary silence descended on the prisoners as they waited for the day to pass.

CHAPTER
17

MISERY

Deep in the heart of the mountain a secret stream bubbled up from deep within a fissure. Guarded by fourteen dragons, this water, source of all things evil and all things good, tumbled down the mountain until it reached the pond where Delgado stopped to drink.

—Traditional Estorian tale

It wasn't easy to tell where the sun was. The only light that came in from outside was filtered through the single doorway to the outer passage, and the only light that entered the outer passage came through the arrow slits. Even in the middle of the day, the interior room where the prisoners stood chained to the wall was dim and relied more on the flickering torches than on sunlight.

After what felt like ages and ages since he had been brought to the tower, Dominique realized that the small amount of light that did filter in was fading. The shadows along the base of the wall grew blacker, and eventually the room was nearly dark save for the pools of light cast by two torches on opposite sides of the room.

Dominique moved his tongue back and forth inside

his mouth, trying to work up a little saliva. But his tongue was dry and his spittle so thick and sticky he choked as he tried to swallow. If he wasn't careful when he coughed, he fell forward so all his weight crushed his wrists against the iron cuffs.

Shasta made him stand, squat, move his arms and legs, and wiggle his fingers so he didn't get so stiff he wouldn't be able to move. Even so, Dominique's arms, shoulders, back, and legs soon ached from the uncomfortable positions he was forced to assume. Every time he shifted, he bumped into Shasta and Alsace, often triggering another coughing fit, so he tried to last as long as possible before moving.

Though his chains were long enough to allow him to sit and stand, Dominique realized that those prisoners unfortunate enough to be fastened to the higher rings were in really miserable shape. They could only stand, and their fingers were swollen and discoloured above their unyielding cuffs.

Several times Dominique thought of Navina. He closed his eyes and willed a vision to come that would give him some idea of her whereabouts, but nothing happened. Dominique soon found that he couldn't think of anything else, not his bird, not the plight of the other prisoners, because always his parched throat and stabbing hunger pangs pushed all other thoughts and sensations away. After a particularly loud rumble, he yanked back against the iron ring as if he might pull it from the wall.

"Your belly will get used to it," Shasta remarked. "Make sure you drink lots when you get the chance later."

Dominique tried again to distract himself by imagining he was back beside his mother's cooking fire. He could practically taste the spicy chibbies she made from chen-wa big beans at the winter camps each year. And, oh, how he would enjoy a bowl of stewed bendahl.

After a time, a new misery began to torment him. It seemed horribly unfair: he hadn't had anything to drink for so long! Nonetheless, the pressure in his bladder was unmistakable, and here he couldn't even use a straw-filled corner.

Dominique had noticed that every so often one of the men would say "Urina vascellum." Then, from somewhere around the circle, a grating sound would start as a wooden bucket was pushed carefully across the stone floor. Being careful not to tip it over, the men nudged this bucket from foot to foot and hand to hand until it reached the man who had asked for it.

Dominique could not imagine standing over the stinking bucket as the others did. Somehow he managed to hang on until after the sun had set and the prison tower was nearly dark. It was only then that he forced himself to say "Urina vascellum" and heard the bucket begin its journey around the circle toward his feet. At least, he thought with some small amount of relief, it was fairly dark. Though he expected a flood, only a dribble splashed beneath him. He held his breath and wrinkled up his nose until he was done.

It was then, as he pushed the bucket aside, careful not to tip it over, that he started to cry, a strange, dry crying without tears. As he sobbed with his forehead pressed against the unforgiving wall, Shasta and Alsace shifted sideways so their bodies pressed against his, supporting him as best they could.

"The first night is the worst," Shasta said.

"Breathe deep, boy," Alsace added. "It won't be long now before they bring our supper. You won't want to miss that."

Though Dominique nodded, he really didn't care whether he ever ate or drank again. He slumped against the wall, the weight of his slight body tugging at the iron cuffs, and wished he were dead.

BREAD AND SOUP

King Pratori raised his staff and declared the city was his. The first story he told his grandson, Prince Pratorino, was that of the great day when his palace colours fluttered above the grand courtyard and his guards marched unimpeded through the streets.

—Campriano palace story

Clang-clang-clang! A staff hammering against a brass bell announced the arrival of food. Those who had drifted into a state of uneasy sleep jerked awake. Dominique drew in a long, shuddering breath and strained to see what the guards had brought. One carried a stack of bowls, two had a cauldron suspended between them from a sturdy wooden pole, and another carried two buckets of water. A fifth guard dropped a basket on the floor and then backed up toward the door and drew his sword.

The guards with the bowls and cauldron set down their loads and then approached the prisoners. With practised movements they unlocked the prisoners' padlocks and the men slowly pulled free of the walls. With groans and cries they moved their fingers and rubbed their wrists, sliding the iron cuffs up and down a little to get at the skin beneath. Many squatted or sat, and a few others immediately lay on the floor, moaning and raising their feet. Those chained to the high rings were in the worst shape. They seemed to have lost the use of their arms altogether and relied on other prisoners to help them.

When Dominique's turn came, he sank to his knees a little way from Alsace and Shasta and gently rubbed at his chafed wrists. The length of chain hung from one wrist, swinging with every movement. He wished he still had some of the leranons' healing potion to sprinkle on his bruised skin. He realized with a start that Amana would have found the vial of potion Kyrie had given him at the leranon cave.

"Here," Shasta said, crouching beside him. He held a bowl of water to Dominique's lips. Dominique's hands felt stiff and awkward as he tipped the bowl and guzzled the water.

"Careful. Don't spill."

Dominique kept drinking until Shasta pulled the bowl away. "Slowly, boy," he said. "You'll make yourself ill. Have some soup and a bit of bread and then drink some more after that."

Shasta nudged Dominique with an elbow and nodded at the stack of bowls being offered to him by another prisoner. He might not have been willing to share secrets, but he seemed happy enough to show Dominique how to take care of himself. Dominique realized then that the guards, who had finished unlocking all the prisoners, had retreated back to the hallway where they were joking and laughing together.

"Let the animals eat!" one said, and another answered with a guttural growl. This brought a fresh round of guffaws.

Dominique took a soup bowl and crawled forward with Shasta and Alsace as they approached the big cauldron.

"Don't the guards watch us?"

Shasta shook his head and leaned in close. "Not all of Emberto's guards are so happy with what has been happening, though even the most sympathetic pretend for the sake of appearances. And they do leave us alone for a short while during our evening meal."

"They don't think we can get up to much trouble," Alsace added with a wink.

The men waited patiently in the line. As each reached the front he measured out his portion of thin soup. It smelled like warm water, but Dominique's stomach growled with anticipation as he slopped a ladleful into his bowl.

"Lovely place, isn't it?" A familiar voice broke into Dominique's thoughts and he nearly dropped his meagre dinner.

"Sir Riley!"

The plump man held a half-full bowl in one hand and patted his ample stomach with the other. "This will hardly fill me," he said with a wink.

Shasta glanced back over his shoulder as he carried his bowl away.

Riley's hand fluttered away from his stomach and he wiggled his pudgy fingers beside Dominique's ear. "You still have your little friend?"

"I . . . yes . . . yes, she's here in the city with me." Dominique had no desire to chat with Riley about his bird. "Why . . ." Dominique couldn't stop himself from pressing on. "Why did you take—"

"Ah, yes. Why did I take the quickest route to Carnillo when I knew I'd find trouble here?"

"No! That's not what—"

"Never mind," Riley said. "We're all in the same boat

now, criminals and innocents alike."

Dominique wondered which camp Riley considered his own.

"Best you eat your gruel, boy."

Dominique nodded and moved away, back to where Alsace and Shasta sat beneath their shared ring in the wall. Riley. How unfair that Dominique should be locked in this place with the same man who had first won his trust and then robbed him blind.

"You know Riley?" Alsace asked Dominique.

"Unfortunately, yes." Then, seeing Alsace smile, Dominique worried he had offended the old man.

"You remind me of my son," Alsace said, slurping a mouthful of soup and smacking his lips. "So indignant."

"I have a good reason!"

"There," Shasta said, "indignant again!"

The two men chuckled, and Alsace nearly spat out a mouthful of soup when he started to cough.

Dominique's ears burned. "Do you know him?"

"Riley?" Shasta asked. "Everyone knows Riley."

"They do?"

"You never know where the old rascal will turn up. He has spent his whole life travelling up and down the archipelago and over to the mainland, working for anyone who will pay him."

"Almost anyone," Alsace said. "I don't believe he's ever worked for our good friend Emberto."

"True enough."

They watched Riley slapping another prisoner on the back. "You know, Riley has always reminded me of a slither fruit," Shasta said.

"Plump, you mean?" Alsace said.

"Well, that, too. What I meant was, slippery on the outside but sweet on the inside."

"Hah!" Alsace laughed and immediately started coughing again.

Shasta slapped the old man on the back. "Easy, my friend. Eat up."

Alsace wiped his teary eyes with the back of his hand and took another sip of soup. On the other side of the room, Riley was talking and joking with several of the other prisoners. One gave him a hearty slap on the back.

Dominique gritted his teeth. Riley's behaviour by the River Epilobium made no sense. What had he been thinking by first helping Dominique and then robbing him?

The first men to finish eating returned their bowls and then began to work. One man, who was normally chained close to the door, carried the urina bucket to the hole in the centre of the room and tipped it out. Another carried the basket forward and drew from it several loaves of bread. He divided the bread up so each prisoner received an equal chunk. A third prisoner reached into the bottom of the basket and pulled out fresh reeds, which he sprinkled over the floor. For a moment, scents of the marsh, the outdoors, and fresh breezes wafted through the room, temporarily masking the other, less pleasant odours of unwashed bodies and excrement.

"Thank you," Dominique said as he took a crust of bread when it was offered to him.

Two other men approached the basket and, keeping an eye on the doorway, reached inside. One man shifted his body to shield the other from view as he pulled something from the bottom of the basket and, so quickly Dominique wasn't even sure he'd seen properly, slipped whatever it was under his shirt.

Without speaking or looking at each other, the two men retreated to their places and began to gnaw on their rations of bread.

Still chewing, Dominique started to get up. What was hidden in the bottom of the basket?

"Never mind," Shasta said, his hand firm on Dominique's arm. He pulled Dominique down to sit beside him as another pair of men approached the basket. "You don't need to—" Shasta tried to distract Dominique by heaving himself to his feet and standing between him and whatever it was the men were doing. He wasn't quick enough, though. Dominique caught a glimpse of the tail end of a rope disappearing under a baggy tunic.

Rope? Why had pieces of rope been hidden in a basket of reeds? *Basket of reeds*—not casket of leaves! Dominique nearly choked on his bread when he realized that somehow someone had got a message to the prisoners about the secret delivery. He turned to ask Alsace about it, but he was hunched over, licking out his bowl, his tongue washing over its already spotless surface. Dominique quickly looked away, uncomfortable watching a man behave that way—like a dog.

Shasta crouched beside him and Dominique watched as the now empty basket was tipped upside down so the last few rushes fell to the floor. Those who had found the ropes said nothing, but moved back to their places around the perimeter of the room. There they sat, their backs against the wall, dipping their bread into the tasteless soup.

"Why did—" Dominique started to ask Shasta.

"Never mind. Just eat."

Dominique could see he wasn't going to have his questions answered. He gobbled what was left of his meal and then looked longingly toward the cauldron.

"There's no more. Don't trouble yourself thinking you might have another portion." Alsace had put aside his bowl and now tore at his chunk of bread. He ate slowly, chewing each mouthful for a very long time. Dominique tore his eyes away. It was rude to stare, no matter how hungry he still felt.

Outside the door, the guards were still talking out in the corridor.

"More trials in the morning," one said. "Though where they'll put them I have no idea. We have too many in here already."

"Why he keeps them alive is beyond me," answered another.

"Lord Emberto must have his reasons."

"More like he's been caught unprepared. He should have known the old man wouldn't live forever. And who hasn't worried about an invasion?"

"Emberto should have hired better spies. He's the one who has been warning us of an attack for ages. He should have found out more about those opposing him."

"Easy for you to say. Would you travel to Ranginoor to spy for Emberto? King Sim would lop off your head faster than—"

"Still—what are we to do with all these prisoners? It's costing a fortune to feed them. Thieves and murderers are overflowing the dungeons and there are hundreds more spies that we couldn't jam in here who are being held over where they used to keep the leranons."

"I know—my brother is a guard there. He said they have twenty or thirty to a pen."

"They deserve no better. We're all in danger if we don't get rid of every last one."

"Not tonight—this lot won't give us any trouble. We've got a game of chillotti to finish. Leave them be for now. We'll chain them up when we're done."

There was no argument from the other guards. The sound of their heavy boots receded down the passageway and Dominique could no longer make out what they were saying.

"They do it every night—have a game or two of chillotti before they chain us up again," Shasta said.

"Thanks to those who are sympathetic to—to us?"

Shasta nodded and lay down on his back, his head resting on a little pile of fresh reeds.

"Why don't we just—" Dominique nodded towards the door.

"No point. The guardroom is at the head of the stairs. We'd never get past them. Besides that, there are guards stationed throughout the tower. Even if we could get onto the stairs, we'd never get through the heavy door at the bottom or past old Blaedusco at the entrance to the passage."

Dominique sighed and put his empty bowl down on the stone floor with a hollow clatter.

Alsace peered at Dominique from beneath a pair of scraggly eyebrows. These pushed together as the man frowned, and his eyes narrowed as if he were assessing the boy before him.

"Not to worry, though—there is a plan in the works."

"Don't give him false hope," Shasta said.

"What other kind is there, in a place like this?" Alsace answered.

Dominique looked at Alsace, but the bony man, whose skin was so thin Dominique thought he could see his breath and blood moving beneath it, said nothing more. Instead, Alsace patted the reeds beside him and said, "Lie down, boy. It will be your only chance to rest properly before tomorrow night. Be thankful that we are given even this short time to rest and stretch. No doubt Emberto would be displeased if he found out we enjoy this much freedom each evening."

Dominique obediently lay down and closed his eyes. Freedom?

He shifted uncomfortably on the hard floor. How quickly he had changed. Only a few days ago he would have found the thought of lying on a filthy floor in a prison filled with sick and filthy men utterly horrifying. Now, these few moments spent stretched out felt deliciously luxurious.

Dominique thought of his mother, his sisters, the

other boys of his clan. Perhaps he could not hear the Stories from Beyond, but he would have some interesting tales to tell if he ever he saw his people again.

CHAPTER

19

SECRETS

The serpent twisted this way and that, desperate to be free.
"Relax," the fisher said, and the serpent slipped through the
net unharmed.

—Traditional Estorian tale

Though Dominique closed his eyes, he did not rest at all. He was amazed to hear some men actually snoring, and many others breathing the deep, regular breath of sleep. Dominique concentrated on relaxing his stiff muscles. He stretched his legs and reached above him with his arms, wincing as the pain in his shoulders intensified. How long would he have to stay in the tower? How would he even survive the first night? There was still no sound of the guards coming back, though every so often a raucous round of laughter drifted into the cavernous prisoners' chamber.

Too soon, heavy boots stomped along the corridor and into the prisoners' room. As Dominique rose to his feet, guards nudged and kicked the men to either side of him, forcing them to stand and be chained to the walls. When the last man had been fastened back into position, one of the soldiers snuffed out the last two flaming torches and darkness flooded the tower.

In the full darkness the clinking chains sounded even louder. Men sighed and shifted as they tried to find positions slightly less uncomfortable. After a heavy door thudded shut somewhere along the passageway, the whispers began. They passed over Dominique's head as plans travelled from man to man around the perimeter of the room.

Dominique strained to hear, but once again Alsace and Shasta excluded him, preferring instead to contort themselves so they whispered over his head. He could make out only a few words, and it was hard to understand what the series of messages meant.

"Someone light . . ."

". . . strong . . ."

". . . enough rope . . ."

". . . tomorrow . . ."

When the whispered conversation had circled the chamber twice, Shasta spoke aloud, his voice echoing in the arched dome overhead. "How shall we choose, then?" he asked.

This question prompted much murmuring and discussion.

"How about you, Alsace? You are skinny as a stick. You'd fit."

"But then what? I'm too ill. Those who go must be fit and strong."

"What about Toranosco?" someone asked.

"I'd agree with that," another answered.

"Aye, he's waited long enough to see his sweetheart."

"Haven't we all!" That comment drew soft chuckles from several of the men.

"Sure enough. Sure enough," Shasta said. "But Toranosco's sweetheart has done more than most."

Nobody disagreed with that statement.

"Thank you, sirs." Dominique assumed the deep voice belonged to the man they called Toranosco.

"Next time you see her, you give the lass a proper kiss, mind," Riley said.

Someone let out a low whistle and Toranosco cleared his throat. "May I suggest someone who might go with me?" he asked. "What about young Sol? He is small, strong—"

This name was discussed at length. Sol didn't sound much older than Dominique, and it seemed he had only a few supporters. The debate progressed in loud whispers.

"You must remember what kind of people are needed on the outside," Alsace said. "Those with ties to outside groups. Those with knowledge of Emberto's court. Those with special powers. Those who are resourceful, willing to work alone, if necessary; those who—" The long speech proved too much for Alsace, who succumbed to a fit of coughing that left him wheezing and gasping beside Dominique.

"Hermano?" another voice suggested from the dark.

"One of Emberto's men? I think not!"

"But a *former* guard," Toranosco pointed out. "Tell us what you know that might be helpful, Hermano."

Another voice answered in a loud whisper from somewhere over by the door to the outer hallway. It wasn't easy to hear, and it seemed to Dominique that every man was holding his breath, straining to keep still so the chains wouldn't clink.

"Well, Toranosco is right—I am no longer one of Emberto's men or I would not be living in these fine accommodations."

A few of the men chuckled softly, but another said, "How do we know he's not a spy for Emberto?"

"Have you seen his back?" Alsace asked.

Now Dominique knew which man was Hermano. He

was chained about two rings away from the door. His back was a mess. His shirt had been shredded by, Dominique guessed, a severe whipping, and the swollen lacerations were still visible beneath the tattered strips of cloth.

"Speak," Toranosco said, and again Hermano answered as loudly as he could at a whisper.

"I know how Emberto organizes his patrols—their routes and schedules. I know locations of secret entrances to the palace, and which other guards and sentries are . . . are sympathetic. Who do you think helped arrange this sympathetic shift each evening? The guards don't hold the game of chillotti in such high esteem they would risk losing their jobs to play. We can't be sure how long this arrangement will last now that I am inside here instead of organizing out there." He sighed before adding, "My back is healing well. I am strong and well versed in hand-to-hand combat."

"He certainly is strong," another voice said. "I can vouch for that. He's the one who arrested me."

"My apologies for that, Tremulo," Hermano said. "You were my last capture before I, myself, was arrested. But, yes, if I am forced to, I can defend myself well with sword, knife, and staff."

Beside Dominique, Alsace said, very quietly, "There has been too much fighting already."

Finally the men decided Hermano had enough to offer that he, too, would be allowed to join the escape attempt.

"Very good," Toranosco said. "Now, we want a third."

Several more names were put forward and each was quickly dismissed. One prisoner was deemed unsuitable because though he was young, strong, and enthusiastic about challenging Emberto's rule, several of the men noted he was lazy when it came to doing the few chores that needed to be completed each evening. Several candidates were rejected because they were chained to high rings or had been incarcerated for too long and wouldn't be strong enough. Another name was put forward, but when it turned out he had once been convicted of robbing a market vendor, several of the prisoners were critical.

"We can't help a petty thief escape!"

"He's done his time. This time he was arrested, like all of us, for crimes against Emberto."

"Still—those on the outside must be willing to help those who remain locked in the tower," Toranosco said. "You know Malia and I have been working hard to help the rebels—both those within the city walls and those on the outside who are working for our cause. Of course, I know that everyone in here has attempted some kind of blow against Emberto, but I find it hard to believe that a petty thief would put the Truth before the protection of his own skin."

"I concur," Shasta's deep voice said, and immediately many voices agreed. "Any other suggestions?"

"May I be so bold as to offer a name?"

Dominique straightened. In the dark, in the echoing chamber, it was hard to tell exactly where the voice was coming from. But the voice itself was familiar. Riley. Thief. Liar. Friend. Dominique steeled himself. He would not be so easily fooled by Riley's easygoing manner this time.

"Sir Riley is my name. Knight of the House of Ronwyn, friend of the Lord of Grenille." This admission elicited another flurry of whispers. "As you all know, there is no love lost between Lord Ronwyn and Emberto. And everyone knows how the Lord of Grenille feels about the presumptuous, wild-eyed man."

In the darkness beside him, Dominique felt movement as Shasta nodded.

"On my journey here, I chanced to meet a traveller

who claimed to know Boris Elnedo."

Dominique recoiled in surprise and yanked against his restraints. Was Riley talking about him? Why? Even less explicable was the fact that the mention of his father's name met with excited exclamations.

"Elnedo, the Speaker of Truth?" Alsace asked.

Another man answered. "The traitor, more like. Speaker of Lies. I'd cheerfully wring his neck if I knew where he was."

Dominique could not move. Apparently many of the men knew who his father was. Although this was precisely what he had hoped for—to find news of his father in Carnillo—somehow his lips would not move. He could not speak the questions racing about in his mind, for even as he felt a mounting excitement, he also felt a swell of anxiety.

"No need to wring the man's neck," another man grumbled. "Far as I know, the deceitful son of a boar is dead. Killed in an ambush in the Festerworlds."

Dominique gasped. *Dead?* In the Festerworlds? Why would his father have been in the Festerworlds? The wasteland between Ranginoor and South Krokoska was home to strange magical beasts and savage warrior tribes without stories. That's what all the Estorian tales said. No man travelled to the Festerworlds and returned to speak of his adventures.

Dominique was not the only one to question this piece of information. Alsace said, "Nonsense. That is another story made up by Emberto and his cronies. Boris Elnedo, if he has returned to the Festerworlds, would be protected there."

Several men agreed with this statement, and one said, "By the power of Unity he would be protected in the land of Truth."

"Truth?" Shasta laughed. "Truth? You think there is truth to any of this? Don't be so naive. Nobody can overcome the forces at work in the Festerworlds. And it is not only Emberto's information. King Krokoska's men will tell you the same thing."

"And you believe anything Krokoska's men would say of the Festerworlds?" Another voice challenged Shasta from the darkness. "Only a fool would not know that Krokoska has vested interests in the region."

"But that doesn't change the fact that there is a strange power at work in the land." Shasta was getting excited. He was no longer even trying to keep his voice down.

Another voice retorted, "And you know this how? You have been there yourself to see?"

Shasta did not answer. Instead he made a noise deep in his throat—a growl or a sneer, Dominique wasn't sure.

Dominique swayed but was caught by his tethers. He felt feverish, then chilled, confused by the strange things the men were saying. He didn't understand either side of the argument that was making the men so angry. He wanted to call out, to speak in defence of his father, though he had no idea what crime he might have committed. A virtual stranger to his own son, perhaps he *was* some sort of traitor. How would Dominique know?

Sobs rose from deep inside. Traitor or not, his father could not be dead! Not after Dominique had come so far. This simply could not be. Dominique pressed his forehead against the wall between his chains so hard his skin felt as if it were tearing. Why couldn't he speak the Stories of Truth from Beyond? If he could only hear the Truth from Beyond he would understand what was happening because those Stories never lied: they spoke only of what had really happened or what would surely come to pass.

But all Dominique heard was the men arguing and the pounding silence between his ears. He was overwhelmed by a longing for his own people, for the certainty in the men's Stories. Among the Estorian people, the men spoke only the Truth. There were no questions like those the men in the prison were asking. He held his breath and vowed not to breathe again until an answer had come to him, until some Story had appeared fully formed in his mind that would explain everything, show him what to do. He squeezed his lips together and his eyes shut and refused to breathe. Crouching in the dark, he waited until his heart started to thud and every fibre of his being screamed at him to open his mouth and suck in a lungful of air. He held his breath until his cheeks bulged and his eyes watered and a deep panic overwhelmed him. His breath burst from him and he dragged air inside with great, ragged gulps.

CHAPTER
20

DECISIONS

Drums called the leader forth, whips drove the followers.
—Campriano story

"Gentlemen, please—" Riley interrupted the heated discussion.

"Let Riley speak," Toranosco said, and the others fell quiet. "You wanted to put a name forward. Does this man have any strengths we should consider? Riley, you said he knew Elnedo, but this alone is not enough reason to send him out with us."

Dominique's throat tightened. He could not imagine what Riley might say that would make the men think Dominique was a good candidate to join the group of escapees.

"I speak of a boy with many strengths. He travelled alone from west Tanga to the Cave of Departure in the Misty Mountains."

"A boy? He crossed the River Epilobium?"

"Aye. Alone."

"Are you saying he has certain powers?" Alsace asked.

"Aye. Or he would never have made it past the old river serpent, Lagrace."

This statement was met with silence from the other men and horror from Dominique. Why did Riley have to lie all the time? Dominique had no such powers!

"Good sirs, while it is true that many of us, myself included, have travelled afar, this boy—and, yes, Dominique is but a boy—this boy is special."

"Special how?" Toranosco said. "Is he a good fighter?"

Riley coughed. "Not exactly."

"Has he wealth behind him?"

"Ahh . . . no."

"Political connections?"

"Not that I know of."

The edge of frustration was sharp in Toranosco's voice. "Well, then—what makes this boy so special? We do not have time to waste debating—"

"I tested this boy," Riley interrupted. "Took his knife and some other things—and he survived!"

Tested him? Stealing from him was a test? Dominique was about to challenge this crazy idea when Shasta spoke.

"Only the intrepid Sir Riley could imagine that stealing from a smallish boy would be a good test of anything."

"And how well do you think you would manage to travel unarmed, without food, without knowledge of the land, in that dreadful place east of the Epilobium?" Riley sounded most offended. "That's not all. This boy is not travelling alone. He travels with a magical kasyapa bird."

In the profound silence that followed this revelation Dominique slumped against his wrist irons. What was Riley doing? How would mentioning Navina help anything? She could be anywhere. He might never see her again. A small sob caught in his throat and he wiped his nose against his arm.

"A kasyapa bird? But nobody has a kasyapa bird!" It sounded like Hermano, though he was no longer whispering.

"Riley is not the only one who says this." The voice was slow, deep. "I was tried right after the boy. A girl spoke on his behalf, said he had a kasyapa bird, though she couldn't say where it was."

"A Bird of Wisdom?" Alsace asked, his voice low and warm with wonder.

In the dark, Dominique nodded miserably.

"Who is this boy? Dominique?"

"Speak up, lad," Riley said.

Dominque's throat tightened but he managed to say, "I'm here." His voice sounded weak. Pathetic. He coughed and tried again. "I'm here between Alsace and Shasta."

In the dark, men murmured and shifted. Dominique heard whispers.

"That little runt?"

". . . no more than a child . . ."

". . . don't believe . . ."

"Dominique," Riley said. "Tell us where the bird is now."

"I'm not sure," Dominique finally managed to spit out. "She came to me in the holding cell but flew away before the guards came. I think she's still in the city but she hasn't . . ." He paused, unsure whether or not to mention the strange visions she had been sharing with him.

"She didn't follow me here."

"An intelligent bird, apparently," Alsace said, and a few men chuckled.

"So Emberto knows about the bird?" Toranosco asked.

"I . . . I don't know if he believed the story. I don't think so."

"Emberto seemed to think the young lady suffered from an imagination too vivid for her own good," the deep voice said.

"A kasyapa?" Toranosco said, still not sounding completely convinced.

"Aye. One and the same," Riley said. "I saw it with my own eyes. And don't we all know that a kasyapa chooses only an extraordinary individual as a companion?"

"That's only a story," Hermano said.

"How can you be so sure?" Alsace countered. "It is said that a kasyapa chooses to help a leader just once in seven generations. Just because none of us can remember the last time a kasyapa came does not mean it has not happened before, nor that it could not happen again."

Dominique now felt quite nauseous. What were they talking about? Navina had been an orphan, that was all. Anyone might have found and cared for her.

"What did you say your whole name was?" Shasta asked.

"Dominique . . ." He hesitated before adding, "Bertolescu." He waited for Riley to correct him, but the knight, for a change, held his tongue.

"Is that not the name of an Estorian clan leader?" Shasta asked.

Dominique nodded and then realized that nobody could see him in the dark. "Yes, sir. My father's name is Roman Bertolescu."

"Doesn't Boris Elnedo belong to the Bertolescu clan?" Shasta asked. "Is that how you know him?"

Dominique swallowed hard and thought a moment before he spoke, battling the turmoil roiling about in his stomach. He wished now he had not guzzled down the terrible soup so quickly. He felt the web of lies he had told tightening around him. Yet for some odd reason that he didn't really understand, he felt that he could not let Riley down. The knight seemed to be trying to help him, perhaps to make amends for his earlier betrayal. Whatever the reason, Dominique knew he had to try to make the men believe him. So he told another lie. "I only knew Elnedo from stories." Lie. "He left the clan before I was born." Lie. "There was some trouble, I believe." Half-lie. "But I never met him." Lie. "And . . . my mother would not speak of him." Half-lie.

Dominique pressed his cheek to the stone wall. The words were out of his mouth now. He could not draw them back.

"You see? Elnedo was not a true Estorian either! What kind of man would abandon his people?"

"Someone like Boris Elnedo belongs in the Festerworlds."

"Son of a boar."

Each derogatory comment about his father bit into Dominique as if he were being lashed. What had his father done to deserve such a terrible reputation? And yet, it seemed the men did not know many more details than he did. Nobody stated a particular crime, nor could they agree on whether he lived or was dead. Those who believed the latter couldn't say exactly where or when his father had died, though there were lots of theories.

The ideas ranged from a hideous battle with a mountain lizard in which his father had come out the loser, to the position held by one or two men that Boris Elnedo had sailed west, not east, and was now in exile somewhere in Great Andalutania. At least being in exile would mean he was alive.

A few spoke of Boris Elnedo in reverential tones, convinced he was very much alive and waiting to lead a triumphant army against evil forces. Some said that he had run away to a fortified island in the Sea of Perfidium.

Of all the stories, Dominique could not decide which

was the worst—that his father was a dead traitor, or that he had fled like some coward.

When the discussion died down a bit, Riley spoke again. "The boy is tough, a good traveller, and he understands the Estorian mind. He has a connection with the kasyapa, and his powers are stronger than even he knows. We would be fools to ignore the signs: we all know the old story. He paused for a moment before adding, "He is also small enough to fit through the opening."

This comment brought about another intense round of discussion that became so loud Dominique was horrified when a torch was thrust into the chamber. He squinted, his eyes temporarily blinded by the sudden glare.

"Quiet in here!" A guard raised the torch and shouted back out into the hallway. "Floggers, come!"

A deathly silence fell upon the prisoners. Heavy footsteps pounded along the passageway and two guards burst into the prisoners' chamber. Each trailed a long whip. Without waiting for additional instructions, they worked their way around the room, lashing each man soundly once or twice before moving on. The lashes landed on the backs and shoulders of the tethered men. They jostled and swayed, cowering against the walls as if they might somehow escape the beating.

The guards The bite of the whip tore into Dominique's shoulders and he cried out. A second blow fell and then it was over. Beside him, Alsace sagged as the whip cracked across his back. He drew in a sharp breath and this started him coughing again.

"Shut up, you!"

Alsace tried to hold his breath, but his shoulders jumped and the cough escaped. The guard seemed to take offence at this insolence and rained several hard blows upon the old man's back before moving on.

As suddenly as they had arrived, the guards left. Once again the darkness was complete.

"Alsace? Are you all right?" Dominique scarcely dared whisper his question lest the guards came back.

"Aye. I shall live. I have suffered worse treatment than at the hands of these beasts." Painfully, he turned his head toward Dominique. "If my son were to find himself in such a hideous place as this, I hope some kind soul might offer some help." Defiantly, he said, "I vote that the boy shall go."

This statement was picked up and echoed by Shasta, who passed it on to his left. The message made it all the way around the circle of prisoners until, eventually, it arrived back at Alsace.

"It has been decided. Dominique, you shall be the third man. Tomorrow at the mealtime we will have enough rope, and you and the others will escape."

"Thank you!"

Dominique's initial excitement quickly turned to worry. Even if they did get out, how would he be able to help those still locked in the tower? Should he admit he didn't have any special powers? What if Navina had been captured or had flown away? Would they still choose him then?

"Enough," Shasta said. "Speak no more of this now. Dominique need not know more until the time comes to leave."

"You are right," Alsace said with a weary sigh. "I cannot imagine the boy would be able to resist should Emberto summon him and—"

"Indeed," Shasta said quietly. "Best for all of us to rest."

The chamber fell silent. With the decision made about the escapees, it seemed nobody wished to risk drawing the guards' attention again.

But rest? Impossible, Dominique thought. Sitting, he

leaned his head back against the wall and closed his eyes. Gingerly he allowed himself to lean against Shasta, who leaned back against him. By propping his elbows on his knees, Dominique eased the pressure on his wrists.

Escape? Dominique longed to ask questions, find out what was going to happen, what he was supposed to do, but he was too exhausted to try to imagine what the men had planned. He felt Alsace slump against his other side and then, wedged between the two prisoners, Dominique drifted off into an uneasy sleep.

21

DREAMS

*With infinite patience, Villo started at one end of the
rope and began to untie the knots.*

—Estorian story

Clear, cool water trickled over Dominique's feet. On the
other side of a stream, his mother gathered peska root,
singing as she stooped to dig up the young plants.
Dominique tried to wave at her, but his arm would not
move. It was stuck in the air above him. He looked up
to see why it would not move and began to scream—a
giant, black incubus had hold of his wrist in its curling
claws.

"Dominique?"

For a moment, Dominique was confused. Why was
Alsace by the stream?

"Dominique—you are having a bad dream. Wake
up."

Opening his eyes, Dominique could see only stone.
He groaned. The pain in his shoulders was hideous, as if
his arms had separated from the rest of his body during
the night. He had tipped sideways while he slept and

could no longer feel his arms. He knew he was awake, but his feet were still in the water, he could feel the trickle of—

Dominique looked down and shrieked. Rats scurried over his toes, searching for crumbs the men might have dropped. He fumbled to pull himself up, kicking a rat aside as its long, naked tail slipped over the top of his foot.

"Shhh . . . you won't be rid of them that way." Alsace coughed and sagged against the wall. The rats continued on their way, oblivious to the prisoners slowly beginning to awaken.

"Ignoring them is best—try not to step on them. You see Donello at the end?"

Dominique leaned back away from the wall as far as his arms would allow. An older man who was chained to one of the higher rings stood on one foot, his head down, hair hanging over his face. The other foot was swollen and discoloured. Dark liquid had pooled on the flagstone beneath him. On its way past, a rat stopped to lick at the sticky puddle. It rose on its back legs, whiskers quivering, and nibbled at the injured foot. Donello didn't even move.

"He won't be with us for much longer. He wasn't able to eat last night and the fever has taken hold."

As Dominique watched, the miserable prisoner jerked against his chains as someone might when first falling asleep. He groaned and muttered something about a deep well and then slumped lower, his fingers contorted above the iron cuffs.

Sickened, Dominique turned away and moved his feet back, out of the path of the rats.

In the black time the rats came
Calling out the dead man's name.

Dawn brought dim, filtered light back to the prisoners' hall. As the men stirred and tried to stretch, they heard loud shouts and curses echoing down the outer passage. The prisoners twisted and turned to see who was coming.

A brawny man with broad shoulders and powerful legs kicked and struggled as four guards, one assigned to each limb, dragged him into the tower room.

"I haven't done nothing, you no-good swamp-suckers."

One of the guards grunted as the prisoner landed a kick in the man's stomach. Immediately, the others tightened their hold and pushed him across the chamber, where he was roughly chained to the iron ring beside the feverish Donello. Donello swung to the side as the guards pushed him out of the way, and a moment later the new prisoner found himself immobilized.

All morning the guards came and went, but they didn't bring food or water. Instead they brought more prisoners, one or two at a time. Some swore and argued, others shuffled in, confused and defeated, their shoulders rounded, eyes downcast. All were boys and men and they ranged in age from as young as Dominique to one ancient farmer with a long, white beard. He moved so slowly, two guards had to carry him in, easily supporting his bony frame between the two of them.

"When will they bring more food?" Dominique finally asked.

Shasta tipped his head to the side as if surprised that Dominique hadn't yet understood the routine. "Tonight."

"Tonight? Like last night? The soup and bread? Not even water?" Dominique's thirst intensified with the thought. *Once a day?*

And what a long day it was. The only interruption to the endless, aching wait was the arrival of new prisoners. With guards coming and going and two sentries taking up their posts at the doorway at dawn, the day was quiet. Only occasional whispers broke the silence, and those comments were generally limited to requests for the bucket or general complaints of discomfort.

The trickle of prisoners slowed and finally stopped in what Dominique guessed was the early afternoon. That left a very long wait until evening fell and the guards reappeared with the bread basket, bowls, and soup cauldron.

Though the number of prisoners had grown by nearly twenty, the amount of soup in the cauldron and the number of loaves of bread remained the same. All afternoon Dominique had planned to savour his meal and make it last as long as possible, but when he found himself holding his bowl and hunk of bread, he was incapable of any restraint. The entire meal disappeared down his throat in a couple of huge gulps and swallows.

Dominique put his bowl down in front of him and stared at it, the empty dish being just a little easier to look at than all the men around him who were still eating. Still, the sounds of the others slurping and sighing with pleasure was nearly too much to bear. After drinking two bowls of water, Dominique's stomach felt a little fuller and he lay down and faced the wall, his hands over his ears. He knew he should sleep, but his mind would not be still.

Ever since the arrival of the food he'd noticed several whispered conversations as men unloaded the basket. These continued between mouthfuls as they ate their meals. Dominique tried not to feel hurt when they excluded him, but the hushed exchanges prickled at him as if a thousand tiny chi-chi flies buzzed around and bit him, making rest impossible. In desperation he tried whispering a story to himself. *With a burst of flames, Cappa escaped, spiralling up and up through the witch's chimney with a shower of sparks and a cloud of acrid green smoke.* But Dominique lost the threads of the story as the sounds of the men around him tugged him back into the Dark Tower of Carnillo.

The planned escape was supposed to happen soon. Maybe that's what the men were discussing. He tried to see whether any more rope had been hidden beneath the reeds, but was shooed away from the basket when he got too close. What if there was some problem getting more rope? What if the good guards, the ones who disappeared each evening to play chillotti, were stationed elsewhere? How many long days without food would he have to endure before they tried to get away? His stomach rumbled and he thought, ruefully, that if he had to wait too long he'd be no use to anybody: he would be as weak as the children of Krokoska after the forty-day famine.

He gritted his teeth at the injustice of being invited along on a great adventure but not being trusted to know anything about it ahead of time. Yes, he understood that he wouldn't be able to give much away if the guards questioned him with the help of whips or boiling vats of oil. But how was he supposed to prepare himself? Given the limitations of his wrist cuffs and chains, he told himself that resting could only help. But his body refused to cooperate, twisting and turning as he lay on the stone floor.

He had just rolled back over to face the wall for about the twelfth time when he felt a firm hand on his shoulder.

"Dominique Bertolescu. We must go now." Hermano kneeled beside him, a coil of rope slung over his shoulder.

"Now?" Dominique was horrified. "Go right now?"

"Hush. There's no time for a long discussion."

Still Dominique could not move.

"Get up. Toranosco is already out in the hallway."

Dominique scrambled to his feet. "But what about this?" Dominique asked, shaking the length of chain hanging from his wrist.

Hermano grinned. "You'll have to take it with you."

"But—"

Shasta appeared behind him. "Suddenly you have a lot to say."

Dominique blushed.

"Come, the others are waiting." Shasta gave Dominique a gentle nudge and the group moved out into the passageway encircling the prisoners' chamber.

Around the corner, out of sight, the guards shouted and laughed over their game. Though Dominique could hear them, the curving hallway to the left was completely empty. Even the marksmen's places by the arrow slits had been abandoned, and Dominique wondered what punishment Emberto would dream up for his unreliable soldiers if he knew the prisoners in his tower were left alone each evening while his men gambled and played games. Silently, Dominique thanked whichever guards were assisting his departure simply by being somewhere else.

Down the corridor and to the right, Toranosco and another man were already hard at work wiggling a large stone at the base of the closest arrow slit back and forth. With a final heave and twist, they slid the stone backwards into the hallway, where it was caught with eager hands so it made no sound. Hermano uncoiled the rope and slipped the end through the crack.

Dominique stepped back. Surely that wasn't where they were going? The hole left where the base-stone had been was scarcely big enough for a tonneck to fit through, never mind three people. He could see now why the prisoners hadn't chosen big men to make this trip. Toranosco was the tallest of the three of them, but he was lanky, one long sack of bones. Hermano was a bit stockier, and Dominique looked from him to the opening and raised his eyebrows. It would be a tight squeeze for a man with a lacerated back.

The small group that was gathered behind them in the passageway made Dominique nervous. There was no room to turn, no way to see down the hallway. Toranosco, Dominique, and Hermano were closest to the arrow slit, their view blocked by others who had come out to watch, to help. Shasta nervously licked his lips, spat on the palms of his hands, and took up the rope. He and the man who had helped lift the stone tested their grip on the rope, bracing themselves, ready to take the weight of those who were leaving.

Shasta dropped the rope and turned to Toranosco. He put his hands on the younger man's shoulders and said, "You will not forget us?"

Toranosco swallowed hard and Dominique saw he was close to tears. "Not for as long as I breathe, my friend."

The two men embraced quickly, and then Toranosco flopped down onto his stomach in the hallway, stuck his feet out the hole, and grabbed the rope. Shasta and the other man held the other end as if they were squeezing the life out of a long, brown serpent.

"Travel well, travel wisely," Shasta whispered as Toranosco squirmed into the hole. The angled chute led through the thick outer wall of the tower. Toranosco wiggled away from the others, his face intent with concentration as he looked up at the men above him until he lay wedged within the wall, his head at the upper end of the chute, his feet somewhere behind and below him.

"Hurry," Shasta whispered, and Toranosco worked his way backwards until all Dominique could see was the top of his head. Then even that disappeared into the darkness beyond the bottom end of the chute.

"There's water below," Shasta said to Dominique as they watched Hermano take his turn and manoeuvre into the opening. Hermano grunted and pushed, turning from

157

side to side as he forced his way into the tight space. Dominique winced as he thought of the ugly whip bites on Hermano's back. Before Hermano was clear of the narrow chute, Dominique heard a faint splash from somewhere outside and far below.

Dominique rubbed his palms against his leggings and made a plan. He would not let go of the rope until he was right in the water. As soon as Hermano's head had passed beyond the end of the crack, Dominique turned and stuck his feet into the sloping opening. The stone walls pressed in against his sides and he breathed faster, perspiration slick on his forehead and upper lip. His palms were slippery with sweat, but he dared not let go of the rope to wipe them. Tentatively at first, he started down, his length of chain slithering down the chute after him.

"Go! Hurry!"

Shasta's face peered down at him but then glanced back over his shoulder. Was someone coming?

It seemed like ages before Dominique felt his toes reach the edge of the stone that indicated the outside of the tower wall. He poked his foot out behind him into the open air. Panting, he kept moving until first his knees were clear, and then his hips. His legs now hung right out of the tower wall and his toes felt for cracks in the smooth stone where he might brace himself, control his descent.

The rope beneath him shook slightly, presumably from Hermano continuing his climb down. What Dominique wanted to do more than anything was just rest a moment, but Shasta's instructions from above were more insistent, urgent. "Go. We can't stay here much longer."

Clamping his fingers around the rope in front of his face and wrapping his legs around the thick cord beneath him, Dominique eased himself completely out of the wall. Below him, there was another splash. The rope swung away from the wall and then back again, bumping Dominique's back painfully against the stones.

He froze there, hanging in the darkness, terrified to move his hands or feet, hitting the wall and then swinging out into space.

"Go," he whispered to himself, and somehow one hand released its grip and then the other, the chain clinking between his wrists, and he began to move again. He heard nothing now—no more words of encouragement from Shasta above and no sounds of any kind from Hermano and Toranosco somewhere in the water far below.

Down he went, the rough fibres of the rope cutting into his palms, his whole body aching with the strain of not letting go. Long before he reached the water, the rope beyond his toes ended, and Dominique realized this was why he had heard the others splash into the water. They hadn't fallen. They had run out of rope.

He dangled there, turning slowly, wondering for a crazy moment if he should climb back up again where he would, at least, be relatively safe. But Dominique didn't have a chance either to start back up the rope or let go and leap into the blackness. Far above, the rope went slack and he soared backwards through the air until the water swallowed him whole, the rope raining in coils around him. For what seemed an eternity he sank down, down, down into the cold water. Fighting the weight of the chain dragging him under, he kicked and clawed his way through the water, struggling to reach the surface. He clung to the rope as he fought his way upwards: tangled coils swirled around him, catching at his legs, wrapping around his flailing limbs.

He burst to the surface and, gasping and sputtering, turned around in the water, wiping his eyes. They were out! They had done it! He pulled in a breath, exuberant, terrified. Now what? He paddled in place and held his breath to listen, peering through the darkness.

"Here. Over here." He recognized Hermano's voice.

Still clutching the rope, Dominique kicked out for the shore, a blacker black than the water around him. When he drew close, Hermano and Toranosco waded into the shallows and each grabbed an arm.

There was no time for celebration. Dominique and the others had no way of knowing whether Shasta had dropped the rope to hide the evidence or because the men had been discovered feeding a rope out of the arrow slit. It was clear that if they lingered by the river-bank, they would be arrested, and this time they might wind up in the dungeons beneath the tower, or perhaps be publicly flogged until they longed to escape into death. As Dominique caught his breath, he started to coil the rope, shivering in the cold night air.

"I'm-m-m al-m-most ready," Dominique whispered through chattering teeth.

"Leave the rope here," Hermano whispered.

"Throw it into the river," Toranosco said. "We don't want to be seen with that."

Dominique nodded and flung the rope as far as he could out into the water. It floated for a moment before sinking into the slow-moving water.

Hermano touched Dominique's arm. "This way."

Together, the three escaped prisoners crept up the riverbank and slipped into the dark streets of Carnillo.

22

VENTNOR'S TAVERN

*The sun turned to climb back down from the sky, but the
ladder was gone.*

—Ancient Estorian story

Hermano and Toranosco seemed to know exactly where
they were going. They avoided the main streets and kept
to the deepest shadows, moving quickly away from the
Dark Tower of Carnillo. The houses and shops were
shuttered against the night, and they saw few other
people. When the prisoners heard guards or patrols, they
ducked into alleys and side streets, weaving their way
through the town, always heading in the same general
direction. A canal ran along the base of the northern
town wall, and eventually Hermano led them to a narrow
footpath running beside the water. The night was
absolutely still—not a breath of air rippled the surface of
the canal.

The water reminded Dominique of a story Uncle
Sethka had once told him.

*From the black depths of the River Em, a hand, then an
arm, and then a skull emerged from beneath the still waters.*

The story had not ended happily. When he was a child, Dominique had felt the same mixture of excited anticipation, dread, and terror listening to that story as he now felt hurrying along Carnillo's streets. His hand reached for the back of Toranosco's tattered tunic. The young man's long, black hair spiralled down his back. He did not turn around when he felt the younger boy's tug. Instead, he and Hermano broke into a jog, hustling quickly along the path, towing Dominique behind.

Twice they detoured away from the canal as they drew close to guard towers standing tall and forbidding on the other side of the water. These towers were placed at more or less regular distances all the way around the city walls, and when Dominique spotted a third watch-tower in the wall ahead, he was ready when his companions turned to the right into a narrow street. This time, however, they did not double back. Instead, they crossed first one street and then, at the next junction, turned left onto another.

Somewhere ahead a dog barked, and Toranosco reached back and grabbed Dominique's wrist. The three fugitives sprinted past two shuttered shops and then, without warning, Toranosco turned and ducked into a recessed doorway. He pressed the others back against the wall, pushed them roughly to the ground, and placed one hand over each of their mouths.

Terrified, Dominique imagined he was going to be robbed, though he immediately realized just how foolish that thought was—he had nothing but the old cotton shift on his back and a pair of ratty-looking leggings. With Toranosco's hand heavy over his mouth, Dominique could barely breathe. Even breathing through his nose seemed to irritate Toranosco, who clamped his hand down harder and hissed, "Shhhh."

Hoofbeats and shouts in the street were enough to make Dominique hold his breath. His eyes began to water and he counted silently—*one, two, three*. How long could someone hold his breath before he'd faint?

Three soldiers on horseback cantered past the doorway, swords drawn. They were travelling quickly, apparently looking for someone. When the clatter of hooves faded, Dominique and his companions warily got to their feet. Dominique took a step toward the street, but Toranosco pulled him back and pointed at a carved wooden sign above the door.

The carving on the sign showed three wooden barrels perched one atop the other, and yellow lines radiated from a lantern held aloft by a beautiful young woman.

"Ventnor's Tavern," Hermano whispered as Toranosco tapped gently on the door three times. At first, Dominique heard nothing but their own heavy breathing. After Toranosco knocked twice more, the door opened a crack.

"Who comes to Ventnor's?" a woman's voice asked.

"Friends of the Conspiracy," Toranosco answered.

"Whence do you come?"

"The Dark Tower of Carnillo. Malia—it's me!"

The door opened a little more and Dominique saw an eye pressed to the crack, peeking out at them.

"Toranosco—it *is* you! Quick. Come inside."

Without further question, the door swung open and Dominique found himself wedged between Hermano and Toranosco and face to face with Malia. The warm glow of the hand lantern she carried lit her face softly, accenting the sparkle in her dark eyes and the plump swell of her lips. Her black hair was parted and two heavy braids framed her face before curving gracefully along either side of her neck and disappearing behind her back.

Dominique coughed and looked at the wall in the narrow hallway, both sides of which were lined with empty coat hooks. The hooks were shaped like coiled serpents, their upturned heads waiting for overcoats, cloaks, and hats.

"I heard tonight was to be the night." The woman beamed at Toranosco and he bent to kiss her on the forehead.

"Ah, Malia. How good to see you again." Toranosco's voice had completely lost its harsh edge. He reached out to touch the smooth brown skin of her cheek and Malia pulled away, closing the door behind them. "Come. Come."

The three prisoners stepped forward into the coatroom but stopped again immediately when Malia turned back to them and said, "We must be quiet. The others are sleeping." Then she caught sight of their chains and said, "Wait here. I'm sure you don't need those any more!" A happy chuckle escaped as she ran off.

"I have so missed her," Toranosco whispered, and Hermano clapped him on the back.

"I can see why!"

Dominique could see why, too.

When Malia returned a moment later she carried a pair of giant clippers and several heavy files. She snipped through the chain links as easily as if they were made of paper.

"Here," Malia said, handing each prisoner a file. She showed Dominique how to cut through the rivets that fastened the cuffs closed around his wrists. They puffed and panted, vigorously sawing the files back and forth until they cut through the rivets and pried off the cuffs. When at last he was free, Dominique rubbed his wrists and wiggled his fingers.

"We'll take these to the canal tomorrow," Malia said, dropping the prisoners' trappings into a barrel of foul-smelling sludge. "When we tip out the slurry from the bottom of the black ale barrels, nobody will be any the wiser! Now, come—but quietly."

The four of them hurried through a large room filled with heavy wooden tables and chairs. They didn't stop inside the tavern but continued straight toward the massive bar at the back. Behind the bar, a large, glass-fronted cabinet reached from floor to ceiling. Tankards, glasses, and bottles filled the shelves.

Malia slipped behind the bar, reached into the cabinet, and then hesitated. "You two," she said, suddenly wary, pointing at Dominique and Hermano. "Turn around."

Obediently, they turned their backs so they faced the empty tables and chairs. Dominique heard a click behind him and the bottles clinked together as something scraped across the wooden floor. The boards beneath his bare feet vibrated and then, just as quickly as the strange noises had started, they stopped.

"You may turn around and come behind the bar," Malia said.

The wall of bottles had moved to the side to reveal an opening two doors wide. A second room lay beyond.

"Careful where you step—and keep your voices down. Nosco, take the others through and I'll meet you in the panarium."

CHAPTER

23

THE HIDDEN ROOM

Late at night while the others slept, young Fritoni lay
awake worrying that the Silencers would come.

—Estorian cautionary tale

"Careful," Toranosco mouthed as he pointed at the sleeping bodies lying all over the floor. The wooden floorboards were almost completely covered by mats and blankets.

Though Dominique did his best not to make a sound, one of the sleepers groaned and rolled over as he passed and Dominique leaped sideways, just missing a stack of chairs that had been pushed against the wall. Both Hermano and Toranosco turned and glared at him before continuing to pick their way carefully around the mounds of blankets and limbs. Dominique followed them toward a blanket covering a doorway on the far side of the room. Behind him he heard the bottles clinking again as Malia moved the secret wall back into place.

Ducking under the blanket, Dominique found himself in a much smaller room filled with sacks of rice and festooned with drying fish hung from lines criss-crossing the low ceiling. Both Hermano and Toranosco had to duck to avoid being slapped in the face by an alabaster or a furthfin. Food! And, apparently, plenty of it. Dominique grinned and ran his finger along the front of a shelf laden with stacks of flatbread.

The blanket moved again and Malia slipped into the panarium. "Nosco," she said and threw her arms around his neck.

"Oh, Malia." He gazed at the woman as if nothing else in the world existed and then leaned forward and kissed her again, this time on the lips. "What a relief you are still here," he whispered. "I do not know where we might have gone, what I would have done if—"

She reached up and put her finger to his lips. "Hush now. I am here and I am not alone. We are stronger than ever. Daily more come to join us. We were worried the ropes might not reach you—there was a problem at the bakery. There were supposed to be more but—"

Malia stopped and looked at the newcomers. "Will you introduce us?"

"Of course. This is Hermano—once a guard with Emberto, but now on our side." Toranosco nodded at Dominique. "And this is Dominique."

"Welcome." Malia smiled and Dominique found himself smiling back at her.

He felt as though he should say something, explain why he was there, why he had been chosen, but he felt like a complete fraud. He cleared his throat and opened his mouth, the now familiar feeling of uneasiness filtering upward from the pit of his stomach. Each time he had to speak he felt he had to spin new lies, and yet he had no idea what lies would keep him safe, or even, he realized with a start, what truths were really truths any more.

"Thank you," he finally offered and was relieved to see Malia's smile widen. She took Toranosco's hands in hers and said, "My guess is you must be hungry. How about something to eat?"

Her suggestion was met with three grins as broad as her own. "Sit down, gentlemen," Malia said, indicating two olio crates with a playful flourish. "Welcome to Ventnor's Tavern!" She twirled around, the bottom edge of her skirt lifting slightly as she turned, finishing with a light kiss on Toranosco's cheek. He caught her wrist as she spun away again.

"Miss, I most sincerely hope you have not been treating all your customers so well," he said, his fierce tone giving way to a warm laugh as Malia tweaked his nose.

"What have you got, Malia? Something to drink and a real meal would do us all good!"

Malia patted him on the cheek and said, "Give me a hand, Nosco. We can have some of this flatbread. Can you reach those smoked tonneck strips for me?" She pointed at several square woven baskets up on the top shelf. "We can't cook anything right now, of course—the smoke from the fire . . ."

The talk of food set Dominique's mouth watering. Toranosco and Malia lifted food and plates from the storage shelves lining the walls. They moved around the barrels and baskets stacked on the floor and ducked under braided ropes of drying bulbs, clumps of fresh herbs, and strips of fish as they worked. After his recent meagre rations, Dominique was nearly satisfied just to sit and stare at the abundance surrounding him. His stomach growled and he clapped his hand over his tummy as if he could silence the rumble.

From the way Toranosco quickly found the packages of wrapped flatbread, it was clear that this was not his first visit to the panarium. And judging by the amount of food stored in the two back rooms, these people were prepared to feed many mouths for some time to come.

The meal of flatbread and strips of tonneck was simple, but to Dominique it tasted as good as any feast he had ever enjoyed with his clan. He delighted in the crunch of the crisp bread, revelled in the way the strips of dried tonneck tasted salty and dry on his tongue. He savoured every mouthful, washing the food down with pale ale.

"Would you like some more?" Malia asked, rapping her knuckles against the staves of a barrel propped on a wooden stand. Both Toranosco and Hermano raised their heavy tankards and nodded, patting their bellies.

"Not too much, my love," Toranosco cautioned. "My poor stomach is not used to such hearty fare."

Malia stopped pouring when his tankard was half full and turned to Dominique.

"Not for me, thank you." Unused to the strong drink, Dominique was already feeling a little wobbly on his olio crate.

"What am I thinking?" Malia said. "Of course you mustn't have any more ale. There," she said, nodding toward another barrel. "You can have as much water as you like."

"Thank you," Dominique said, holding out his cup. He flushed hotly when he realized he was supposed to help himself. Dominique made his way unsteadily to the water barrel as Malia sat on Toranosco's knee. Her hand strayed to his shoulder, touched his hair, his arm. Dominique tried not to watch them, but the room was small and it was impossible to ignore their obvious affection for each other. He took as long as he could to fill his cup with water, but soon enough he had to turn around again—just in time to catch the end of a kiss! His hand shook and water splashed onto the floor. The ale he had consumed made his blush seem hotter, but he didn't dare leave the panarium to sit in the room with the sleepers for fear he would offend his hosts.

It was Hermano who saved Dominique from further embarrassment.

"That was a fine meal, Malia. I do thank you. But I need to ask for more."

Malia looked up in surprise and Dominique wondered what else Hermano could possibly want.

"You are still hungry? I think Toranosco is right. Too much food too fast will just make you—"

"No, no. I have had plenty to eat—and drink." He raised his tankard as if making a toast to Malia, the shelves laden with food, the ale barrel. "What I am after is information. We heard so little of what was happening in Carnillo while we were in the Dark Tower. I know that the Elder has died and that, ever since, the number of arrests and trials has increased—but what has made Emberto so suspicious?"

"Suspicious?" Malia sniffed. Dominique watched, fascinated, as she pulled her two long braids over her shoulder and began to fiddle with the decorative clasp that fastened the two thick ropes of hair together at the bottom. "Paranoid. The man has become completely paranoid. Everyone is a spy. Everyone is helping spies. Every day he expects an invasion."

"From where, though?"

"The mainland. King Sim. King Sim and the forces of the Festerworlds. Lord Ronwyn. The Estorians. According to Emberto, everyone is poised to invade Carnillo. And if none of that happens, then he tells us there will be a full-scale rebellion within the city walls. Nobody can be trusted. Oh, I curse the day his father died. Things were bad enough before, but now . . ."

"What are the tellers saying?" Hermano asked.

"You can hear for yourselves tomorrow night. They come every evening, sent by Emberto to *inform* the people. He decides what stories they will tell, which endings to choose." A sneer of disgust darkened her voice.

"They come to Ventnor's, visit the other taverns, spread their so-called news through the marketplaces."

Toranosco grunted and Malia stroked his head. They both smiled.

It made perfect sense to Dominique that the Campriano storytellers told their tales in the places where people gathered: his own people did the same thing. But he wasn't sure he had understood properly what Malia had said about Emberto. "What do you mean, Emberto decides what endings the stories will have?" he asked.

Malia's eyebrows pushed together. "Where are you from?"

"Tanga. I was born on Sedna."

Malia slowly shook her head. "That's not what I mean."

"He's an Estorian," Toranosco said, as if that explained everything.

"Ah. No wonder. Your people believe each story has only one ending." Something in the way Malia tilted her head and regarded him with open curiosity made him think she didn't believe this could be possible.

"Yes," he said firmly. "That's how it is. If these tellers change the stories they're not doing it right." Dominique had an uneasy moment wondering about Amana. While they had been together, nobody had told her what stories to tell and she had never hesitated at the end of a tale. Of course, she had never repeated a story, either.

Malia smiled again. "I didn't mean to offend you. I only meant to say that there are many stories to tell and many ways to tell them. And, in a sense, you are right, too. Some stories are more malleable than others."

They couldn't both be right, but Dominique wasn't going to argue with someone who was being so kind. Besides, he'd always been told the Camprianos had some strange storytelling traditions: this just proved it.

"Much as I dislike them all, I think we have to listen to the tellers," Toranosco said. "We can't afford not to. We must know what is happening."

Malia and Hermano nodded. "Aye," Malia said. "Father hates to do it, but he pays them well to come and speak each evening."

"Good business for old Ventnor," Hermano said. "I'll bet plenty of people come in and buy dinner and more than a fair share of ale or wild water."

Malia blushed. "It's true. My father is not a stupid man. Speaking of wild water, did you hear what happened to the Wild Water Station?"

"Remember where we've been," Hermano reminded Malia. "We know little of what has happened out here over the past weeks."

"Bim Scarpio refused to admit Emberto's tellers into his tavern. He said his customers wanted to sing and dance and hear tales of adventure, not be made to worry about invasions and conspiracies."

Hermano laughed at this. "Conspiracies, yes. Frightening lot, those conspirators." He winked at Dominique and pretended to parry with an imaginary foe, a wicked sword dancing before him.

"Shh." Toranosco held up his hand and Hermano's invisible sword drooped. "Go on, Malia."

"Bim refused to let the tellers in. The next night, his tavern was burned to the ground."

"Wild Water Station is no more?" Hermano sounded truly horrified. "But that's where I first—"

"Never mind," Malia said. "Best not to think about it. Best to let the tellers in and try to understand what game Emberto is up to."

"And Bim? What happened to Bim?" Toranosco said.

Malia did not answer right away. She shook her head and closed her eyes.

Toranosco covered her hand with his. "Bim was such a gentle man. I told him so many times to join us, but he believed . . ." Toranosco's voice broke. "He wanted to believe that things would get better on their own."

"These are terrible times." Malia sat down heavily. Suddenly, she seemed exhausted. She put her head in her hands and rubbed her thumbs in slow circles over her temples.

"What are the latest plans?" Hermano asked. "And weapons! We need weapons!" He wasn't joking any more.

Malia sighed and then rose to gather the empty tankards. "The plan right now is to sleep for what little is left of the night." She took Dominique's mug and gave him a long, hard stare. "You are so fair. We'll have to dye your hair."

Dominique reached up and touched his hair. His mother would be appalled at how filthy and matted it had become.

"Tomorrow we will talk when Father is here. We have many decisions to make. You two—" She looked from Hermano to Dominique. "You two will have to introduce yourselves properly, tell the others how you can help our cause."

Dominique avoided her eyes. He had no idea what he would tell the conspirators. A wave of exhaustion overcame him and he swayed.

"Poor thing," Malia said, more gently. "You must all be so tired."

Toranosco nodded. "Where shall we lie, then?"

"In the other room. Find a space on a mat. There are blankets by the door—take one as you go back in. I'm sorry it's not more—"

"Nonsense," Toranosco said. "Think of where we have been for the past weeks."

Malia nodded and bit her bottom lip. "I have thought of nothing else for as long as you have been away," she said, and the two sweethearts hugged briefly before Dominique, Toranosco, and Hermano ducked back under the blanket into the room where all the others slept. They crept to empty mats in the middle of the room and Dominique watched as Malia slipped through the false door and out into the tavern beyond. She slid the shelf across the opening with the now familiar rumble and clink.

Dominique lay down on a mat beside Toranosco, who was busily arranging his blanket. Weary though he was, the minute he lay down, Dominique's head began to spin with questions. He longed to ask who all the sleeping people were, what was going to happen, how long he could stay with this odd group.

The puzzle of the changing Campriano stories bothered him. They must have their own stories, he reasoned, the kinds of tales they shared in the evenings after their meals were finished. Surely they didn't change those whenever they felt like it. The listeners would notice. Those Campriano stories had to come from somewhere—if not from Beyond like those of the Estorians, then from other tellers . . . surely not just from Emberto. Malia didn't mean that one man could control the stories people told, did she? Again his thoughts turned to Amana. What about the stories the Campriano girl had told about Clio the Goddess? Surely they were the stories of her people, stories that even a man like Emberto could not control?

The more Dominique twisted and turned the questions in his mind, the less sense it all made. It was strange that the Campriano tellers came to Ventnor's, where they weren't particularly welcome. Then again, Dominique wondered if they even knew that Malia's father didn't want them there. Listening to the steady sounds of breathing all around him, Dominique suppressed a shiver as he thought of the Wild Water Station. That must have been the burnt-out shell he had seen when he had ridden into the city with Amana. Malia had not mentioned any survivors. What if there had been a room full of sleeping people trapped inside that building, too? He wondered if he should take his bedding and move into the panarium, closer to the door Malia had said led to the outdoor courtyard.

Beside him, Toranosco shifted and sighed as he tried to get comfortable, and Dominique resigned himself to staying where he was. Moving outside now would disturb the others. The night was almost over: chances were that any fire would have been set by now. It was completely unnecessary to move, he told himself firmly. He would just rest his eyes for a time so he would be stronger the next day.

As the pull of sleep began to soothe his thoughts and slow his breathing, Dominique allowed himself to recall his mother's voice and the stories she told so well—the great tales of Tara, the goddess who brought fire to the Estorian people, the strong woman who wove fishing nets from the long, straight hair of young maidens. *Tara drew herself tall and turned her back on the warriors. "To be strong is to be still," she said.* As he imagined her voice speaking the familiar words, Dominique realized the face he was envisioning was that of Malia, who seemed to possess the same grace and power as the goddess.

This thought made him blush and smile at the same time. What harm could it possibly do to think of Malia's face, her impossibly long braids clipped together behind her back, as he remembered the story of Tara raising her arms skyward, calling for warm weather so her people might travel to a new encampment? Still smiling, he heaved a deep sigh and fell asleep.

CHAPTER
24

QUILT OF THE REBELLION

When he stood alone at the top of the tower, he found himself wishing he could lift his arms and fly away, leave the troubled city behind him.

—Campriano story

Dominique awoke to what sounded like a thousand melodic whispering voices. As he lay on his mat, half dozing, still exhausted, gradually the mumblings began to sort themselves out into distinct conversations. A woman sang quietly. Hermano's voice rose and fell in conversation not far from where Dominique lay. Dominique rolled over onto his side and half opened one eye.

He scarcely recognized the man who sat cross-legged on the mat. Hermano had washed, cut his hair, and shaved off his beard. He looked quite respectable.

An older woman about the age of Dominique's mother smoothed thick yellow paste over the scabs and cuts on Hermano's back, and though Hermano occasionally flinched, he seemed more interested in something on the floor.

The woman working on Hermano's back did so thoughtfully, gently, her eyes half closed. As she worked, she hummed a sweet, soft melody, the same melody Dominique had first heard upon wakening. Dominique sat up and took in an older man who squatted beside Hermano. His bony knees jutted up and pressed against his shoulders. Both men leaned forward, studying what looked like a patchwork blanket they had spread on the floor.

Dominique propped himself up on one elbow and tried to see what they were looking at. It was, in fact, a blanket, but unlike any Dominique had ever seen before. It was made of many squares of off-white cloth, fine woven and soft. Not all the squares were blank, though. Some had other pieces of fabric, wool, or fur stitched to them. These additions were cut in shapes that looked like mountains, rivers, buildings, people, and animals.

Dominque crept closer. "What kind of blanket is this?" he asked, aware now of people staring at him. The looks, he noticed uneasily, were not entirely friendly, and he suddenly felt as if he'd been caught spying.

The old man didn't seem as leery as some of the others. He rocked back on his heels and gave Dominique a broad wink. "Ah, our Estorian guest is awake at last. Come. Join us!" The old man moved over and patted the mat beside him.

"Don't be shy," Hermano said. "This is Ventnor—owner of the tavern. And this is Dominique."

"Hello."

"Welcome, Dominique." The men made room for Dominique to sit between them. "I believe you met my daughter last night."

Dominique nodded, remembering the way he had told himself the Tara story as he fell asleep. He blushed when he thought of the way he had imagined Malia's features as those of the goddess. He glanced around the room but could not see Malia. Perhaps that was just as well.

"Have you seen a Quilt of the Rebellion before?" Ventnor asked.

"No. Never."

"Strange," Hermano said. "I thought Boris Elnedo had one."

Ventnor grunted. "Perhaps he felt unsafe showing it to the clan?"

Dominique shook his head, confused.

"No matter." The old man's face crinkled into a smile. "The boy has never seen one before. He has now and, no doubt, will again."

This statement didn't seem to endear Dominique to the others. A grey-haired man with a hooked nose scowled and shook his head. Dominique swallowed hard and looked down at his worn leggings. He poked his finger inside a large hole, touching the skin drawn tightly over his bent knee. The way they talked made Dominique feel vaguely guilty for never having seen such a blanket before. He wondered whether it was true that his father had one. He tried to remember if, on his father's infrequent visits, he had ever shown him such a thing. Dominique didn't think so, though his main concern during those fleeting visits had always been to make his father notice him. It hadn't mattered to Dominique what things his father might have brought back from his travels.

"You and Hermano will have to work on your squares," Ventnor said. "And Toranosco will probably want to add something to his, too."

"Where is Toranosco?" Hermano asked, looking around the crowded room.

"Don't ask!" Ventnor said, putting up his hand. "I'd rather not know what he and my daughter are up to!" Though he tried to contort his face into a fierce scowl, the twinkle in his eye made Dominique think he wasn't really too angry about Toranosco spending some time with Malia.

Though the sleeping mats still carpeted the wooden floor, nobody in the room was asleep. A mixed group of at least a dozen men of different ages, women, and youngsters about the same age as Dominique seemed to live in this one large room. They had all gathered around the quilt, and when they weren't shooting suspicious glances at Dominique, they studied the quilt's intricate designs.

Doing his best to ignore them, Dominique asked Ventnor, "What do you mean, I have to work on *my* square?"

"Everyone comes to this revolution with a story," Ventnor said. "And this collection of stories—" he waved his hand over the quilt, "—is just one of many such blankets spread throughout the known world."

Dominique raised his eyebrows. That was a lot of stories.

"If we don't record these stories, they may be lost. Emberto is not likely to have his tellers recite tales of insurrection, is he?" Ventnor ran his fingertips along a wrinkle in one of the blank squares. "You must choose one of these and then stitch in your story."

"Stitch in my story?" Dominique had never heard of such a thing. "But how—"

"The tools are simple. Needle and thread and scraps of fabric. You may cut the cloth into shapes and then fasten them to the blanket—here inside your first square. Later, as the rebellion progresses, you will add to other squares, too, maybe on other quilts, as your story changes."

"Unless you die," Hermano interjected.

Ventnor bobbed his head. "Yes, Hermano. Then someone else must stitch in a black circle. Like this one over here. That means the person's life journey has come to a close."

He pointed to a square near the centre of the quilt. It showed a small boat at the foot of a rugged cliff, a series of huge waves, fish shapes, and a tiny house perched on the side of a mountain. In the very centre someone had neatly stitched a black circle using thread so thick it was more like string.

"This was the story of El Madrical," Ventnor explained. "Madrical was a fisher who died in a dreadful storm. He was guiding a ship carrying revolutionaries to shore. The ship arrived safely, but a great tidal wave swept El Madrical out to sea. His wife still lives in their house on the cliffs."

Ventnor sat back and sighed. "There is another sad part to this story. They say that on the same morning El Madrical went out to save the ship, he and his wife had a terrible argument. Her square is over here."

The colours in this second square were muted, sombre. The same little house on the cliff overlooked a raging sea. "Sonya Madrical never had a chance to tell her husband of her love for him and he went to his grave suffering the same fate. Sonya has never forgotten why her husband died. She carries out his work to this day, working the lights on the cliffs to guide the ships in, and she will continue until we are free to live without fear and can own our stories once again." Ventnor touched the fabric house and drew a deep breath.

Then, as if bringing himself back into the present, he winked at Dominique and said, "Obviously you don't need to worry about adding a black circle to your square."

Dominique nodded but still wasn't sure exactly what the old man wanted him to do.

"Do you have a story about it?" Dominique asked.

"A story about making a quilt square?" Ventnor asked.

"He's an Estorian," Hermano said. "They have a story for everything."

Dominique wished he hadn't said anything. "Or I could watch someone else do it . . ." His voice trailed off and he picked absently at the hole in his leggings.

"Dominique, we have plenty of stories about these quilts. But most learn by doing. It's the best way. So, yes, you must watch. We will all watch so we will all understand each other's part in our story. And when it is your turn, you, too, will have an audience."

Dominique didn't feel too happy about that.

"Not to worry, my boy. There is no wrong way to fill in your square. And later, when your story has changed, you may add to your square or start another one in the next Quilt of the Rebellion you encounter. Remember, though, that you may never take away what is already there."

Dominique leaned over and examined the quilt more closely. Some of the squares had very little in them, while others were crammed so full of carefully cut cloth shapes the images overlapped each other in an exuberant display of colour and form.

"Do you have a square?" Dominique asked.

"This one here." The old man pointed to a square adorned with many, many scraps of cloth.

"I was born in Carnillo," Ventnor said, pointing to a piece of grey cloth cut in the shape of the Dark Tower. "My father, like his father before him, ran the tavern." A shield identical to the one hanging outside the tavern was represented in miniature. Golden threads radiated from the profile of a dark-haired woman.

"Who is this?" Dominique asked, fascinated by a delicate rendering of a woman sitting in a rowboat. A lock of real hair cascaded over her shoulders.

"Francesca," Ventnor said, his voice cracking. "Malia's mother. And here—this is Malia." A tiny white bundle lay in a cradle. Dominique didn't need to ask about the black circle over the woman's head. Ventnor looked sad enough.

"Does everyone here have a square?" Dominique asked.

"Yes. We are all part of this rebellion." Ventnor scratched the beard under his chin, his discoloured fingernails rasping back and forth several times before he leaned forward again. "This area of the border is the tavern. Those who pass through only briefly add a small mark." The border was so cluttered with fabric representations of people that some were fastened over others, flaps that, when lifted, revealed more faces and figures beneath.

"When you leave, collect scraps from your journeys, and when you visit us again you can add them to the quilt. Or if you travel far away, you may add something to other quilts."

Dominique sat back on his heels, in awe of the incredible collection of stories spread before him.

"It's important that you keep your story safe somewhere, share it with others so it will not be lost."

But what of those whose stories *were* lost? This idea, that the struggles of those in the prison or who died in battle would never be heard, stirred a deep sadness in Dominique. And what about his own people? Had they ever known stories of rebellion? He had no way of knowing. What about his father? Was he part of all this? Did he have a square somewhere? What did his mother know of these things? Was her story captured on a quilt somewhere?

These thoughts shook Dominique. What did he know of his mother's own story? Little more than he knew of his father's, he realized with a start. How could he have let that happen? Why hadn't he asked more questions? Demanded answers?

But that wasn't the way of his people. To be an Estorian meant to accept whatever stories others chose to tell, to learn from the wisdom of those stories, understand them, and pass them on. Where, in all of that, was there room for asking questions?

"Dominique? Are you feeling unwell?"

"No—I'm—I'm fine, thank you."

A noise from the panarium caught Ventnor's attention. "Toranosco! There you are!"

Toranosco hooked the blanket to one side of the doorway. The panarium behind him was empty. He, too, had cleaned up while Dominique slept. He looked even more handsome with his beard neatly trimmed and his hair tied back.

"What have you done with my daughter?"

Toranosco turned nearly as red as Navina's crest. "Nothing, sir!"

"Where is she?"

"At the fruit market, I think—she was away early this morning."

Ventnor's face creased with concern. "Up late. Up early. She'll fall ill, she will. Not that she'll listen to me—who am I but her old father? But you, young man, you'll do as you're told, won't you?"

Toranosco grinned. "Of course, sir. You know I shall do your bidding should I ever hope to wed your daughter!"

Now it was Ventnor's turn to blush. "Enough of such talk. Come and change your square, show the young lad here how it's done."

Toranosco grunted. "I suppose I must add something about the tower. I'd rather just forget about it."

Ventnor waggled his finger at Toranosco. "No, no. Others must know what has happened. Tell us the story as you stitch."

With a shrug, Toranosco reached for one of several

tightly woven baskets, each with a snug-fitting lid. He peered inside and then rooted through hundreds of scraps of cloth of all colours and textures.

"Nothing nasty enough for that place," he said, finally settling on a coarsely woven piece of fabric of such a dark grey it was nearly black. As he began to cut out the shape of a tower, he described how Emberto's men had arrested him back near the beginning of winter.

Selecting a needle from an assortment stuck inside the padded lid of the basket, Toranosco stopped talking only long enough to lick the end of a piece of black thread and poke it through the needle's eye. Dominique watched with admiration as the man's big hands deftly stitched the tower onto the quilt.

"I was one of the first to be arrested." He nodded at Ventnor and said, "Could you please get some yellow thread ready?" As Toranosco continued to sew, Ventnor prepared the next needle. Without finishing the tower, Toranosco took the yellow thread and stitched five short, straight, vertical lines on the outside of the tower. "Alsace was already incarcerated," he said, sewing a round bead at the top of the first stick.

Dominique was so intrigued with what Toranosco was doing that he was barely aware of the others gathering around to watch. "Cassidy Burke, the redhead, was also there when I arrived." Toranosco added an orange bead to the top of the second stick.

"I remember that, when he was arrested," said a young man with dark eyes and a quick smile. "Where is he now?"

"Dead." Toranosco shook his head and stitched a black circle of thread below the orange bead head. He continued to add beads and then black circles for three more men who had died inside the Dark Tower. Suddenly, the story Toranosco was telling stitch by stitch was no longer so fascinating. It made Dominique ill to think that so many had perished or remained chained up while so few had escaped.

Dominique's eyes flicked to Toranosco's face and he wondered if he, too, was thinking of poor Alsace, so sick and still inside.

"Why did they spare you?" asked another man with flecks of grey sprinkled through his hair. He shifted the leather tool belt that he wore over his tunic and cocked a questioning eyebrow.

Toranosco shrugged. "Not easy to know, Zeff, why some are spared, some not. But my guess is, I didn't break any law of any kind—I inquired about renting a boat."

Several of those gathered in the hidden room nodded knowingly. Toranosco selected a strip of blue cloth for a canal and then cut a boat from some yellow silk. He placed the water and boat on his square and moved them from one part of the square to another. He touched some of the other shapes already stitched there: the barrels adorning the sign Dominique now recognized as the one outside the tavern, a yellow dog, and a woman with two long braids clipped together behind her back. His fingertips lingered on the figure's face and he sighed wistfully before picking up his needle again.

"Not to worry, lad," Ventnor said, patting Toranosco's shoulder. "She'll be back soon. Now, get on with it. There's much to add before we put the quilt away."

As he said this, Ventnor looked from Dominique to the scrap basket. "You might as well get started, Dominique. You can select your cloth and start cutting while Toranosco's finishing up."

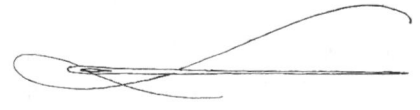

25

STITCHING STORIES

When Elanora saw her son dive into the enchanted river,
she wailed and wailed until the water turned to ice.

—Traditional Estorian tale

"Where do I start?" Dominique asked, feeling lost as he stared at the wide expanse of quilt spread on the floor in front of him. "I can't put everything that has ever happened to me, everything that I am, in the square."

"Of course not," Ventnor replied. "Why don't you start by telling us a little about your journey, how you came to join us, what strengths you bring to our cause. We can help you choose what is most important."

Dominique couldn't think of what to say. How much did he really want recorded in this quilt for everyone to see?

"Sir Riley—he's here in Carnillo—was brought into the tower on the same day as Dominique. He said the boy travelled alone across the River Epilobium," Toranosco said, trying to help.

"Really?" A youth a little older than Dominique spoke, his dark eyes shining. Then, as if remembering his manners, he added, "I'm Breska. From Crestio. What happened? How did you get across the river?" At least he didn't seem to mind Dominique's arrival.

"I . . . I, um, I swam." Though Dominique kept his eyes down, studying a particularly detailed area of complex stitching, he sensed the others shifting, falling quiet as they edged closer to listen.

"And you didn't hear anything in the water?" Hermano asked. "Didn't you know how Lagrace lures her victims with her music?"

"Yes, I did." Dominique blushed again, this time because he was ashamed he had been so easily fooled by the river serpent's enchanted melodies.

"Why didn't you get pulled under? Why didn't you see one of the river serpent's faces?" Breska asked.

Dominique shook his head and closed his eyes, remembering, though he didn't want to. "It was terrible. Lagrace tried to drag me down, tried to make me open my eyes—her singing was—was . . ." There were no words to describe the strange music of the two-headed river serpent. It had been so beautiful, nothing to be afraid of at all. And yet, he had resisted: he had not opened his eyes.

"Do you have magic?" The intense gaze from an old man who leaned forward behind his question stopped Dominique short. He considered his answer. Perhaps it wasn't such a good idea to let on that he had no magical powers.

"I didn't need to use my magic. I just sang."

"Sang?" Hermano was now staring at Dominique with open astonishment. "A particular song? A magical song?"

The woman who had been working the salve into Hermano's back now rubbed her hands together. She stopped humming and waited to hear what Dominique was going to say.

"No! No, nothing like that. It was just a simple song— sometimes without words—just humming. I think it was the noise—when I made noise it was as if the sounds of her music couldn't get into my head and make me look at her."

"Can you make the noise—sing the song—again?" Breska asked, and several of the others nodded, eager to hear him sing the song that had vanquished the deadly river serpent.

"I don't remember exactly. I was shouting . . ." Dominique felt utterly foolish.

"Go on—tell us," Ventnor said gently. "What did you shout? What kind of incantation?"

"I think at first I was just screaming—no words or anything."

Ventnor nodded as if this made perfect sense.

"And then I think I yelled at her to go away, that I was swimmmmming."

Breska laughed. "And she listened?"

"Not really. She chased me the whole way across the river. I felt her tongues slithering around my ankles . . ." Dominique shuddered at the thought of it. Everyone else, though, seemed most impressed.

"But you didn't open your eyes?" Another of the younger boys couldn't seem to believe this was possible.

"No. So I didn't ever see either of her faces." This, Dominique knew, was what had saved his life. "And when I was humming or singing I couldn't hear her music, so somehow I got all the way over to the other side."

"It sounds as if you have some kind of magic, maybe magic that you don't know about," Ventnor said, and both Hermano and the woman beside him nodded. The woman began to hum again, very softly.

"Riley spoke very favourably of—"

Ventnor interrupted Hermano. "I'm not certain just how seriously we can take anything Riley says."

"He has helped the cause over the years," Hermano countered.

Ventnor snorted. "The cause Riley is most interested in is his own."

"Hermano's right, Ventnor," Toranosco said. "Riley was charged with trying to poison Emberto."

"A shame he didn't succeed," Hermano said.

Toranosco went on. "Whatever you think of Riley, he isn't the only one who knew that Dominique here was travelling with—"

"I could start with Lagrace," Dominique interrupted quickly. He guessed Toranosco was going to say something about Navina, and Dominique felt uncomfortable talking about magic he didn't understand, a bird that had disappeared. "Though I don't really know exactly what Lagrace looks like. I . . . I . . . didn't see much of her—a bit of her side, her scales."

"That would do," Ventnor said, smiling. "How about some blue for the water?"

"It was more grey, maybe with a bit of green . . ." Dominique said, rooting through the baskets of scraps, running his fingers through more types of fabric than he had ever imagined existed. His fingers slipped easily over some, lingered on the coarse bumps of others, stroked the soft finish of fine-spun wool, the firm diagonal ridges of rough twill.

"This is more like the river," he said, pulling out a piece of blue-grey fabric the length of his arm. "But it's too big . . ."

Toranosco handed him the shears and gave him an odd look. To Dominique's relief, he didn't pursue the matter of Navina. Dominique snipped off a strip of the cloth with a gentle curve to represent the mighty River Epilobium. He lay the piece at the bottom of the square he had chosen and then selected a piece of pale greenish fabric with a delicate sheen that made it look as if it were wet.

From this he cut another curve, stronger than the one

he had made for the river and about as thick as his smallest finger. He ignored the shape of the serpent's head completely by making the shiny curve rise in and out of the river water, the smooth bend of the serpent's back the only thing visible above the surface of the water.

"Here," Ventnor said, offering Dominique a pre-threaded needle.

"Thank you." Dominique waved the needle back and forth over the fabric, unsure how to start.

"Do it like this." Ventnor covered Dominique's hand with his own and guided him as he poked the needle through the layers of fabric. "You have to push hard—that's the way. Watch your hand underneath or you'll poke yourself. Good. Keep going."

At first, Dominique was tentative as he pushed the needle in and out of the fabric, but as he worked, he grew more confident. Ventnor helped him start stitching the serpent, and then Dominique added a few more details of his terrifying crossing.

"I thought I'd never reach the other side." Stitch. Stitch. "I could feel her slipping through the water underneath me." Stitch. Stitch. "I kept going, shouting, singing, kicking." Stitch. "Water came into my mouth and—" Stitch. "I thought I was going to die!"

"I've never met anyone who has beaten old Lagrace in such a way," Toranosco declared and patted Dominique on his back. "So that's where you met Riley, is it?"

Dominique nodded and knotted the end of the thread. How would he show Riley in the picture?

As if reading his mind, Toranosco said, "Just show a stick with a bead, like I did."

Dominique made several long stitches and then bent over the quilt again.

"What are you doing?" Breska asked.

Dominique added a round bulge on one side of the

stick. The stitches were uneven so the bulge looked a bit lumpy. "Hah!" Toranosco laughed. "You are right, lad. If there was ever a man who could not be drawn as a stick, it would be Sir Riley!"

Several others chuckled and Toranosco said, "The man has a belly as large as a woman with child!"

Breska whooped with laughter and was roundly hushed by a dozen angry voices. He clapped his hands over his mouth, his black eyes huge and dark in a face suddenly drawn and pale.

The mood had definitely changed, and Dominique knew he would not be able to distract Toranosco this time when the young man asked, "What about the kasyapa, Dominique? Riley said you were travelling with a kasyapa bird."

Ventnor squinted, his eyes nearly disappearing into the heavy wrinkles of his face. "A kasyapa? Hmmmm." Dominique waited for Ventnor to say more about the bird, but instead the old man asked, "Is this true?"

Dominique nodded.

"No wonder Riley was keen to get the boy out here to us."

Dominique put the needle down. He didn't want to add anything more to the quilt. It felt dangerous, as if he was exposing more about himself than was safe.

Ventnor stared at him. Breska's jaw hung slack and the singing woman went quiet again.

"And where is this bird now?" Ventnor asked, his expression as much challenging as questioning.

Dominique studied the hole in his leggings. It seemed to have grown a little since the night before. How could he say when he did not know? Would they make him leave or, worse, turn him back over to Emberto when they realized not only did he lack special powers, but also he no longer had the bird that everyone seemed to find so extraordinary?

Without warning, soft bells tinkled. The sound was pleasant, but the reaction among those within the room was dramatic. Spinning around, Dominique saw a string of tiny brass bells suspended from an overhead beam near the false wall leading into the tavern. As he turned, Hermano and Ventnor each grabbed one of his arms and reached out to cover his mouth. Hermano was quicker, and Dominique squirmed as the man's strong fingers clamped against his cheeks.

Hermano's eyes widened with an unspoken question. Dominique nodded, barely able to move his head, he was held so snugly. Yes, he understood. Everyone in the room stared at the blank wall, frozen in place. From the tavern beyond they heard voices—several men and then a woman. The woman's voice was light and cheerful, but loud, loud enough they could all hear it was Malia.

"We aren't open for business yet, gentlemen. Will you come back later? I've just come in with the fruit—I need to put it away."

Boots clomped over the wooden floor and then a door slammed. Inside the hidden room, all the heads turned slowly, following the sounds of the footsteps as they travelled farther away. "Courtyard," Ventnor whispered so softly Dominique wasn't sure he had heard properly. "They are checking the tavern courtyard."

A moment later, the boots grew louder. "Can you get us a drink of ale?"

"But we aren't open—"

"Ale!"

Something in the tavern smashed and Ventnor stiffened. He took a step toward the hidden door, but Zeff put his hand on Ventnor's shoulder and stopped him. Zeff's other hand went to a mallet in his tool belt. Toranosco also stood, and two other men immediately rose and moved to stand on either side of him, careful not to make a sound. Ventnor raised his arm as if to brush Zeff aside when Malia spoke again.

"Very well, gentlemen. I'll make an exception—but just this once!"

Dominique heard the dull scrape of glasses being pulled from the shelf and then Malia began to sing as if she had all the time in the world to serve the unwelcome guests.

When men shall sail across the sea,
Let them take the ale of bees.

Ventnor's arm slowly dropped to his side.

"Will Honeywell's suit you both?"

"That would be excellent!"

"Very well then. Will the tellers be coming tonight as usual?" Malia asked.

"I have not heard otherwise. Ahhhh—this tastes good!"

"Thank you. Only the finest at Ventnor's. May I ask, have you heard whether we'll be able to get our shipment of Verescian wine released from the harbourmaster today?"

"That, I couldn't say. Lord Emberto is reassessing tariffs, as you know."

"Yes. Yes, I know."

Another man's voice interrupted. "Where is your father?"

It was only when Ventnor's grip tightened on his arm that Dominique realized he was still being held firmly from both sides. The old man's eyes darted from the wall behind the bar to the little bells that had warned them someone was coming into the tavern. Dominique, too, looked around, but toward the panarium. Was there a way out through the back?

"My father? He is at the fish market. He should be back very soon. Would you like to speak with him?"

"Aye."

"Could I tell him why you've come?"

"No. Our business is to deliver a message from Emberto to all business owners."

"In that case, you may speak with me. My father and I run the tavern together."

The two men conferred, though too quietly for their words to be heard. "Very well. We come with a warning. Dangerous criminals have escaped from the Dark Tower."

Malia gasped.

"I'm sorry to alarm you, miss. But it is important you alert us immediately should any strangers come to the tavern or if you notice any unusual behaviour in your clients."

"Of course. Oh, how awful! I will certainly report anything unusual right away."

"In the name of Emberto, we thank you."

"But it is I, in the name of Emberto, who must thank you for warning us of this terrible danger."

CHAPTER

26

VISITORS

"If each of you brings me a thousand stories, I still won't know enough about my people. But that would be a start." With that, the king sent his armies out across the land to listen.

—Campriano palace tale

Ventnor's breath hissed in and out of his nostrils, unnaturally slow and even as he listened to the conversation out in the tavern. Glancing up, Dominique watched the muscles in the older man's jaw clench and unclench as he stood, motionless, staring at the wall.

"I shall tell my father you called."

"Indeed, give him our regards."

"Please let us know if there is anything else we might do to help protect the great and benevolent Lord Emberto."

"We will let Lord Emberto know of your loyalty."

"Thank you. Now, gentlemen—I don't like to rush you. But I must be off to the bread market or I'll miss the best loaves. With the tellers here each evening we do a brisk business and for that my father and I are grateful.

Still, the customers would be none too happy to be eating stew without good bread."

It was amazing how controlled Malia sounded. Dominique, with only a thin bit of wood and a few glasses between him and the intruders, felt anything but calm. Sweat trickled down his back, though he hadn't moved since the men had come into the tavern.

The men in the tavern didn't say anything else, and not long after, their boots clomped away from the wall and the little bells tinkled again as the front door opened and closed. Dominique listened hard but didn't hear Malia's footsteps, though a few moments later there was a soft *tap-tap-tap* on the other side of the wall.

Everyone in the room let out a long breath. There were a couple of soft chuckles and whispers, but the easy chatter was gone. They listened intently to the bells tinkling once more as Malia let herself out of the tavern.

"She has to go for bread now—whether we need it or not," Ventnor said.

Toranosco strode to the wall, put his ear to it, and then turned back to the others, nodding. "All quiet." He touched the wall longingly as if he could melt it away.

"We'd best roll up the mats and put away the quilt for now," Ventnor said, and the others quickly set to work to tidy up the sleeping room. Remembering how the tower prisoners had despised the lazy boy, Dominique watched carefully to see how the others put away the bedding. He, too, rolled his mat, tied it with the bindings lashed to one end, and slipped it into a space under the floorboards at the back of the room. Without being asked, he helped pull tables, chairs, and benches away from the walls.

When the room had been set up and the others had settled into chairs, Ventnor gestured for Dominique and Hermano to follow him into the panarium. "Toranosco has been here before," he said. "So he knows it is possible to leave without going through the tavern."

Ventnor opened a heavy wooden door at the back of the panarium and waved Dominique out into a tiny walled yard. In one corner was a stone fireplace, unlit, but large enough to bake bread or smoke fish. Dominique turned to ask a question, but Ventnor put his fingers to his lips and pointed to the wall at the back of the courtyard. He pulled Dominique back into the panarium and pulled the door shut behind them.

"There is an alleyway on the other side of the back wall," Ventnor whispered. "Behind the wall to the left is another courtyard where my customers sit when the weather is good. Not many use the alley, but that's not to say someone could . . . " Ventnor didn't finish the sentence. "Obviously, it is not safe for us to come and go through the front door—except in an emergency like last night when you arrived. Out in the courtyard, did you see the fireplace?"

Dominique nodded.

"The fireplace stands just a little away from the wall," Ventnor continued, punctuating his words with short tugs at his beard. "Behind the fireplace, right at the base of the wall, are several loose stones. Remove them and you will be able to crawl into a hole that extends beneath the wall and out into the alleyway. Once you drop down into the hole, look up. There's a grille on the alley side of the wall. From out there it looks like a drain, but in fact, the drain goes nowhere. Generally, though, it's best if you wait for a signal from my sleeping room in the boarding house—Malia or I will throw a stone onto the roof should a quick escape be necessary. That way you'll know nobody is out back. We have quite a good view from upstairs."

Seeing Dominique's confused look he added, "We also own the boarding house next door. The three back rooms overlook the courtyards, though you can't actually see into this one because of the roof. One of the rooms is mine, one is Malia's. The third we use for storage, though if the soldiers demanded it, we would have to let them in."

"Why would soldiers want the room? Don't they have houses here in the city?"

"Yes. Emberto's men live here—there are barracks, and of course the older ranking officers have quite nice residences. But the others who have come to join forces with Emberto—"

"Like Lord Andalon?"

"How do you know about Andalon?" Ventnor's bushy eyebrows dipped into a frown.

"The Campriano girl who caught me and brought me here to Carnillo—she told me after we met some of Andalon's men on the road. I don't think she liked them much."

"It's not surprising a Campriano didn't think much of Andalon and his men being here. Not all of the Camprianos are happy that Carnillo is crawling with soldiers from other islands. Andalon is not the only one who has come to help Emberto. But you won't hear anyone complain out loud. Those who speak against Emberto are tried for treason."

Dominique didn't need to be told what happened to those Emberto believed to be his enemies. He had no desire to return to the tower. He wondered how Alsace and the others were faring, how many new prisoners had been brought to the tower after the morning's trial, how much trouble the guards were in over the missing prisoners.

"What do we do now?" Dominique asked.

Ventnor's face crumpled into a sad smile. "We wait. Our forces are gathering, but we must be careful. And right now, I must slip out the back way and return via the front door with a load of fish. I'm sure Emberto's cronies have an eye on the place. We must all be extra careful. And then—" He sighed and scratched his beard. "Then I suppose I'll have to thank those kind soldiers for warning me about the dangerous escaped criminals." He winked and patted Dominique on the cheek. "And at some point you'll have to finish your part of the Quilt of the Rebellion. I'm sure we'd all like to learn more about your powers and your bird. But that will have to wait until later."

Dominique watched as Ventnor opened the door to the courtyard, paused a moment to listen outside, then closed the door behind him. He swallowed hard and then looked at Hermano. The closest he had ever come to having a magical talent was when Navina had somehow spoken to him from afar. But that was not his power, it was hers. He could no more control the visions than he could control Navina. Thinking of her made him want to cry. Where was she? Had she, too, been captured?

"Would you like to meet everyone properly?" Hermano asked after Ventnor had gone. "I know I would."

Dominique nodded. Learning who everyone else was would be a good distraction until he could figure out how much he should share about himself.

"Come. Toranosco will introduce you to the others. But first, let me show you where to wash up, so you will be presentable."

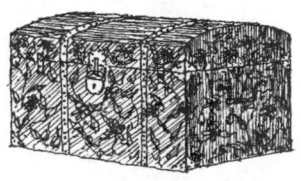

27

INTRODUCTIONS

Tara's maidens kneeled in the ashes of the cold fire,
weeping.

—Estorian Tara story

Toranosco started at the table closest to the panarium. "This is Ontocki—he's a metal worker and woodcarver from Corposcia." Ontocki was the grey-haired man who had glared at Dominique with something close to open hostility earlier. Now he crossed his arms over his chest, leaned back in his chair, and pursed his lips.

Toranosco ignored his apparent bad mood and turned to the stocky man with big ears who sat beside Ontocki. "And this is Zeff, a Campriano—"

"He can't help the way he was born," Ontocki interrupted, slapping Zeff soundly on the back. Zeff was quite a bit younger than the grouchy Ontocki and dressed like a herder with baggy trousers and a colourful woven scarf wrapped around his neck.

"Your upbringing didn't do much for your manners," Toranosco said.

"Good to have you back, too, Toranosco, you old

son of a boar," Ontocki said.

"Behave yourself or we'll cut your rations in half," Toranosco threatened.

Ontocki clutched his stomach and rolled his eyes. "Just you wait until I get my workshop back from Emberto's carrion-pickers. When you come to visit you can eat out back with the swine!"

"Better than dining in your company," was Toranosco's quick retort.

Listening to the pointed banter, Dominique couldn't decide whether the two men liked each other or not.

Turning back to Dominique, Toranosco continued with the introductions. "Breska here you have already met."

Dominique nodded at the lean, wiry boy whose dark eyes and quick grin he had noticed earlier.

"His father, may he be long remembered in story," Toranosco went on, "died in a skirmish with a raiding party sent out by Emberto."

Dominique felt a twinge of jealousy that Breska had a father whose memory he could be proud of. Immediately that feeling of envy was replaced by remorse: how could he be jealous of this boy who knew for certain his father was dead?

"Hermano you already know—but some of the others don't. Hermano here is from Verescia originally, though you've lived here in Carnillo for years now, yes?"

"Yes. True."

"And, yes, Hermano used to work for Emberto as a guard."

"Ahh," said an old man sitting at the next table. "I thought I recognized him from the palace."

"Indeed, but he is one of us now. I don't need to tell you all to treat him accordingly. And for those of you who weren't paying attention when Dominique was starting his story square, our newest arrival is an Estorian. What he didn't tell you is that he is a member of the

Bertolescu clan. Roman Bertolescu is his father."

This piece of information was met with nods and murmurs, and Dominique noticed that everyone was watching him. He blushed and shifted from foot to foot, staring down at his shabby outfit. The hole in his knee was even bigger. He would have to find a way to fix that. He knew now where to find a needle and thread.

"Over here," Toranosco moved to the next table, "we have Erma and Nina. Say hello, girls."

Girls? Dominique had another look at the two young people he had assumed to be boys who were sitting at the table in front of him.

"Hello," Nina said. She was the younger of the two, with short, dark brown hair and a big smile. Now that he looked at her more closely, Dominique guessed she was about the same age as he was. Both Nina and Erma wore the leggings and loose shirts common for Campriano men and boys. Erma also wore a heavy leather belt containing the tools of the carpenter's trade—a hammer, charcoal stick, measuring band, and square.

Estorians had little use for carpenters. Dominique's people lived in simple huts and tents that could be taken apart each time the clan moved. But Dominique's visits to villages and towns over the years had introduced him to carpenters and potters, weavers and metal smiths. Whenever a cart broke or the men of his clan were unable to mend a cooking pot, the Estorians would trade stories for a new cart axle or a sharp knife during a visit to town. Otherwise, they lived simply, making most of what they needed from reeds, saplings, or leather harvested from tonnecks or wild boars.

"Welcome," Erma said. "It will be interesting to hear a Story from Beyond." She smiled sweetly, but Dominique sensed a challenge in her words, and he looked away to the next table where Toranosco was already standing beside a very tall, elegant woman whose long, black hair hung straight down her back, unfettered and streaked through with long strands of white. Her grey eyes gazed directly at Dominique as she assessed the boy standing before her. She was so tall that her eyes were nearly level with Dominique's, even though she was sitting. Dominique recognized her as the woman who had smoothed the healing balm onto Hermano's sore back.

"Brigitta," she said, not waiting for Toranosco's introduction. "From Ticabella. I, too, tell stories. I sing them." She smiled and reached out to touch Dominique's arm. Her hand was warm, her fingers long, and Dominique felt comforted by her. She was unafraid to reach out to him and he wished she would never remove her touch. She did, though, folding her hands together on the table as Toranosco introduced the old man sitting beside her.

"And this is Grembal—an artist."

"Yes," Brigitta nodded. "He tells stories, too—through his glorious mosaics."

Grembal seemed a little embarrassed by the praise and ducked his head. He was completely bald on top. The pink moon of skin was covered in freckles, which made his head look like a gigantic egg. "Welcome, Dominique."

The third person at the table was huge. His shoulders and chest were massive and his hands seemed strong enough to break even the thickest saplings. Dominique assumed he was a warrior or a knight, but Toranosco introduced him as Meath Boru from Hespa, a man of powers.

Dominique bowed before the imposing presence. He had never before met anyone who admitted to possessing magical powers. In fact, it was only through the stories that he knew such people existed at all. Meath Boru didn't speak but merely nodded his head and then gazed straight into Dominique's eyes.

It was as if a great hand reached deep inside him and pulled something out into the light to examine it more clearly. "Ahhh . . ." Dominique groaned, and Brigitta tut-tutted.

"Leave the boy alone, Meath. Give him a chance to get to know you."

The strange feeling of invasion faded, and Dominique stepped back from the table and looked up at Toranosco, who was watching him closely. The room was silent and Dominique felt every eye upon him. "And the others?" he asked, his voice shaking.

The rest of the introductions went quickly. Dominique met Scillio, a herder from Timpah; Cleppeno, a well-dressed young man in a fine silk shirt and thick wool trousers; and Flinta, a former advisor to the Lord of Grenille. Flinta, the last to be introduced, was the first to rise and extend his hand to be shaken.

"Welcome, Dominique. I once met a man from your clan. Boris Elnedo."

Dominique hoped Flinta wouldn't notice how his hand went rigid and his palms instantly began to sweat at the mention of his father's name. Flinta continued to pump his arm up and down.

"Very pleased to meet you. Do you have news of Boris?"

Dominique shook his head. How could he? He had plenty of questions, but no answers. "No. No, he has not returned to our clan in some time."

Flinta seemed disappointed and dropped Dominique's hand. "A shame. He did some good work for the Lord of Grenille."

"Yes. Good," Dominique stuttered. Flinta didn't seem to despise his father the way so many others did. When Flinta sat back down, the sense of loss was so intense, Dominique wanted to cry. He dared not say anything for fear of giving himself away. He was Dominique

Bertolescu, son of the clan leader, Protector Roman Bertolescu, he reminded himself firmly. Until he understood more about his father's work he had to be careful. It was bad enough to be an Estorian in the land of Camprianos. To be the son of a man many called a deceitful son of a boar was even worse.

"So," Toranosco said with a clap of his hands. "Who is ready for a morning meal?"

If they had not been in hiding, Dominique suspected the question would have been greeted with a round of rowdy cheers. As it was, the others answered with loud whispers of "Yes!" and "High time!" and "Bring it on!"

Dominique joined Nina and Erma at their table, and Breska dragged his chair over to them.

"Lift your chair, boy," Flinta said, reaching over and giving Breska a cuff on the back of his head.

"I know, I know," Breska said with a laugh. But he was quiet after that, speaking in an exaggerated whisper and pulling such ridiculous faces it was all Dominique and the girls could do not to roar with laughter.

"Should we be helping out there?" Dominique asked, pulling himself together and pointing at the door to the panarium.

"No room," Nina said.

"What a shame," Breska whispered.

"Grembal, Brigitta, and—" Erma looked around. "Who else is over there?"

"Toranosco," Breska said. "Remember how he likes to eat?"

Nina giggled. "He didn't take long to volunteer for a shift in the kitchen, did he?"

It wasn't long before platters of steaming wedges of flatbread served with small dishes of sweet sauces were delivered to each table.

"Eat as much as you can," Nina advised. "The midday meal is hours away."

She dipped the pointy end of a piece of flatbread into a dainty bowl filled with thick, lumpy sauce, deep maroon in colour.

"Mmmm," Erma said with her mouth full. "Dragonberries."

With a pang, Dominique thought of Navina and the way the kasyapa bird loved to gorge on fresh dragonberries until her red breast feathers were streaked with dark stains.

He tore a wedge of bread in half and dipped it into the dragonberry sauce. The taste was sweet and tangy at the same time, delicious on his tongue. Despite his hunger, Dominique chewed slowly, closing his eyes and savouring the flavour, relishing the memories of warm afternoons spent plucking plump, ripe berries from the tips of dragonberry bush branches.

It was a lovely image, warm and reassuring, but even as he took another bite and indulged himself with another memory of an afternoon spent lying in the sun on a flat boulder near his family's camp at Tivarnen, the image in his head began to change.

No longer was he alone, watching Navina swoop and turn against a huge empty sky. Now he looked down into a narrow street crowded with beggars, children, peddlers, and soldiers. The street was flanked on both sides by higgledy-piggledy buildings, each pressed up against the next, as if vying for a little extra space.

There was no pain this time, just an overwhelming sense of relief that Navina was still alive, and then a steady pressure in his head as if the images he saw were just a little too large to fit comfortably inside his skull. The view shifted slightly so now he could also see the upper windows and small balconies of the buildings, laundry flapping from lines strung across the street, wisps of black smoke escaping from stone chimneys.

Looking up and over the rooftops he saw the Dark

Tower of Carnillo in the distance, an ugly round sentinel glowering over the city. From this vantage point Dominique could also see the city walls extending west and south from the tower at the northeast corner of Carnillo. If he could only turn around, he might be able to follow the walls in the great rectangle that protected the bustling city within.

He tried to turn, but it was as if great hands held his head and shoulders immobile and he was powerless to see anything other than the vision in front of him. In front of Navina, he corrected himself.

From wherever Navina was safely perched high up on a rooftop, she turned her gaze back to the street below. Dominique watched as three soldiers rode abreast up the narrow road, forcing everyone else to jump aside and press themselves against the walls or scurry into doorways.

A woman with a basket atop her head raised a fist and shouted something. Without slowing down, one of the men on horseback slashed at her basket with his sword, sending it and its contents tumbling to the ground. The woman dropped to her knees and scrambled to gather the fruit that had spilled, snatching at lemons and olios as they rolled away from her. She was not quick enough to save them all from the eager hands of the beggar children who leaped forward to scoop up as much fruit as they could carry before darting off into the crowd.

Navina then leaped from the rooftop and Dominique's stomach pitched as she swooped along the street to a corner where several vendors had set up temporary stalls. One man sold shoes, another piles of rags, and another strips of dried fish. One woman, as bent and gnarled as the story sticks she sold, had a second line of products—large clay pots with swollen bellies, the types of urns and containers one might use to store rice, pinta beans, or pickled yentle root.

Navina flew a little closer and Dominique squirmed in his seat, anxious that Navina might get too close, that someone would see her and try to catch her. "No!" he cried out, but the bird did not seem to hear him.

"Dominique? Are you feeling unwell?" Erma stood and put her hand on his shoulder. Dominique opened his eyes, unaware he had even closed them. The whole group stood around his table, watching him.

"I . . ." He tried to wave the others away, but his hands were shaking. He dropped them beneath the table and squeezed them between his legs so they might be still.

Meath Boru leaned forward and touched his fingers to Dominique's forehead.

"He is warm," he said. "Best he lies down for a time."

Anxious whispers filled the room.

"Fever?"

"Tower sickness?"

"He hasn't eaten very much . . ."

"Should he stay? What if he brings illness?"

"We can't cast him out. Where would he go?"

"Hush, everyone," Meath Boru said. His deep voice had a steadying effect on everyone, even Dominique, who felt as if he were still half asleep and struggling to be released from a dream. The piece of flatbread he held in his hand fell to the table and, dazed, he meekly followed Meath Boru to the corner of the room farthest from the false wall.

Meath Boru pulled a blanket from a shelf and flicked it open. "Lie here."

Dominique nodded and lay down without argument. Stray images passed in and out of his mind—a child crying, a woman with her head covered rushing past the clay pot vendor, a snatch of blue sky, a swallow darting by and disappearing between the feet of a statue standing atop a stone building.

"Allow your visioning to continue here," Meath Boru said so softly nobody else could hear. "I shall keep them away and tend to this sudden 'illness' of yours."

Dominique nodded weakly, already slipping back out into the streets. He even managed a smile. Meath Boru *knew* and he wasn't trying to stop Dominique or make him explain what was happening. As Dominique drifted away, he was vaguely aware of the old man telling the others that he needed to rest, that he was suffering from stomach distress caused by the poor food consumed during his imprisonment.

The others did not argue. They left Dominique to lie on the blanket, where he closed his eyes and lost himself once again in the world Navina could see somewhere beyond the walls of Ventnor's Tavern.

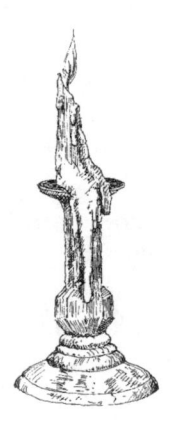

28

THE DRAGON POT

Even the great King Nerion had never possessed a kasyapa bird.

—Campriano story

Unlike the hidden room with its hushed whispers, the streets outside were noisy with the shouts of vendors, soldiers, and children.

"Best price on trumpfish, fresh from the Sea of Chanmari!"

"Glass beads, all kinds—imports and domestic!"

"Buy! Sell! Trade!"

"Sharpen up! Sharpen up! Bring your knives, axes, spearheads, arrow tips!"

"Clear the way! Emberto's men are coming!"

Hoofbeats, the rumble of handcarts trundling over the rough stones of the streets, children shrieking, a baby screaming, two women arguing, dogs snarling and barking—Dominique heard all of this as if he were behind a wall or under a blanket. The sounds were slightly muffled but still loud enough that they drowned out the soft voices in the hidden room, Brigitta's gentle singing, the *whisk-whisk* of Erma whittling at a piece of wood to help pass the time.

Slowly, deliberately, Dominique relaxed his arms and legs and stretched out so he was more comfortable where he lay. With his eyes shut he gave himself completely to the vision that continued to play out in his head.

Navina had flown to a higher perch and Dominique watched from above as the old woman with the pots lifted those she had displayed on the ground onto her handcart. Once everything was loaded, she looped long cords around her wares and secured the ends to the corners of the cart.

"Get out of my way, brats!" she said as she took the push handles at the rear of the cart and gave a mighty heave to get it moving. A skinny girl snatched up her baby sister and dodged aside as the cart gained momentum and rattled off down the street. Navina followed the old woman's progress, staying well above the street and out of sight.

"Pots! Jars! Canisters! Story sticks!"

Every so often the woman would stop at a shop and bang on the door, repeating her cry.

"Pots! Jars! Canisters! Story sticks!"

Every time she stopped, her hand went to her lower back and she straightened up, her face twisted with pain. Few bought her pots. None purchased her story sticks. She turned another corner and the road seemed familiar. Dominique recognized the corner where he, Hermano, and Toranosco had turned to reach the street where Ventnor's Tavern was located.

The old woman turned down the narrow road and Dominique hoped for her sake that no horsemen would gallop past, for her jars would surely be sent tumbling to the ground.

No horsemen were about, but the pot woman was not alone. Approaching from the other end of the street was a familiar figure. Malia, with a basket of bread balanced on her head, hurried along toward the entrance to the tavern. She and the old woman reached the sign at almost the same time.

"Pots? Jars? Canisters? Finest quality. Excellent crafts-manship."

Malia fumbled with her keys and Dominique gasped as Navina leaped from her perch and dove straight toward the two women. Dominique squeezed his eyes more tightly shut but could not stop himself from plunging straight at the cart of pots.

"They are lovely," he heard Malia say, though her back was to the cart. Navina dove right into the neck of a large blue urn decorated on the outside with a red dragon. Once Navina was inside the urn, the old woman's voice sounded strange, distant.

"Please, miss—surely you might need a fine new pot?"

Dominique heard the clink of keys, the creak of the front door, and the soft jingle of bells.

"Let them in!" he shouted and several people rushed to his side.

"Quiet!" Toranosco slapped his hand over Dominique's mouth.

Dominique struggled wildly, trying to push away the stronger man's hand. "Let me go," he tried to say, but the more he shouted and squirmed, the harder Toranosco held on. Several others grabbed at his flailing legs and arms.

"Navina!"

"Be quiet!"

The bells tinkled again as the door was shut. Panting, Dominique listened with the others as Malia's footsteps came across the tavern floor. The false wall slid to the side and she entered the room, lifting the basket of bread from her head.

Her eyes widened with surprise when she saw four people sitting on Dominique who, seeing her standing there alone, renewed his struggles. Already Brigitta and Erma were sliding the false wall back into place. In desperation, Dominique bit Toranosco's hand as hard as he could.

"Owww!"

"Stop! Let the pot lady in!"

Though Dominique tried frantically to escape his captors, he was no match for the strong hands holding him down. He lay on the blanket, panting. "Please! Let her in!"

"How do you know about the peddler?" Malia said, coming toward him. She placed the basket on the table and kneeled beside Dominique.

"Let him go," Meath Boru said. Though the hands holding his wrists and ankles relaxed a little, they did not release him.

"I said, let him go."

Reluctantly, they did, and Dominique jumped to his feet, realized he did not know the trick of how to open the false wall, and spun around, considering whether he could reach the panarium, slip out into the courtyard, and escape through the hole behind the loose bricks before he was caught. With the others crowded around so closely, he knew that would be impossible.

"Please—you must let her in. She has—something of mine."

Malia tipped her head to the side. "How can that be?"

"Malia—the boy has visions," Meath Boru said, touching his temples with the tips of his fingers.

Dominique hardly cared what they were saying about him now. Navina was so close. All they had to do was go outside, call the pot lady, and get that pot! He closed his eyes again but all he could see was darkness. Did that mean Navina was still in the pot? Or did it mean she had flown off again and was no longer letting him see what she saw?

"You must believe me—my—the—the thing is in the pot with the blue glaze—the one with the serpent design. About this size—" He showed Malia with his hands.

Ontocki interrupted. "How would the pot lady know you are in here? What lies have you been telling us?" He shook his head. "We shouldn't open the door. He's speaking nonsense."

Cleppeno folded his arms over his chest and said, "These are dangerous times. I don't think we should trust him."

"Gentlemen!" Meath Boru spoke and the others were quiet. The old man placed his large, gnarled hands on Dominique's shoulders. He looked into the boy's eyes and once again Dominique felt the strange sensation of invasion, as if Meath Boru could draw secrets from his heart that even Dominique did not know were there. Something shifted inside him as if Meath Boru had pulled aside a curtain and found a hidden chamber.

"Purchase the pot," Meath Boru said, releasing Dominique.

"You are certain?" Malia's voice quavered. "Cleppeno is right. It's so dangerous. Are you sure?"

"Go. Purchase the pot. Offer to trade for wild water and a pot of stew plus a few silver kinnels."

Still Malia hesitated, but Meath Boru insisted. "I would go myself but that would be utterly foolish. Malia—have I guided you wrongly yet? Go quickly, before she is too far away."

"Very well." Malia pushed the wall aside, then closed it behind her with the now familiar rattle and clink of bottles. A moment later the others heard the jingle of bells as the front door opened.

Dominique alternately opened his eyes to see if the

wall was moving again and closed them, hoping to catch a glimpse of whatever was happening outside. There were no more visions, however, only silence and darkness. He swayed and Meath Boru helped him sit down on the blanket where, hardly daring to hope, Dominique waited.

"Dominique?"

Dominique stirred and opened his eyes. Meath Boru, Brigitta, and Malia kneeled beside him at the edge of his blanket. The others stood behind them, peering at him anxiously.

Meath Boru spoke again. "You had us worried! No sooner had Malia gone off to do your bidding than you disappeared into the sleep of a dead man!"

This time, the vision had completely drained Dominique. He fought against the weariness that pinned him down as effectively as a hundred hands, but the effort of holding his head up was too much and he slumped against Meath Boru, who put his arm around Dominique and gave him a squeeze.

"Malia was able to find the pot vendor," he said. "She has brought the pot for you."

"Where is it?" Dominique managed to ask, suddenly terrified that maybe he had been wrong, that the vision had been a mistake, that he had seen something else and not what Navina had seen. Or that he had seen correctly, but that Malia had bought the wrong pot. He pulled away from Meath Boru as Malia turned and reached behind her. The pot she held out to him was smaller than Dominique had thought, but then, he had been seeing it through Navina's eyes. To her it must have seemed huge, large enough to hide inside.

The pot was lovely. Glazed a deep blue, it had a glistening black rim and a fine painting of a red dragon encircling its rounded belly. Dominique blinked. If Navina was, in fact, inside, it must have seemed to her that the dragon had swallowed her.

Dominique took the urn and pulled it toward him. He tipped it and peered inside.

"Navina?" he whispered. Breska cocked his head to the side, watching. The inside of the lacquered vessel was painted deep black and it was hard to see past the slightly narrower neck. Slowly, gently, Dominique slid his hand inside. There, right at the bottom, huddled to one side, he felt the familiar soft feathers, the plump, warm body of his bird. He smiled, a huge, wide smile.

He withdrew his hand: his fist would be too large to fit through the opening if he held onto Navina. Dominique was hardly aware of the others watching him as he tipped the pot onto its side, leaned over, and whispered, "Navina. Come out. It's safe here."

He straightened up and watched the opening. First a beak, then the familiar scarlet crest, and then the rest of the kasyapa bird crawled out of the pot's mouth. Brigitta gasped, her hand flying to her mouth.

"A kasyapa!" Meath Boru said, sounding as if he were trying to convince himself that what he saw was no illusion.

As Navina walked in a most dignified manner over to Dominique, everyone else in the room froze, gaping at the glorious bird. She reached Dominique's knee, tilted her head to one side, and examined the hole in the knee of his leggings. Navina's beak darted out and tweaked the edge of the torn cotton, and Dominique laughed.

"She's trying to tell you something," Breska quipped.

Realizing everyone in the room was now staring at the hole in his leggings, Dominique flushed. "I—I must mend that . . ."

Seemingly oblivious to her rapt audience, Navina hopped up onto Dominique's leg and then, using her beak and claws, climbed all the way up his loose shift until she was perched securely on his shoulder, exactly where she belonged. Dominique's fingertips automatically moved in a slow circle behind her head.

"It really is a kasyapa, isn't it?" Brigitta said.

Meath Boru nodded. "Yes. I've never seen one before."

"Kasyapa? I didn't think it was possible," Toranosco said. "I thought Riley had been mistaken," he admitted. "I always believed the kasyapa was a bird of myth."

"Apparently not," Erma said. "A myth doesn't tug on someone's ear like that."

Dominique's cheeks ached as he beamed at the others. He tipped his head sideways so Navina could nibble her way around his entire ear. She tugged and pulled, clearly enjoying the reunion as much as Dominique.

"The kasyapa's power is immense," Meath Boru said. "It is remarkable this bird is here. Remarkable."

The others could not seem to think of anything to say. They sat in silent awe, watching Navina's every move. For once, Dominique didn't care that he was the centre of attention. He took a huge breath and let it out with a shudder. Navina had found him. Lightly, he kissed the top of her head, pressing her crest feathers flat.

Brigitta swayed, closed her eyes, and started to hum. The melody rose and fell, filled the silence, and so moved Dominique that he swallowed hard two or three times so he wouldn't cry. Then Brigitta began to sing.

And in the hands of one small boy
The kasyapa lies . . .
The bird of wisdom, grace, and hope
Will lead the boy to war
And when he throws his sword away,
Peace will come once more.

Her voice was like that of a goddess—pure and clear

and nearly as magical as that of Lagrace. But instead of the sense of dread he had felt in the pit of his belly when he'd heard the serpent music, this singing made Dominique feel warm and comfortable. Surrounded by the conspirators in the hidden room, in that moment, his bird on his shoulder, he even felt brave.

Dominique leaned back against the wall and, still smiling, looked from face to face. Something had changed. Gone were the wary glances, the residual suspicions. Now there was curiosity, admiration, and concern. Even Ontocki gave him a grudging nod. And there was something else, especially in the faces of the younger ones—Erma, Nina, and Breska. They leaned forward, shoulders tense with anticipation, as if they expected Dominique to say something profound. Wanting desperately to please them, he opened his mouth and heard himself saying, "Please don't stop singing."

Brigitta smiled, a genuine, warm smile, and pressed her fingertip to her lips. "If I'm not mistaken, soon the doors will—"

Just then the bells tinkled and she nodded and her eyes sparkled.

"Brigitta's right. That will be Papa," Malia whispered. "I must go. The others will show you how to listen to the stories."

With that, Malia rose to her feet, took up the large basket of bread she had brought in earlier, and moved quickly to the hidden wall. Two sharp raps sounded from the other side and only then did she push the wall aside and slip out into the tavern. The wall rattled back into place and left the others silent behind it.

Malia and her father spoke in loud voices out in the tavern.

"Those are lovely fish, Papa. The soup will be good tonight."

"Indeed. The fish soup is always fine at Ventnor's."

Dominique wondered who else they were hoping to fool, for their words were obviously not meant for those in hiding. A moment later, a loud banging at the front door rang through the tavern so loudly that even those in the back room could hear it clearly.

"Father—the patrons have arrived," Malia said, and Ventnor's footsteps moved away to open the door.

29

FRIENDS IN ODD PLACES

The little boy picked up the pebbles and dropped them in the basket. How could he have known that others, too, needed to follow the path home?

—Estorian story

Once the patrons started to arrive in force, it was nearly impossible to pick apart the voices. Every few minutes the bells jingled and another three or four voices joined the ever-louder rumble of talk. Behind the wall, the hidden ones paced quietly back and forth, sat at the tables and played hupsula with pebbles, or dozed.

Soon, smells of cooking began to drift into the room from the tavern and Dominique's stomach rumbled. In the early afternoon, the three designated cooks, Grembal, Zeff, and Ontocki, ducked under the blanket and disappeared into the panarium. Before long, delicious smells assaulted Dominique from both directions and set his mouth watering.

The meal in the back room was consumed in near silence. Occasionally someone whispered something, but only when the noise level next door was loud enough that there was no possibility they would be overheard.

Dominique remained in a daze for the rest of the morning, so relieved and delighted at the return of his bird that he temporarily stopped fretting about his place with the others. Throughout the day, various members of the secret group came to sit beside him and admire Navina. Breska tried to make friends by offering Navina a bit of his flatbread, but the bird refused to take anything from anyone other than Dominique. Certainly nobody tried to touch the kasyapa.

After lunch, Erma emerged from the panarium carefully carrying a shallow dish of water. She placed it on the table in front of Dominique and Navina and then sat down and watched as Navina fluttered to the table and had a drink. Erma's smile was so wide she could have been serving a queen or a goddess. When Navina had finished drinking, she eyed the water and then stepped up onto the side of the dish. As Dominique and Erma watched, she tipped forward into the water, chest first, and proceeded to have a bath right there on the table, rocking the dish and splashing water everywhere as she fluttered her wings and scooped water up and over her back with quick flicking motions of her head and beak.

Erma clapped her hand over her mouth to stifle her giggles, and Dominique had to hold his breath to stop himself from bursting out laughing.

With her bath finished, Navina strutted to the centre of the table where she fluffed up her feathers and settled in for a good long preening session. Dominique would have been quite content to watch her all day, and might have done so, if Zeff, his big ears poking out sideways, hadn't sat beside him and said in a hushed voice, "Dominique. As a member of the Ventnor Conspiracy, you have a job to do."

Dominique looked up, searching the Campriano's face for a clue to the nature of his task. He imagined hand-to-hand combat with one of Emberto's guards, or a secret spying mission to learn of some plot to capture leranons, or—

"You have been added to the duty roster," Zeff said. "You must go to the panarium and help clean up after the midday meal. Tomorrow you'll take a turn to help with preparing the food."

Dominique nodded. It was no longer so strange to think of helping with the cooking and cleaning. These might have been women's jobs with his own people, but here, being asked to pull his weight meant the others were expecting him to stay.

Zeff cuffed him lightly on the side of the head and winked. The friendly swat didn't hurt, and Dominique felt a delicious sense of belonging. Zeff would not have cuffed a stranger's ear. When he had lived with his own people, a cuff from one of the other boys was merely another way to torment him. He had never felt the easy sense of camaraderie he now enjoyed.

He didn't quite dare to give Zeff a playful punch back—he was an adult, after all—so instead he grinned in reply and held his wrist out to Navina, who stepped up readily and let him put her on his shoulder. There she resumed her preening as Dominique took his place in the panarium with Zeff and Scillio.

Two large wooden tubs stood on the floor in the panarium.

"Come with me," Zeff said. "But be quiet out in the courtyard."

Dominique nodded, remembering the warning from Ventnor.

With exaggerated caution, Zeff showed him how to work the pump handle to collect water in a smaller bucket. A fire crackled in the outdoor fireplace, and someone had already filled two copper kettles with water that heated over the flames. Worried that someone would see the smoke, Dominique looked up but could see only the battered metal roof.

"What about—"

Zeff motioned for Dominique to be quiet and then pointed up and gestured—at the fire, the roof, and then in the approximate direction of where the upstairs of the tavern should have been. Zeff's increasingly animated gestures only baffled Dominique, and finally Zeff gave up on his silent explanation. Instead, he left Dominique to fill the buckets.

Dominique pumped water and then carried a dozen bucketfuls into the panarium. His labours filled only one of the large tubs.

"What were you trying to tell me out there?" he asked on one trip inside.

Zeff laughed. "That the only people who might see the smoke would be Ventnor and Malia—they have the rooms above the courtyard. On the other side of the alley out back there's a walled garden and then a canal—anyone farther away would just think it was the cooking fire for the tavern. To those in the tavern courtyard it would seem as if the smoke was from the boarding house next door."

Despite the reassuring words, Dominique still felt uneasy, and on each trip out to the courtyard he concentrated hard, careful not to clank the pump handle or bump into anything with his full buckets. As he hauled water, Zeff and Scillio scraped the wooden plates and heavy mugs and stacked them neatly, ready to wash. Then they cut open a large sack of peska root and began to scrape the thick roots clean.

"Only half full," Zeff said softly when Dominique tipped water into the second barrel. "We'll use the boiling water from the kettles to fill that one."

Arms aching, Dominique carried another five buckets of water. By the time he poured the last bucket into the barrel he could hardly lift it high enough to clear the rim.

"Take a rest," Zeff said, and Dominique crouched beside the two men where they sat on two low stools, cutting the peska roots into thin disks and dropping them into a large wooden bowl.

"Do your people eat princha root?" Zeff asked.

It took a moment for Dominique to realize he was talking about the peska root in his hands.

"Oh, yes—yes, we do," Dominique answered, keeping his voice low. "But we call it peska root. And we—well, the women—grind it up and use it to make flatbread. Or sometimes they use it in tonneck stew."

Zeff nodded. "Princha root is the Campriano name. What do you call it on Timpah, Scillio?"

"We have two different names. Some call it princha—mostly those who live in the villages—but the herders call it shy root because it's hard to find."

Dominique didn't care what it was called: peska root tasted good. Though he had eaten so recently, Dominique was already looking forward to the evening meal.

"Can you manage to lift the kettles?" Scillio asked. He wasn't a tall man, but he was powerful. Each time he twisted his wrist to slice off a piece of peska root, the muscles in his arm flexed and bulged.

"I'll try."

"Use the tongs out by the fire," Scillio said. "We wouldn't want you to burn yourself."

Outside, Dominique lifted a huge pair of long-handled iron tongs from their hook on the wall and manoeuvred them toward a smoke-blackened kettle handle. On his first attempt to lift the kettle, he was caught off guard by its weight. His arms shook so much that water splashed onto the fire below. Clouds of steam hissed up and Dominique froze, anxiously staring at the back wall of the courtyard.

A roar of laughter from the other side of the wall dividing the longer side of the courtyard from the outside eating area reassured him. With all the clattering of dishes and mugs, the shouts and cheers of Ventnor's patrons, there was little chance anyone would hear him.

Dominique braced himself with his feet far apart and his elbows closer to his sides. "Careful, careful," he whispered to himself as he lifted the bubbling kettle from the hook. Setting his burden swinging, he headed back inside the panarium, proud to find very little water was sloshing out.

"Well done," Scillio said with a nod. "Set it down there." Dominique put the kettle down and straightened up. "Your mother won't know you when you see her again."

Dominique's blush was hot and immediate: the pride he felt for carrying the boiling water without spilling evaporated instantly. It was one thing to help these strangers who worked together in so many ways. But it was quite another matter to think of the humiliation it would bring to his mother if he returned to his clan knowing how to prepare peska root and tend cooking fires. He had not been banished for a year to learn to do the work of women. The Stories he sought, the Stories from Beyond that would earn him a place among the Estorian men, were still out of his reach. He sighed and Scillio and Zeff looked up from their work.

"Only one more to carry in," Zeff said, waving his knife toward the courtyard. "It's not that bad a job. You haven't had to scrub the cooking pots yet."

Dominique didn't set him straight. It was easier to let them think he was unhappy about the work than to explain what was really troubling him.

Zeff winked and then twirled his knife with a dramatic flourish before resuming the rhythmic *snick-a-snick-a-snick-a* of the chopping. How could Dominique possibly say anything about his embarrassment without being rude? He took comfort in Navina's warm body snuggled close to his neck and went back outside for the second kettle.

CHAPTER

30

BRIGITTA'S SONG

The story's truth lies in its usefulness.

—Campriano proverb

Washing and drying the dishes, slicing peska root and sweet avamorn for stew, and working a fresh batch of dough for bread seemed to take ages, but when Dominique, Zeff, and Scillio finally finished their work and returned to the hidden room, Dominique wished there had been more to keep them busy. The afternoon was only half finished. Inside, the others rested or sat at the tables, silently playing hupsula and whispering. Meath Boru paced quietly back and forth in front of the wall with the secret entrance, his hands clasped together behind his back and his lips moving as if he were telling himself a story.

From the other side of the wall the noises in the tavern sounded so enticing. Men and women shouted and laughed, glasses clinked, and at some point, someone began to play an instrument Dominique had never heard before.

"What is that?" Dominique whispered to Grembal,

who was sitting with Brigitta at a table near Meath Boru's well-worn path.

"A fourteen-stringed zlavott, I think."

Brigitta nodded in agreement. While there were people in the tavern she couldn't sing, but she tapped her fingers lightly on the table as the zlavott's music drifted through the wall.

Grembal went on quietly, "I had one myself—I loved to play when I was resting in the afternoon after a morning working on a wall."

"Did you see Grembal's mosaic at the palace?" Brigitta asked softly.

"Where is it?"

"There are two. One runs along the outer wall."

Dominique nodded. He remembered the yellow palace wall adorned with the intricate mosaic work showing the city and its towers.

"The other one is in the grand dining hall on the wall above and behind Lord Emberto's seat."

Dominique smiled. "Lord Emberto didn't see fit to invite me to dine with him."

"Of course not," Brigitta said. "But should you ever dine in the palace, you are in for a treat. Excellent food, of course, but Grembal's work is incredible."

"Were you a prisoner there, too?" Dominique asked, wondering how she had seen Emberto's dining room.

Brigitta chuckled. "Not at all. I was invited to perform for Emberto. And, for a time, he very much enjoyed my songs and stories. That is, until I told the story of four armies, each approaching Carnillo from a different direction. Emberto didn't like it and asked me to leave the city."

"But you didn't—"

"No. I didn't leave. But it's a good thing he doesn't know that. After the first attack, he would have had me arrested."

"First attack?"

"You don't know?"

Dominique shook his head.

"Midwinter last, fourteen ships sailed from Castle Donemicci, very much the way my song predicted." Brigitta closed her eyes and began to sing so softly Dominique had to lean close in order to hear her.

Tall ships shall sail from shores afar
Beware your men are ready.
They shall sail in winter's dark,
Weapons drawn, fine swords sharp.
Risk not the lives of man nor wife,
For with those ships come weeks of strife.
Beware you take good heed of me
Or lose the City by the Sea.

Brigitta sat back and Dominique let out his breath. "Carnillo was attacked last winter?" he asked.

"It was very much as I sang. Emberto's left arm suffered a dreadful wound in the battle with Donemicci's ships. Many lives were lost on both sides. If he had chosen to listen to my warning, perhaps he would not have been so badly injured. Perhaps fewer would have died."

"Had he not listened at all, he might have been killed," Meath Boru countered, joining them at the table.

"Hmm. We will never know. I might have made a terrible mistake by warning him."

"But how did you know of the invasion?" Dominique asked.

Brigitta's grey eyes studied Dominique thoughtfully. "You are a teller. You know how these things come to pass. The greatest talent a teller possesses is the ability to listen to whispers and from them construct the spoken truth."

Did she mean that she heard whispers from Beyond? Dominique picked uneasily at the edge of the hole in his leggings. The idea that a woman might be able to do such a thing seemed too outlandish to consider. Perhaps Brigitta meant that a man had whispered the story to her. Maybe she had met an Estorian man who had been to Donemicci and returned with news of ships being readied for battle. Amana had been taught quite a few stories, not all of them tales of the earth, the seasons, the goddesses of all living cycles. Yes, someone must have told Brigitta.

"In the song it says Carnillo would be lost," Dominique said.

Brigitta smoothed her hands over her long skirt. "Yes. That was the story I told. But that's not exactly the truth."

"You didn't make it up, did you?" But the minute the words were out, he knew that wasn't the case—she had *known* what was going to happen and she had chosen to tell the story differently.

"Does a story need to be entirely true to work as a warning? The Estorians tell special stories that warn of danger, don't they?"

"Yes, we have special Stories from Beyond." Dominique hesitated. "But the Stories from Beyond are never lies."

With one eyebrow raised, Brigitta asked, "If a story served to protect or help someone, wouldn't that be a special story, too?"

"Well . . . in some manner, I—I suppose—"

"And if the story was only partly true, but it still served its purpose, would that make it a lie? Or, perhaps it would be better to say, would that make it any less special?"

Dominique didn't know what to say. Was she mocking the way the Estorians told their finest Stories? He longed to tell her a Story from Beyond so she would understand how special they were. But he couldn't do that, and his failure was why he had ended up here.

Snatches of the Stories from Beyond, the ones the men had told when he had been with his own people, now drifted through his thoughts. He would never forget the way the flickering light of the evening fire reflected on a teller's face, or the looks of wonder as the listeners drank in every word, enraptured. Dominique frowned. Those Stories had power. Surely that power was rooted in their unalterable truth?

Meath Boru tipped his head toward the base of the false wall. "Speaking of storytellers, the Campriano tellers will arrive soon. Shall we show our young friend here how to view?"

Brigitta touched Dominique lightly on the shoulder, a firm but gentle gesture that told him all was well between them. "We must prepare now before the tellers arrive and the crowd quiets down. Then we won't be able to move a muscle back here."

"You are right about that," Erma said, coming up beside Brigitta and giving her a quick hug.

"Too bad for anyone who isn't ready," Breska said, nudging Dominique with his elbow. "Come on. We'll show you what to do."

31

THE TELLERS

Three children sat listening to the storyteller. Into the first child's head galloped a fine, white horse. In the second child, a dragon rose from behind a low hill. To the third child came a new ending. And that child became the Grand Teller.

—Campriano Recitatorium tale

"Here," Breska said, tossing a blanket to Dominique. All along the wall with the sliding door, those in the hidden room were flipping blankets open onto the floor. Breska waved Dominique over to a spot to one side of the secret door and spread out his blanket at the base of the wall.

"Down here," Breska said, patting the space beside him. Dominique spread out his blanket and, like the others, lay flat on his belly with his head toward the wall. Navina perched on top of his head, her spindly toes buried in his thick tangle of hair.

"She could make a nest in there," Breska whispered.

"We should cut some of that," Erma said, stifling a giggle as she settled on Dominique's other side.

Self-consciously, Dominique touched his long curls.

Maybe she was right. The men here all had shorter hair than he did.

"Don't listen to her," Breska said. "She's just jealous!"

Dominique's cheeks flushed. "Leave me alone!" he said, but he didn't really mean it. He liked the gentle teasing, especially when Erma did it.

Scillio squeezed in on Erma's other side and Meath Boru waved his arm to indicate everyone was ready. Then Ontocki moved from lantern to lantern and extinguished all the lights. The room was momentarily thrown into complete darkness.

Suddenly, Dominique felt the movement of air on his face. The chatter and laughter from the tavern became much louder and a strip of light appeared before him. When he tentatively pushed his hand forward, it did not stop at the wall, and Dominique realized a long piece of wood at the base of the wall had been lifted out of the way. At first he thought he was meant to look directly into the other room, but when he wiggled forward to peer through the gap he saw that would be impossible. The back of the large bar opposite where they lay blocked the rest of the room from view.

As Dominique watched, two pairs of feet moved back and forth, in and out of view. One pair belonged to Malia, who chatted and laughed with the customers as if she hadn't a care in the world.

"Why, if you have another cup of wild water now, you'll be under the table before the tellers arrive! Slow down, Tigano! A bowl of soup for you, Malwin? Just a minute—one or two pieces of bread with that?"

The other pair of boots moved a little more slowly, but Dominique recognized Ventnor's voice as he, too, served customers.

Dominique wiggled closer, rested his cheek on the blanket, and waited. Erma and Breska also settled into more comfortable positions. Perhaps they would just listen to the tellers. Maybe they weren't going to see anything after all.

The bells tinkled and a man's voice boomed into the tavern.

"Be still! Be still! Tellers ho! Tellers ho!"

As the tavern patrons fell quiet, something moved below the row of bowls stacked on the bottom shelf of the bar directly opposite Dominique. A black cloth slipped up, pulled by cords set at equal distances along its length for as far as Dominique could see. Behind the cloth, a smooth, reflective piece of glass angled up from the floor. In the glass, Dominique clearly saw a good section of the room, tables filled with food and drink, patrons sitting and standing as they watched the tellers arrive. There had to be another mirror somewhere, he reasoned, one that looked down on the room and, in turn, was reflected in the mirror opposite those lying behind the false wall.

The sensation of looking down on the room even though he was lying on the floor was similar to seeing something through Navina's eyes. He reached up and gave his bird a scratch.

The strip of mirror opposite was not large enough to take in the whole room, but from where he lay, Dominique could easily see a small platform opposite the bar. A man dressed in a bright jacket and tight breeches stepped onto the platform and bellowed, "And so begins our evening of entertainment. Listen well!"

Malia and Ventnor clapped enthusiastically and the patrons joined in.

"Our first teller tonight is Brocheno Chella, a young man with considerable talent and knowledge of the Conspiracy tales."

More applause greeted the plump man whose black hair was slicked back and shone in the lantern light. He stepped onto the platform and bowed deeply as the crowd clapped.

"And so my tale begins . . ." The young man turned slowly on the platform, making eye contact with many of those in the room. "There was once a great city by the sea . . ."

"Carnillo!" the crowd shouted back.

"Carnillo. Prosperity came to all who lived there."

The young man spoke of great wealth and peace within the walled city, and Dominique wondered whether the poor children and beggars who swarmed the streets were recent arrivals or whether Chella would mention them later.

"And then the day came when ships sailed from Castle Donemicci and a great battle raged in the waters of the Sea of Chanmari."

Brocheno Chella went on to relate several dramatic battle scenes during which he threw himself from side to side on the stage as if he were being run through with curved blades. He died forty times over as he related details of losses, mostly of Donemicci's men, and the heroic acts of Emberto's soldiers and sailors.

His technique was good, Dominique had to admit. Brocheno Chella's face contorted with agony and smoothed into serenity as one particularly brave fighter met his end. But talented though he was, he was still a lying Campriano who neglected to mention the heavy losses on Emberto's side and who never once mentioned Emberto's injury.

The stories continued, changing from tales of the battles to stories of conspiracies and invasions. Brocheno Chella was soon drenched with sweat and his eyes were wild as he gestured toward the dark corners of the tavern with his story stick. "Dangerous spies and conspirators lurk in every corner. Trust nobody in these terrible times. Your neighbours may be your worst enemies. Have you heard of the Wild Water Station burning?"

Several in the crowd nodded.

"The leather worker Tona Billiamo, who kept a stall at the marketplace, was a spy and an arsonist with a grudge against the good citizen Bim Scarpio. Tona Billiamo burned the place to the ground!"

Dominique stiffened. That certainly wasn't true. Emberto's men had burned the tavern as punishment for not allowing the tellers to perform there. Bim Scarpio had died because of Emberto's soldiers. Surely the patrons wouldn't believe these ludicrous stories!

Several men in the tavern banged their fists on the tables. "Death to spies!" one shouted, and another answered, "I'll set the sons of boars on fire myself!"

On his stage, Brocheno Chella nodded. "Fear not. Tona Billiamo was duly arrested and justice was done. But his betrayal, his fervent denials, his declarations of innocence are warnings to us all! We must all be careful."

"Aye! Aye!"

"Tell us more!"

The storyteller swept his dishevelled hair from his eyes and bowed. "Enough today. Return tomorrow for more news of the latest threats and to hear what the Great Emberto is doing to secure our safety, well-being, and wealth."

Many in the tavern cheered, and even Malia and Ventnor clapped and stamped their feet. Dominique was furious. He wanted to barge through the secret door and tell the crowd—what? He had not been at the battles. How did he know that Brigitta's version of what had happened was any more accurate than Brocheno Chella's? How did he know that it was Emberto's men who had burned down the Wild Water Station?

After all, the people hidden in the back room had no love for Emberto and his men. That made them conspirators. And lying on the floor, secretly watching Emberto's tellers at work, made all of them spies. Dominique swallowed hard. He hadn't come to Carnillo a criminal, but no matter how he looked at it, he certainly was one now.

When Brocheno Chella took his final bow, Dominique assumed the evening's entertainment was over and began to wiggle backwards away from the wall. Two hands reached for him and Breska patted the blanket on the floor. From the other side, Dominique felt Erma's hair tickle his cheek as she leaned close and whispered in his ear, "There is usually a second teller. Stay still."

Dominique didn't want to hear any more stories, but he felt hands pushing firmly on his back and he lay down again.

The man with the fancy clothes stepped up onto the platform. "This evening we have a special treat. As you know, the finest tellers are invited to study with the Grand Teller of Carnillo in the Recitatorium."

Murmurs of approval moved through the crowd.

"This evening it is my pleasure to present to you not just any teller from the Recitatorium, but the First Teller Born."

Dominique pushed forward so his forehead was wedged against the bottom of the wall. First Teller Born?

The crowd reacted to this statement with wild cheers.

"It has been said that this teller may someday become the Grand Teller of Carnillo."

At this, many banged their empty bowls on the tables and stomped their boots so hard that Dominique felt the floorboards vibrating beneath him. Malia scurried out from behind the bar and weaved her way between the tables, collecting the empty dishes and asking if any of the customers required fresh drinks.

When the crowd had settled, the introducer cleared his throat. "And now, please welcome the great Amana Elnedo."

CHAPTER
32

AMANA'S STORY

The story's usefulness lies in its truth.

—Estorian proverb

The tavern erupted with a great burst of cheering, whistling, and shouting.

Behind the wall, Dominique was glad he was already lying on the ground or he would have been in danger of collapsing. Amana? She wore her blood eagle cloak, her quiver of arrows slung over her back, and her dagger at her side. Her hair was twisted into a single, thick braid that hung straight down the middle of her back. As she turned on the platform, greeting the tavern guests, her cloak fanned out, the bottom edge lifting as if blown up from below by a swirling wind.

She raised one hand and the crowd fell quiet. "The great Lord Emberto does, indeed, rule during difficult times," she said, her familiar voice slicing right through Dominique. Shocked though he was by her presence in the tavern, he now also recognized a quality in her voice that he had not fully appreciated before. Hers was a voice that commanded attention, he knew that. But the effect she had on the crowd was nothing short of magical. Even though she had not yet begun to weave a tale, the tavern was silent and all eyes were fixed upon her, eager to hear what she might say next.

"Perhaps you expect me to tell a story of how Emberto came to rule the City of Carnillo."

Several patrons nodded as if this was exactly what they had hoped to hear.

"Or perhaps you expect another tale of great battles led by the wise Lord Emberto."

Several others nodded at this suggestion, and one man raised his cup and shouted, "Say whatever you will and we shall listen!" His drunken comment was greeted with howls of laughter and general agreement.

Amana nodded in his direction. "Then you shall be pleased to hear me tell you a story of the great kasyapa bird."

In the near darkness of the hiding place, Dominique felt Breska and Erma reach for him, their hands moving to his shoulders as if to keep him quiet.

In the tavern, Amana reached over her shoulder and withdrew her story stick from its place among her arrows.

"A foundling prince once drifted along an ancient river, cloaked in a simple wrap of fine-spun silk."

As Amana described the baby, adrift on the current, she moved the story stick, her hands, and her arms, and they became the waves, then the tightly woven basket, and then the baby's hands grasping at the edge of his floating cradle.

As Dominique listened, her words blurred and faded and he found himself watching the prince wandering the wide open grasslands of western Tanga where the child's adoptive family lived. These shepherds cared for the boy they found in the river and raised him as if he were their own.

Amana wove a word spell so powerful that not a soul moved, all whispers ceased, and for as long as she spoke, all those in the tavern and in the hidden room stayed absolutely motionless, even when limbs began to stiffen and backs to ache.

The story went on and on. Amana changed her voice, her posture, and became the prince as he learned to fight. She threw herself into each battle as the prince defended new lambs against the attacks of white wolves and incubus alike. He grew up to become a fine shepherd and a strong fighter, unaware of his true parentage. Shortly after his surrogate father died, the boy made a discovery.

"I walked to the top of the hill behind my family's house," Amana said, speaking in the voice of the young man grieving the loss of his father.

"At first, I believed I was alone and I stood close to the cliff edge." Amana leaned forward as if she were peering down into the valley below. An uneasy recognition pulled Dominique forward and he ground his forehead against the bottom of the wall.

"I believed I was alone until—" Here Amana paused, rigid and terrified, and it was as though Dominique could hear the strange fluttering, the desperate wheezing from the ground behind him, as he had that day when he found Navina.

Amana whirled around, her arms flung out sideways as she tried to frighten away what the young man believed was a demon, or a Silencer.

She can't do this, Dominique thought as Amana continued to relate how the shepherd-prince had followed the mother kasyapa bird who, flailing her wings in the dust, desperate to capture his attention, led him to her only chick. This is *my* story, he thought, furious. She can't just take it and pretend it's hers. He could have told the rest of the story right along with her—the scramble up the strange rock formation, on top of which the glorious bird had made her nest, the nasty bite on the hand the big-headed baby had given him, the way he had used his trousers to wrap up the baby and take her home.

Dominique blushed when the patrons laughed at this last description. He should never have told Amana about that. Never.

"With the coming of the kasyapa, bird of visions, bird of peace, the boy's mother knew the time had come for the young man to seek the crown that was rightfully his."

At this point Amana took several deep breaths and wiped sweat from her forehead as if she herself had scrambled up to the nest and rescued the orphaned kasyapa. Her gestures abruptly changed now that the bird had become her constant companion. With easy familiarity, her hand rose to scratch the back of her imagined companion's head, and Dominique's hand rose of its own accord to find Navina's sleeping form, her head tucked beneath her wing, one foot lifted, toes curled against her breast.

When Amana had caught her breath, her voice dropped low and serious and she carried on as if she were sharing an intimate secret with her closest friend. Everyone that Dominique could see in the mirror and those lying to either side of him listened as if stunned, jaws slack, eyes wide, ale and soup completely forgotten. "For there is none among us who does not know that the kasyapa comes only to one destined to lead. To see such a boy is to see your future king."

Immediately she retreated back into the story, once again becoming the young man with his kasyapa, who first marched on the City by the Sea and then headed east to the mainland to regain his kingdom in the Festerworlds, the land cloaked by dark magic.

The final image in the story was one of the boy standing on the bow of a sailing ship, rising and falling with the waves as he set out on his journey.

When she had finished, Amana bowed her head. For a moment there was silence. And then the response came like a thunderous wave as the listeners whooped and whistled. Banging their fists on the tables, they demanded to know where the boy went, the name of his father, the king, whether he ever claimed his rightful place as head of state, whether he survived the curse of the Festerworlds.

Amana's head remained bowed and the introducer stepped up onto the platform beside her.

"Please, please—we understand how you have enjoyed this wondrous tale. But the great Amana is clearly exhausted." Indeed, Amana was still out of breath and seemed dazed. She tucked her story stick back into her arrow quiver and kept glancing at the door as if eager to leave the crowded tavern. "The tellers will return tomorrow evening."

The man bowed deeply, sweeping his arm before him in a wide flourish as if he had been the one to tell such a marvellous story and not the girl beside him.

"The time has come for us to depart. Amana must rest well now. Good evening!"

The man took Amana's arm and guided her from the stage. Her face was flushed and she swayed slightly as she stepped down. Brocheno Chella fell into step behind them and they moved through the crowd, beyond the view of the mirrors. Malia's feet moved past Dominique and a moment later a narrow slat of wood flapped down over the viewing hole, plunging the hidden room back into complete darkness.

Dominique lay motionless on his stomach, stunned. He stayed there, vaguely aware of someone behind him lighting a lamp, the others shifting and stretching as they moved away from the wall.

CHAPTER
33
NEWCOMERS

Three children sat listening to a story. The first child heard wind when the teller whispered, "Whoooosh." The second child tasted sweet syrup when the teller spoke of dragonberries. The third child, a boy, listened and heard a Voice from Beyond. When this child became a man he travelled far and wide. His wife and children were always plump and healthy and lived in the biggest hut in the encampment.

—Estorian tale for boys

It was very quiet on the tavern side of the wall until someone shouted, "Another round of wild water for my friends here!" and the conversation started again. Only then was Dominique able to push himself to his hands and knees. Navina, woken by Dominique's movement, stretched her wings and yawned. Slowly, the hidden ones made their way back to the tables where they would consume their evening meal in silence. Then they would wait the long hours until the tavern closed and they could move the tables and chairs to make room for the sleeping mats.

When the tinkling bells rang for the last time after the final customer's departure, those in the hidden room began to speak softly among themselves.

"So, we have a foundling prince among us," Erma joked, though Dominique thought she looked at him a little differently.

"The girl is a fine teller, indeed," Brigitta said. "So, she, too, has heard the story of the boy with the kasyapa." She turned to look at Dominique and said, "Perhaps you have more stories to tell than you know."

Dominique blushed. He hated this, the way they seemed to expect things from him that he didn't understand. Yes, he had once found a kasyapa bird, young and alone in a nest, abandoned by her dying mother. But that didn't make him a prince. Amana had made that part up.

"But I'm not—" he began to protest.

The hidden wall slipped aside and Brigitta turned away. Malia and Ventnor joined the others in the room.

"An interesting night of tales, for a change," Ventnor said. "At least, the second half was interesting."

"Yes, Amana is good," Brigitta agreed.

"Not like that fool, Brocheno Chella!" Ventnor waved his hand as if he were brushing away an annoying insect. "Those stories he tells are ridiculous! No new information from him!"

"Do you think anyone believed him when he said Tona Billiamo had burned down the Wild Water Station?" Ontocki asked.

Ventnor snorted. "I don't think anyone was *that* drunk!"

"They say Amana Elnedo will someday be the next Grand Teller," Malia said.

Dominique didn't know whether he should mention that the Campriano girl who had brought him to the city was actually the exalted performer who had enthralled the tavern patrons. Being chosen to be the Grand Teller sounded as if it was a great honour. It intrigued him that Amana had never mentioned she might one day become so famous. He thought of Roman Bertolescu, the Protector in their clan, the elder who made sure all the boys received their training, heard Stories from Beyond when it was time, and if they didn't, cast them out to find their voices. Was this what the Grand Teller did? "Do the Campriano tellers also have a Protector?" he asked.

Zeff nodded. "In a manner, yes. The Tellers Guild works like the other guilds. If you show any promise at all when you are little, you become an apprentice."

"Your family doesn't teach you anything?"

"No more than any child learns of the family stories at a young age. The children who are chosen to be sold to the guild to learn the serious craft of telling leave their families and go to live at the Recitatorium. They have lessons, they train with the masters, they spend time with the ruling families. They practise their skills in places like the tavern and in the market square. The best of them are sent on solo journeys to learn—"

Zeff stopped when someone rapped at the front door of the tavern.

"Quick!" Ventnor said, pushing Malia out through the opening.

"Who comes to Ventnor's?" Malia shouted as the wall slid back into place.

"Who?" Dominique mouthed to Breska, who shrugged and shook his head. Nobody seemed to know who would be coming so late at night. Dominique strained to hear what was happening beyond the wall but could make out only hushed voices. The warning bells tinkled as the front door opened. Footsteps crossed the floor out in the tavern and then the wall slid to the side. Everyone took a step back. Two men staggered into the room, panting hard.

"Shasta!" Dominique said, recognizing the shaggy

prisoner whose red-rimmed eyes squinted and blinked in the filthy strip not covered by his heavy beard or the tangled hair falling over his forehead.

"This is Berolino—member of the Fishers Guild." Shasta panted as if he and the boy had run a great distance. Dominique recalled his own terrified flight from the tower. Both newcomers were spent but could not tear their eyes away from the wall, as if someone might break down the door to the tavern and come after them. A long chain remained shackled to each prisoner's iron wrist cuff. Without saying a word, Malia opened the wall enough to slip out and returned a moment later with the cutters.

"Why tonight?" Toranosco asked after the wall had been closed again. "I thought the plan was to wait at least five nights—"

"I know—oh, what a mess," Shasta said, still breathing hard. "More rope arrived—we thought the plans had changed."

"We didn't send rope," Malia said. "It was too soon after—" Her hand started to reach for Toranosco and then dropped to her side.

"So who . . ." Ontocki glared at Hermano, who nodded.

"Yes. It is possible that someone, perhaps one of the guards, grew suspicious. Or maybe it was a trick, a betrayal."

"What matters most now is, were you seen?" Ventnor asked.

Shasta nodded.

"Don't say there was a third this time . . ." Ventnor said.

"There was another fisher."

A sharp intake of breath was the only response from those inside the room.

Then Berolino spoke. "It was my older brother. Dorian." He pushed the hair out of his eyes and looked away. He blinked and swallowed hard and Dominique could tell he was trying hard not to cry.

"He fell," Shasta said. "Guards were chasing us, and . . ."

Shasta could not finish. He put his arm around Berolino and the boy buried his head in the man's shoulder, unable to control the tears any longer. Shasta's gaze caught and held Dominique's and he nodded a silent greeting before turning his attention back to the distraught boy beside him.

Breska darted forward and tugged at the door. Malia and Ventnor rushed to help him and the door slid closed.

The room seemed smaller and no longer so safe.

"Did anyone see you come in here?" Meath Boru asked.

Shasta shook his head.

"I'm too old for this," he said. "Old—but not a fool. We must have run half the way around Carnillo to get here."

"Shasta—sit down," Malia said. "Breska, Scillio—get them chairs."

Berolino collapsed into the chair he was offered. His slender body crumpled forward, wretched with sobs. "Dorian . . . they caught him . . . we have to . . ." He buried his face in his hands and wept, inconsolable.

Meath Boru turned to the others who stood immobilized, watching the boy's misery, uncertain what to do.

"If the young man has been caught . . ." Meath Boru started to say, but he didn't finish aloud.

Nobody said anything, but Dominique could imagine what they were thinking about. Emberto's men had quite an arsenal of intimidation tools at their disposal.

"How much did he know?" Dominique surprised himself by asking the question.

Shasta put his head down and made a strange, gagging sound, so wretched Dominique thought the man was going to be ill.

"He insisted . . ." he started to say and then groaned.

"You told him?" Malia asked, her voice tight with disbelief, fear. "You told him where you were going?"

"He said I was too old," Shasta said miserably, "that if we were chased I would not be able to run quickly enough . . ."

Shasta raised his head, his matted hair soaked, Dominique now saw, not just from his plunge into the canal but sticky with blood.

"I'm sorry," Shasta said. "I'm so sorry."

"Shh," Brigitta said, stepping forward. "What's done is done. Perhaps he will not break . . . or, not quickly."

"Papa," Malia said, "we must find another place to hide."

Ventnor nodded, looking from face to face. "We will make preparations for a quick departure, should it be necessary. But perhaps, as Brigitta says, Dorian will hold up long enough for me to make other arrangements."

"Maybe," Berolino said, still sniffling, "my brother will give them wrong information and they will never come here." The boy sounded so desperate that nobody spoke up to say otherwise.

Malia kneeled beside him and touched his cheek. "Your brother was brave to attempt to escape. I'm sure he will do everything he can to keep the rest of us safe."

34

PREPARATIONS

When Obriamo lifted the lid of the basket he saw a mass of undulating spiders. They huddled together, their hairy abdomens distended and quivering. This was not what he expected, so he slammed the lid shut and replaced the rock on top, but not before the queen of the spiders had escaped.

—Campriano story

"What now?" Erma asked.

"Now we barricade the wall," Ventnor said. "We must prepare travel bundles in case we have to make a quick departure out through the back."

"We'll keep watches," Toranosco said. "One out in the courtyard—one in here while the others sleep."

"From now on, no more chit-chat," Malia added. "Talk only in an emergency."

"I will leave at first light," Ventnor said, "and see whether I can find somewhere else to hide everyone, though chances are we'll be split up. I can't think of anywhere large enough for all of us to hide together. And once they learn the tavern was used . . ." He didn't finish the thought, but Dominique noticed the shadow of grief flicker over the old man's face.

Toranosco moved to stand behind Malia, his arms slipping around her waist. She turned her head to look up at him and, despite everything, gave him a quick and lovely smile.

Ventnor cleared his throat. "If you two could please restrain yourselves—"

Brigitta put her hand on Ventnor's arm. "Leave them alone. Who knows how long any of us have together."

Malia gently pushed Toranosco's hands away and said, "We have much to do, and I know you two," she smiled at Shasta and Berolino, who wiped his nose on the back of his hand, "will want something to eat and drink. We have plenty of dried tonneck, flatbread—"

"But I'm not—" Berolino began, but Shasta cut him off.

"She's right," he said. "We don't know when we will eat again. Come—I know tonight's soup didn't fill that young belly of yours." Berolino still didn't look convinced. "Come along. Not eating cannot help Dorian now." Shasta's words sounded cruel, though Dominique knew he was right.

"Go on," Dominique said to the boy. "You will feel better after you eat."

Dominique's words seemed to be the encouragement Berolino needed. He rose from his chair like a very old man and followed Malia and Shasta into the panarium.

"You know what you must do?" Ventnor asked when the others had gone.

"Aye," Toranosco said. "There will be little sleep in this room tonight."

The older man nodded. "No doubt you are right. I know sleep won't find me before first light." He paused a moment, one hand on the sliding door. "Toranosco. If . . . if something should happen . . ." He blinked several times before continuing. "Look after my Malia."

"Ventnor, you know I shall—but don't speak like this. You will return with news of where we shall move next. And before long we will be ready to strike—"

Ventnor held up his hand. "We must not speak of this now. If we can merely survive this night and perhaps another, I shall be happy." With that, he pushed the door aside and slipped into the darkened tavern.

As soon as the wall had clicked back into place, the rest of the group jumped into action. Silent, focused, they pushed furniture in front of the tavern wall, stacking tables and chairs right up to the ceiling beams and wedging them tightly to make it as hard as possible for someone to push into the room. While Dominique and Breska carried another table to jam in behind the other furniture, Zeff and Meath Boru packed food into bundles and then arranged the bundles, two per person, at the back of the panarium.

There was no more cheerful banter, no more teasing from Breska. Brigitta pulled the quilt from its place and arranged an assortment of fabric scraps in a pile in the middle. Dominique wondered what was so strange about her as she added the scissors, needles, and thread, and then rolled everything into a bulky bundle. She worked as she always did, with elegance and calm and no sign of feeling rushed or pressured. Then it struck him how it was that she had changed. Brigitta was completely silent. She didn't sing or hum as she worked, and this silence filled Dominique with a sense of sick dread.

When the last of the furniture had been moved, Dominique and Breska joined Zeff and Meath Boru in the panarium.

"Here," Meath Boru said, handing Dominique a ladle so he could fill empty bladders and skins with fresh water. Dominique scooped and poured, soon finding a rhythm. *Dip. Splash. Drip. Pour.* When a container was full, Breska spun it so the neck twisted shut and Dominique tied it closed with a length of leather cord. The boys hung the full containers from hooks on the wall beside the door to the courtyard.

With so many helping, the packing was accomplished in remarkably little time. When the last water bladder was full and it seemed that the food packing was under control, Breska tugged at Meath Boru's sleeve and then, eyes closed, tipped his head to the side.

"You won't see any sleep before dawn," Meath Boru whispered so softly that Dominique hardly heard, though he only stood on the other side of the water barrel. The shelves were nearly empty. Dominique couldn't imagine what else they might need to pack.

Back in the other room, Ontocki squatted in one corner with Hermano beside him. Ontocki pulled a tool with a sharp, hooked blade from his belt. Both men hunched over, staring intently at something Hermano held in his hands.

"Come on." Breska mouthed the words and moved closer, not waiting to see if Dominique was following. Meath Boru gave Dominique a gentle push from behind.

"Go," he whispered. "You'll need one, too."

"Need what?" Dominique turned to ask, but Meath Boru had already ducked back into the panarium.

Dominique crouched beside Breska, who was on his knees, watching Ontocki. "What—" Dominique started but stopped when Ontocki's eyebrows came together like a prickly minion branch above the bridge of his nose. Dominique stayed quiet, not just because of the carver's warning, but also because he had caught a glimpse of the object Ontocki had taken from Hermano. It was a brand new name ring.

35

NAME RINGS

*Without a name, the sickly baby was left to die
beside the river.*

—Estorian story

The knife bit into the hard wood. Ontocki added the final side of a square he was notching into the ring's surface. He then picked up one of several sticks, each about the length of Dominique's forearm and the thickness of his forefinger. One end of the stick had been carved so it tapered to a hollowed-out flat part, the end of which had been sharpened to a crisp point. Dominique could not imagine what the strange tool was used for.

"That first square shows what guild the person belongs to," Breska whispered.

Dominique now noticed that most of the others already wore name rings. Hermano had removed the one he had worn in prison, and Ontocki appeared to be carving him a new one.

"How can you tell what guild someone's in? Everyone has a square."

"Different colours. See? Grey is for the Fighting Arts Guild. That's for guards. Soldiers. They all have a grey square."

On Hermano's old name ring, the square closest to the place where the ring came apart was grey and had a smaller red circle inside.

Ontocki dipped the pointed end of the stick into a shallow dish filled with thick, yellow liquid the consistency of smooth mud. The colour collected in the hollowed-out part of the stick, and when Ontocki tipped his hand, the liquid oozed into a narrow channel and down to the end of the pointy tip. One drop at a time dribbled from the end as Ontocki touched the tool to the groove he had cut into the wooden ring.

"What does yellow mean?" Dominique asked.

"Fishers. There are lots of fishers—it's a good guild because they come and go, are allowed to own ships."

When the square had been coloured yellow, Ontocki added a green circle inside and then carved another line to the right of the square. This line was short and angled up and to the right.

Dominique nudged Breska, who whispered in Dominique's ear, "A line that goes up like that means a man—down would be a woman. Ontocki will cross it in a minute because Hermano's old enough to marry."

Sure enough, Ontocki added a second, shorter line slashing across the first. He then left a space, made a small nick beside it, and carved a five-pointed star at the end of the wooden ring.

"Hermano was a member of the Carnillo court. That's why he has a red circle. If he was really close to the ruler, he'd get a second, smaller circle inside the first. The inside circle would be black. Can we see the old one?" Breska asked.

Hermano handed it to him and Dominique saw Hermano's old symbols. A grey square because he was a member of the Fighting Arts Guild, an angled slash crossed by a smaller mark to show he was an adult male, and a red circle inside the square indicated Hermano was a member of the court but not particularly close to Emberto. A green star was the last thing carved into the wood.

"What's this for?"

"The star? Right of passage. It means you can go in and out of Carnillo."

"And what about this part?" Dominique pointed to a strange, rough squiggle between the circle and the star.

"Personal mark. That's how you can tell one guard from another. You choose that one and carve it in yourself when you get your ring."

Dominique wished he'd paid more attention to the markings on the ring he'd found, the one that had caused him so much trouble. When he'd first found it, he had innocently thought the marks were merely unusual decorations.

"We all have one," Breska said. "You can't move around Carnillo unless you do. The way things are these days, someone would turn you in."

Hermano had taken the ring and was notching the space beside the star with a shape that looked a bit like a fish tail.

"Why is his circle green?"

"Fishers can't be a member of the court," Breska said, as if this should be obvious. "But they can sell to the court if they have a green circle."

"How do you remember all this stuff?"

"It's not that hard. There aren't *that* many guilds."

When Hermano had coloured his fish tail with black, Ontocki motioned for Dominique to sit beside him. He tried several blank wooden rings of different sizes on Dominique's ankle until he found one that snapped together snugly.

"Brigitta?" Ontocki waved Brigitta over. "What guild do you think?"

Without hesitation Brigitta said, "Storytellers. That

would make sense."

"Of course," Ontocki said and carved a square. This he coloured with brown. Beside that, Dominique was given a slanting mark to show he was a boy, but unlike Hermano's, his was not crossed by a short slash: he wasn't old enough to marry.

There was no circle for court membership, but Ontocki did carve a star, his skilled fingers guiding the hooked carving tool with swift, tight strokes. Dominique's star was green—he had just earned right of free passage to Carnillo.

"How do people usually get these?" he asked.

"You are born to registered parents in Carnillo," Breska said. "Otherwise it's a serious offence to wear one."

Dominique had already discovered that.

"Add a personal mark yourself right here," Ontocki directed, "and that should do the trick." Then he added, "But you'll have to do something about that mess before you walk through the streets." He pointed at Dominique's head.

"I'll take care of that," Breska said, reaching for a pair of shears in Ontocki's tool belt.

"Do I have to—" Dominique said, his hand touching his thick curls.

"Move your hand or I'll lop off your fingers," Breska joked.

"Shh," Ontocki said. "Work quietly." He handed Dominique a knife and his new name ring. "Go ahead. Make your mark while Breska cuts your hair."

Dominique turned the wooden ring in his hands, careful not to smudge the wet colour. He knew exactly what he was going to carve.

With the tip of the blade he scratched two wings spread wide and between them a curved chest and belly arcing in the opposite direction. Another curve showed the top of Navina's head. On top of her head he dug three short grooves to show her crest feathers. Once he had marked out the design he went over it again, making each groove and line deeper, more distinctive.

His forehead furrowed with intense concentration, not just to avoid making a mistake, but also to distract himself from the matted blond curls showering onto his shoulders, his lap, and the floor around him.

"What do Estorians use instead of name rings?" Breska asked, a clump of hair in his hand.

"We don't have anything quite like them," Dominique said, smoothing his thumb over Navina's carved wings. "Babies get these."

He reached inside his baggy shirt and pulled out a soft pouch hanging from a slender leather thong. Tugging open the drawstring at the top, Dominique tipped the bag until an oblong stone slid out into the palm of his hand. He held the reddish brown stone out so Breska could see. "That's my Namingstone. See all these marks?"

The surface of the stone was broken by many slashes and nicks—some heavy and deep, others barely scratching the stone's surface. "The people of my clan— mostly the women—mark the stone on the day the baby is named. No two stones are the same."

Brigitta overheard Dominique's explanation. "It's beautiful," she said, touching the stone.

What Dominique didn't add was that his stone was incomplete: his father, Boris Elnedo, had never added his mark.

"It may be beautiful," Ontocki said, "but it's dangerous."

Brigitta nodded. "I'm sorry, Dominique." Before he knew what had happened, her graceful fingers had closed around the stone and taken it away.

"You can't!" Dominique reached out.

"Quiet!" Ontocki's glare could have paralyzed a

leaping hickletoad mid-leap. Ontocki gestured for him to hand over the leather pouch in which the stone had been kept safe for almost as long as Dominique had been alive. Hands shaking, Dominique did as he was told, blinking back tears as if he were watching someone die.

"From now on you are Dominique the storyteller, born right here in Carnillo to mixed parents—that will explain your light skin colouring, even if we dye your hair. Do you understand?" Ontocki's whispered question left no room for argument, and Dominique knew that to protect himself and the others, he had no choice.

He snapped his new name ring around his ankle and met Ontocki's gaze. "I understand."

"You'll run into less trouble in the city if your hair is dark," Ontocki said. "I'll get some bucket black." He disappeared into the panarium and returned a moment later with a jar containing a thick, sticky, black paste.

"What is that?" Dominique said, wrinkling up his nose at the sharp odour.

"Bucket black. We use it to coat the insides of the wooden water buckets to stop leaks. It's very sticky—"

"And very black," Breska added, scooping out a glob with his fingertips.

"Do we have to—"

"Shh. This won't take long. You don't have much hair left."

Dominique sighed but didn't argue. Anything they could do to make it safer for him to move about in Carnillo seemed like a good idea.

"Good. Very good," Ontocki said, watching Breska smear the bucket black through Dominique's newly cropped hair. "Now, where is Toranosco? I'll modify his name ring and then make new ones for Shasta and Berolino."

"Weapons?" Meath Boru asked, coming back into the room.

Ontocki nodded. "Out in the panarium. Can you send Toranosco in here next? He must still be working."

When Meath Boru returned, both he and Toranosco carried an odd collection of knives and a couple of short swords.

"Breska, you know how to use one of these, don't you?" Meath Boru asked, holding out a sword.

"Yes, sir. So does Zeff."

"So, that's settled. Zeff will get the second one. Well—" Meath Boru said, taking a good look at the new haircut. "I must say you look handsome as a Carnillian teller with Campriano blood. But stories won't help you in a fight. Choose a knife, Dominique."

Meath Boru held out a fish cleaver, a bread saw, and several smaller knives from the panarium. Dominique took a short but very sharp paring knife. "Could I please have my cord back?" he asked Brigitta.

"You're going to hang the knife around your neck?" Breska asked, covering his mouth with his hand to muffle his snicker.

"No."

Brigitta cut the leather cord from the pouch that held Dominique's Namingstone. It felt as if she were cutting away a part of him, and his hand shook as he reached for the cord. He wrapped it twice around his calf and knotted it securely.

"There," Dominique said, carefully sliding the knife blade under the cord. He practised sliding it in and out a couple of times.

"If you cut open the pouch that held your stone," Ontocki said, "you can stitch the leather behind the cord to protect it so you don't slice through. Like a simple scabbard."

Brigitta took the Namingstone out and handed the pouch to Dominique. He pushed the tip of the blade into the seam and tore it open, biting his lips so he didn't cry out with the pain of destroying the last thing that connected him to his people.

I'm sorry, Mama, he thought, hoping she would understand. Ontocki handed him a heavy needle and thick thread.

"The leather's soft," he said, "but if you have trouble sewing, I have a punch you can use." The carver reached over and placed a hand on Dominique's shoulder. "You're still the same boy inside," he said kindly.

Dominique squinted through lashes wet with tears, took up the needle, and started to sew.

It was well after first light before they decided that everyone should get some sleep. Watches were organized and Dominique found himself among the first group to lie down. Maybe, he allowed himself to think as his eyelids grew heavy, maybe Dorian had been stronger than anyone had dared to hope. Maybe the boy had lied to the guards, sent them elsewhere. Despite everyone's worst fears, the soldiers had not come. Maybe they would all be safe in the hidden room for a little longer.

36

TRAITOR

*Look at the child who holds your hand the tightest for she is
the one who will turn on you the fastest.*

—From the Campriano story
"The King Who Trusted Innocence"

Dominique slept until Erma nudged him awake, her
finger on his lips to remind him not to speak aloud as he
fought his way back from a dream. Opening his eyes to
the flurry of muted activity around him made him wish
he really was back by the fire in the leranon cave. In the
dream, his big worry was whether he could speak loudly
enough to be heard by Kyrie and the other young leranons sitting at the very back of the cave.

Dominique stretched as Erma took his place on the
mat. He joined several other bleary-eyed conspirators
where they crouched on the floor near the door of the
panarium eating a cold meal of flatbread and dried dragonberries.

The afternoon dragged by with little change. The
only excitement was when the warning bells tinkled and
everyone froze in their places, relaxing quickly when
Ventnor's voice sang out, a slow, sad song about a man

who must wait a hundred years for the return of his lost bride.

"He has not found us a place yet," Malia whispered. "We can do nothing but wait."

Brigitta unpacked the story quilt and Berolino and Shasta added their stories of near capture. Dominique added a flying bird and a name ring. Malia stitched images from Amana's story into the border reserved for tales of Ventnor's Tavern. It seemed an eternity before a bundle of flatbread was unwrapped for the evening meal—they still did not dare to light a fire, even out in the courtyard. The tavern opened as always, and the smells of broiled peska root and smoked trumpfish tantalized those in seclusion behind the wall.

During the afternoon, Malia crept out the back way and joined her father in the tavern while the others waited and waited, hoping against hope that Dorian had not given them away.

That evening, two new tellers appeared at Ventnor's. When one of the patrons asked about Amana, the slick introducer who had been there the night before declared, "The great Amana is unwell. She will not join us this evening."

This announcement was met with hisses and boos from the crowd. Behind the wall, Dominique felt uneasy—what had happened to Amana?

"Ladies and gentlemen—please be assured that we offer only the finest tellers for your enjoyment. Let us now welcome Sobrino Carena, who will entertain you with a tale of Emberto the Great as he conquers the villains responsible for the inland uprising."

Polite applause greeted the introduction, but it was quickly obvious that the thin young man with large eyes was not in the same league as Amana. He droned on and on, relating one battle after another in which Emberto was always a hero, defeating his opposition with brilliant strategy and incredible bravery. Dominique could hardly stand to listen. What he wanted to know was whether or not Amana was all right, but about this, Sobrino Carena had nothing to say.

Late that night after the tavern patrons had gone, those in the hidden room pulled out their sleeping mats and posted another watch. All was still ready in case a hasty departure was needed, but the whispered conversations focused more and more often on the possibility that Dorian had managed to hold his tongue and not give them away. Ventnor even seemed a little more relaxed, whistling as he tidied the tavern, and when Malia pushed open the secret door, the others pulled aside some of the furniture so she could come and go once again.

The mood as they settled in for another night was strange—not exactly carefree, but the sense of panic had subsided, and Brigitta was humming once again as she spread out her mat and blankets.

It made no sense to Dominique when he thought about it later, but the telltale jangling of the bells came as a complete shock.

Eyes wide, Erma whispered, "Do you think it could be Dorian?" and Berolino's eyes lit up with a desperate hope, even though the suggestion was ridiculous.

Brigitta pressed her finger to her lips and all was silent.

"What are *you* doing here?" Ventnor sounded angry. The tavern door slammed and bottles and glasses on the other side of the wall clinked in sympathy.

"Come in." Ventnor spoke again, loudly, evenly. Those in the secret room dared not breathe for fear of giving themselves away. Toranosco made as if to move the furniture back into place, but Malia caught his sleeve and stopped him.

"You frightened me," Ventnor said. "With all the soldiers

in the streets these days you can't be too careful. Spies, you know. They are everywhere."

Two sets of boots moved about in the other room. "Is there something I can help you with, miss?"

"Thank you. Yes. I know they are here." The voice was unmistakable. Amana Elnedo had returned.

"Who? I am here alone. Except for my daughter, Malia, of course. But she has already retired to her chamber."

All eyes went to Malia, who most certainly was not in her bedchamber. She stood, poised, as if she might flee out through the panarium.

"I saw the prisoners come in here last night. I followed them. I believe you have the boy, too—Dominique."

"I cannot imagine what you are—"

"Hush!" Dominique heard the distinctive rasp of a dagger being drawn.

"Oh!"

"Don't think that just because I am a teller, I am not skilled in the use of my blade."

Dominique's tongue flicked over his lips. How well he knew the speed with which Amana could draw and then use her short dagger. His hand went to his shoulder and the place she had wounded him.

"Where are they?"

"Ow!"

Several of the men inside the hidden room stepped forward but stopped again when Ventnor said, "There is no need to wound me. If I am dead, what will I be able to tell you then?"

"I apologize." Amana's voice softened. "I am accustomed to dealing with Emberto's men."

"Understandable. Apology accepted—but please put your weapon away. There is no need for it here."

Those in the hidden room visibly relaxed but remained silent, attentive.

"I am here to help the boy, Dominique. Not hurt him."

Dominique drew a breath as if he might shout out to Ventnor. But what would he say? A warning? A welcome? Dominique's gut twisted with uncertainty. Had Amana helped him, really? So far, she'd been unable to protect him.

"I understand why you might not trust me," Amana was saying. "Let me speak and then you can decide whether to help me. I tried to see Dominique in the tower—it was not my idea to imprison him there. In fact, I didn't want to see him jailed at all. It is true that I thought he could be useful as a source of information about the Estorians—but I meant for him to stay at the palace. Until I returned from my journey, I didn't know the Elder had died, that so much had changed. And besides, it was obvious that the boy was harmless."

Dominique stiffened. Harmless?

"But now Emberto has gone mad. He's arresting everyone!"

"You are telling me nothing new," Ventnor said.

"I am the First Teller Born during Lord Emberto's rule. You know the tradition."

Ventnor said something Dominique couldn't quite make out.

"Exactly. It is my duty—my destiny—to support the Lord of Carnillo, act as a liaison between the ruler of Carnillo and the Grand Teller at the Recitatorium."

"Miss Amana, I am hardly in a position to discuss your destiny—"

"You must listen! I've heard the full story of the kasyapa—the ancient myth. The Grand Teller told me." Her words poured forth, a desperate torrent of pleading and explanation. "Dominique has one—a kasyapa bird. At least he had one. Emberto must not find him. Emberto will want him dead if he captures him again, because the story says the boy with the kasyapa is destined to be a great—"

"I know what the story tells us. My grandfather told me the tale. I've never forgotten. To be honest, I was surprised to hear you tell it here."

"For a long time I was prepared to go along with Emberto's foolishness—he does support the Recitatorium—but there comes a time when certain stories must be told, no matter what the consequences might be. You know the kasyapa story, so surely you can appreciate why Dominique must not die?"

"If what you say is true—that the boy had a kasyapa—what happened to it?"

Dominique admired the way Ventnor was thinking on his feet. He really sounded as if he had never seen a kasyapa bird in his life.

"I don't know!" Dominique was shocked to hear that Amana was on the verge of tears. "I had her in my care but I let her go and she flew away. I thought she would recognize me, stay with me until I could get her back to Dominique. The way Dominique talks to her, treats her like, I don't know—like a friend—I thought she could understand what I said. That was foolish—she's just a bird. I should have kept her locked up—I—I—"

"Calm down, Miss Amana. Sit here and let me pour you a glass of ale."

"Oh, I don't know what to do. If Emberto knew I was here, he would . . ." Her voice trailed off and she sounded to Dominique very young, vulnerable. "The only person Lord Emberto will listen to is the Grand Teller, but if she tells him the story of the kasyapa he will—he will—oh, I don't know what he might do."

"Here you are. Drink up. You'll feel better." A full tankard thunked against the bar.

"Thank you."

"Lord Emberto," Ventnor said carefully, "must by law at least seem to listen to the Grand Teller, correct? And if he listens and does not act to protect himself, his people, then he would be a poor leader, would he not?"

Ventnor seemed to be testing Amana without actually saying anything incriminating.

"Some stories must be told, but not necessarily to a leader who will use them in the wrong manner," Amana said quietly. Then, more firmly, she added, "This is very fine ale."

"Imported—from Crestio. Without the bird, such a boy as you describe would hardly be worth bothering about, isn't that so?"

"Please—if you know where he is, you must let me see him. I can help him get out of the city. Dominique must leave Carnillo."

"Why do you think I would know where he is?"

"Because I found out some things." She paused before continuing, more quietly. Dominique strained to hear. "I still have friends among the tower guards. After the Grand Teller spoke with me, I asked one of the guards to find out where Dominique was. I wanted to get word to him about Navina—the kasyapa. I thought maybe I could help him somehow. But my friend told me he was no longer among the prisoners."

Dominique's knees buckled and he staggered forward, just catching himself before he fell right over. First Erma and then Brigitta came to his side. Brigitta's warm hand guided him to a chair at the closest table.

"Don't worry," Amana said out in the tavern. "I would not speak to just any guard. This one knew—" She stopped and then proceeded slowly as if choosing each word carefully. "The guard knew what—what had happened. And he said it would happen again—though he couldn't tell me when."

"Why are you so interested in the whereabouts of a prisoner?" Ventnor asked.

"Because he is not an ordinary prisoner. Dominique is not a criminal. And because things have changed here.

Emberto doesn't care what happens to the prisoners—or to anyone else. When I was waiting outside the tower, the guards carried two bodies out. There was no burial—they just . . ." Amana's voice shook. "They just wrapped the dead in heavy chains and threw them into the canal."

"We have seen better times in Carnillo," Ventnor said.

"And we will see better times again," Amana replied. "But not until Emberto is gone."

Brigitta's long fingers stopped stroking Dominique's arm and tightened around his wrist.

"The words you speak are treasonous," Ventnor said. "You could find yourself a prisoner if the wrong ears hear."

"I know. That is why I've come to you. I feared I would have to return night after night to wait outside the tower until someone else tried to flee. It was fortunate indeed that the three escaped last night, though most unfortunate that one of them was recaptured. I followed the prisoners here, but there were guards everywhere in the streets, searching. I didn't dare come in just in case I had been followed. Please believe me, I mean the boy no—"

Fierce banging on the tavern door interrupted whatever Amana was going to say.

"Who's there?" Ventnor shouted.

"Emberto's patrol! Open up or we'll take the door down!"

"Hold on! No need for that!" Ventnor shouted back even as the wall began to slide open.

CHAPTER

37

ATTACK

The great warrior, Perpetano, never let anyone see the fear in his eyes. Instead, he lowered his visor at dawn and left it down until night fell. Nobody knew and that was all that mattered.

—Campriano tale

Several things happened at once. Ventnor thrust a shocked-looking Amana into the hidden room. Malia darted forward and rushed past her father out into the tavern. The others stepped back away from Amana, who still clutched her dagger. Dominique, terrified, slumped forward over the table, and Navina fluttered upwards, where she alighted on an open beam above his head with a startled *peep!* The wall rumbled shut and furniture was shoved roughly against it.

"I'm coming! I'm just an old man! It's the middle of the night!"

The door bells tinkled and a loud crash was followed by several bangs and a thump. Dominique's body jerked as if he had been hit.

"There's no need to do that!" Ventnor said. "What do you want? We are closed for the night."

"We have orders to search every shop, every house, every tavern."

"For what?"

Another crash made Dominique jump.

"Prisoners, you old fool. Dangerous sons of boars who would slit your bony old throat and have their way with your daughter if they had half a chance. We are here to protect you, old man."

Heavy footsteps crossed back and forth out in the tavern. It was hard to tell how many guards there were— at least three, Dominique thought. He squeezed his eyes shut, horrible images filling his mind; of Malia and Ventnor being clubbed to death or being hauled off to the tower where they'd be left to die.

Then he saw an equally disconcerting image. It was the hidden room from above. All the others stood facing the sliding wall, ready to fight. Erma had freed her hammer from her tool belt and was smacking the head silently into her open palm. Several of the men and Nina gripped chair backs, ready to brandish the chairs as weapons. Others readied cooking knives, and Breska and Zeff raised their swords. Even Amana was poised to do battle, her dagger at the ready.

Only Dominique slumped on the table, his paring knife stiff and cool against his leg. Brigitta stood at his side, watching over him. But the way she held his wrist, eyes glued to the false wall, there was no doubt that if the soldiers came through the secret door, she would use her own body to shield his.

Feeling Navina's gaze upon his prone form, and at the same time seeing his unmoving body from above, Dominique slowly drew his arm back. Twisting his wrist, he pulled his hand away from Brigitta and sat up.

Ignoring the way his head swam and his heart pounded madly, he stood. As the heavy footsteps of the soldiers thumped back and forth in the rooms upstairs,

270

he reached down and drew out his knife. The weapon seemed pathetically small in his palm, but it was better than nothing, and Dominique faced the stacks of furniture, a ludicrous barrier against armed soldiers. Amana motioned with the tip of her dagger and Dominique moved to stand closer to her. If there was going to be a battle, he might as well be beside someone who knew how to fight.

The group behind the wall was so used to keeping quiet when others were in the tavern that nobody screamed or shouted when the wall suddenly slid aside and several guards forced their way past the stacks of chairs and tables, swords drawn.

For one long moment, everyone, guards and conspirators alike, assessed each other. Dominique took in the guards' wide eyes, their surprise at the number of people in the room. Nina and Cleppeno flanked the opening, both gripping the backs of chairs, and Breska, Hermano, and Scillio, all brandishing weapons, stood between Dominique and the guards.

Three of the guards stepped forward, swords flashing.

Nina and Cleppeno swung their chairs at the same time, striking the two guards closest to them squarely across the shoulders. The guards turned and their swords sliced the air. One knocked the chair from Nina's hands. Then everyone in the room moved. Breska leaped forward, jabbing at a guard advancing on Nina. He slashed the guard's back, but the knife, hitting a thick leather doublet, didn't hurt him. The attack from the rear did slow the big man enough that Nina had time to dart to the side and snatch up her chair once again. In one smooth motion she swung the chair and hit the guard on the side of the head, opening a gash over the man's eye. With a roar, the man lunged at Nina, who dove beneath a table and then tipped it over in front of her.

Though the counterattack did no damage, it was a

distraction and Toranosco swiped at the guard's neck with a heavy meat cleaver. The blow landed solidly, spraying blood over the wall.

The other guards fought viciously against the conspirators, who surged forward. Fighting side by side with Amana, Dominique managed a hard poke with his paring knife. He aimed low and wedged the blade between the attacker's boot and his thigh wraps. The man howled and reached down to remove the blade, dropping his short sword from one hand and swinging his long sword wildly with the other. From behind, Erma delivered a glancing blow to one guard's head with her hammer. Another kicked at her and Erma fell backwards.

"Oh, Tara!" Dominique cried, leaping out of reach. He crashed over an upturned chair and scrambled away, diving under a table at the back of the room near the panarium door. The hideous noises of the battle assaulted his ears as furniture smashed, swords and knives clanked and slashed, bottles shattered, and voices rose in angry shouts, cries of anguish.

From where he lay, cowering under the table, Dominique could not see which side was winning. The guards were well armed and protected with light armour, but they were outnumbered by the conspirators, who fought like crazed hoarcats.

Do something, Dominique muttered to himself, wishing he'd had the good sense to keep hold of the paring knife. He crept forward on his hands and knees, looking for something else to use as a weapon.

Crack! A great weight fell or was thrown onto the table. His shelter creaked under the strain and Dominique dove back out into the room. As he did, a story flashed into his mind. Elixor in the tale of the War of Grummond turned the tide of battle by claiming he heard the thundering hoofbeats of the king's men approaching.

272

The fight had moved deeper into the room and Dominique had to dodge between Toranosco, grappling with one guard, and a second man who was holding off blows from Breska, Ontocki, and Erma. Dominique screamed at the top of his lungs, "The others are out back! I'll get them!"

Heart galloping like a whole stampede of wild horses, he threw himself toward the panarium still yelling, as if there really were more conspirators hiding out in the back. "Emberto's guards are here! Hurry! Grab your weapons!"

A glancing blow caught the back of his head and Dominique fell forward, scrambled into the panarium, and grabbed at the closest shelf. It came down with a crash as pots and jars tumbled to the ground. It sounded as if a hundred people were throwing things around in the panarium, which gave Dominique another idea.

He reached up and snatched whatever he could from the shelves—empty glasses and tankards, cooking implements, the brass kettles. He threw everything against the walls, the floor, out into the back courtyard, making as much noise as possible. Drawing a deep breath, he shouted, "Hurry! Come help us!" Then he dove behind a stack of baskets and slithered under the lowest shelf in the panarium, waiting for the guards to follow him into the back room and slice him to ribbons with their glistening blades.

Instead, a dagger clattered through the doorway. As Dominique reached for it he recognized the carving on the hilt. Amana's dagger! He'd have to go back out and fight, to help her, help the others.

When Dominique lunged through the doorway, confusion reigned in the main room. The guards had been backed against the stacked furniture on the opposite side of the room, but they slashed viciously with their swords, still managing to hold the conspirators at bay.

Dominique roared, as much to give himself courage as to scare anyone. To his amazement, one of the guards looked in his direction and yelled, "Watch out!" and Dominique waved Amana's dagger from side to side, trying to look menacing.

Something whizzed past his ear and he ducked out of the way. The same guard who had shouted out the warning now staggered backwards as an arrow buried itself in his cheek.

"Get out of the way!" Amana yelled. Turning in time to see Amana putting another arrow to her bow, Dominique threw himself to the floor.

"It's Amana Elnedo!" the second guard yelled as the arrow narrowly missed the side of his head.

"They have Hermano, too! And more help coming from the back!"

Breska threw a bottle and it shattered over the man's head, dripping dragonberry wine over his face in garish streaks.

"Back! Back off!" the first guard screamed, his face contorted in agony as he tugged at the arrow stuck in his cheek.

Another shrieked as an arrow bit into his shoulder. Dominique hadn't even seen Amana shoot again.

"We'll be back!" the first guard shouted as he retreated, still thrusting his sword at the conspirators as he went.

A loud crash followed the soldiers' departure through the tavern. Then the bells tinkled and Dominique heard nothing but his own rapid breathing.

"Dominique?" Amana's voice was tentative. "Dominique, is that you? Your hair! Are you all right?"

"Yes—I—I think so. What about you?"

"I'm all right."

"Good shooting."

"I thought you were a dead man," Breska said, offering his hand to help Dominique to his feet.

"One of them whacked you pretty hard," Amana

said. She touched Dominique lightly on the back of his head and he flinched.

"Ow!" A good-sized lump was already forming beneath his fingertips when he reached up to feel the damage.

Gradually, Dominique became aware of what the others were doing. Meath Boru seemed to be chanting something, his voice a deep and steady rumble beneath someone else's sobbing.

"Is everyone . . ." Dominique began to ask. But even before Breska shook his head, Dominique knew that was impossible. There was no way all the conspirators had escaped the melee unhurt.

Toranosco had followed the soldiers out into the tavern. Now he ran back into the hidden room shouting, "Go!" He waved his hand toward the panarium and the safety of the courtyard and alleyway beyond.

"But—" Dominique made a move toward Meath Boru and the others.

"Go!" Toranosco insisted. "You've done well—but there's nothing more that you can do here. The soldiers recognized Amana and Hermano. You all have to go—now!"

Toranosco dashed into the panarium and Dominique thought he had fled. But a moment later he was back with a dripping rag, heading for the others who were huddled around someone on the floor—Brigitta.

"Maybe Toranosco's right," Breska said softly. "We should leave. There's nothing you can do, Dominique."

"Amana—do you have my sack?" Dominique asked.

Amana shook her head. "I burned it," she said. "I'm sorry. I couldn't risk being caught with it. There wasn't much inside," she said. "Just this thing—" From her own sack slung over her shoulder, Amana pulled the vial the leranon, Kyrie, had given Dominique in the cave.

"This is it!" Dominique jumped forward, snatching the vial from Amana. "This is what I wanted!" Ignoring her shocked look, Dominique pushed into the circle.

CHAPTER
38

FLIGHT

When Tara found the baby by the river, she could not walk past. The moon would have to wait, for the baby was hungry.

—Estorian story

"Brigitta!" Dominique whispered. The older woman's black hair flowed away from her head and shoulders like a dark river.

"They will be back before long," Toranosco said, dabbing desperately at the gaping wound in Brigitta's stomach.

Ventnor, a bloody hand wrapped in his apron, nodded. "We must leave here. Everyone—out through the back."

Nobody moved.

"Brigitta—can you hear me?" Toranosco asked. Erma moved behind Brigitta and lifted her head into her lap.

Kneeling beside his friend, Meath Boru continued to

chant, his hands moving slowly back and forth just above Brigitta's still form.

Dominique pushed beside Toranosco and crouched down. He touched her cheek, startled at how cold she felt. "Brigitta?" He squeezed the leranon's vial and shook it, willing its contents to work. There were only a few drops left, and a quick glance at the others told him he would not have nearly enough to treat all the injuries, perhaps not even enough to save Brigitta. Nobody had escaped without some bruise or cut. The apron wrapped around Ventnor's hand was already darkening as blood soaked the heavy fabric, and Amana had been nicked across the cheek by the tip of a sword.

Very gently, Dominique tugged Brigitta's loose blouse aside enough so he could better see the extent of the gash across her stomach. "Oh," he gasped, and his hand shook so hard he feared he would spill the precious healing drops. He took a deep breath and steadied himself. "Please," he whispered. "Please let this heal as I know it can heal."

Three golden drops of liquid dribbled onto the wound. He bent closer to Brigitta's silent form. "Think of golden light," he whispered. "Can you feel it working? Can you see it flooding into the wound?"

At first there was no response. Toranosco jumped up when he thought he heard a noise outside the back door. Though it was only a cat, he could no longer stay still and hovered around the others, shifting a long, curved knife from one hand to the other. "Quick," he said. "We must hurry. It won't be long before the guards will return."

"Close the door," Ventnor said, gesturing toward the hidden wall. "Barricade the wall with the tables and chairs."

"We don't have time!" Toranosco shouted. "There's no point—they'll just break it down again!"

"Do it," Ventnor insisted. "It will give us some protection. They don't know how many are still here. For all they know, Dominique really was calling for more rebels to come and help us fight. They won't barge into an ambush."

Toranosco drew a breath as if to argue, but then changed his mind and barked, "Help me, then."

While Dominique held Brigitta's hand and spoke to her of the golden, healing fluid, warm and sweet as honey, the others hurried to secure the secret entrance as best they could.

Brigitta's eyes opened and she took a moment to focus on Dominique's face. Her hand moved to the wound on her stomach. Already the bleeding was slowing.

"Dominique," Meath Boru said. "You must go. Ventnor and I will stay here with Brigitta."

Dominique shook his head and waved his hand at the group crowding into the panarium, ready to flee through the secret tunnel behind the stone oven and escape out into the alley.

"I will stay here until Brigitta can move. It should only take a few more minutes."

Toranosco and Ventnor exchanged glances. "Go," Ventnor said to Toranosco. "Lead the others to safety. Try the fishers—they will help. We will join you shortly. Take the Quilt of the Rebellion. The bundle is by the door."

"Leave me here," Brigitta said, her voice weak, her breathing laboured.

"Nonsense, my dear," Meath Boru said, and he held his hands over her stomach, closed his eyes, and began to chant so softly Dominique could not make out the words.

Toranosco hesitated only a moment and then beckoned for the others to follow him. Dominique watched them go and then turned his attention back to Brigitta.

The three drops of liquid were not going to be enough to heal her wounds even with the help of Meath Boru's magic. And Ventnor, Scillio, Amana, and several others could benefit from a drop or two of the golden liquid.

"Amana," he said, pleased she had stayed at his side and not followed Toranosco. "I need more of this." He held up the empty vial.

"But where do you get it? You told me it came from a healer you met—"

"Yes. A leranon healer."

Amana stiffened. "Leranons? Beasts of burden—they could hardly—"

"Listen to me. They are not just beasts of burden. They sheltered and protected me when I was lost. And they healed me with their golden liquid. You live here. Where do they keep the leranons?"

Amana tightened her grip on the bow. "I can show you," she said at last.

"Thank you."

Dominique and Meath Boru helped Brigitta to sit up. She was very weak and her head drooped as she slumped sideways, leaning heavily against Meath Boru.

The bells tinkled and Dominique and Amana jumped to their feet. Meath Boru stopped chanting and said, "Come, Brigitta. Be strong. We must leave now."

"Navina!" Dominique shouted.

"In here," Amana said, holding her travel sack open.

Navina swooped down from her high perch and sailed straight into the bag. Amana slung it over her shoulder and Dominique realized he would have to trust her for now—there was no time to argue.

With Dominique on one side and Meath Boru on the other, Brigitta struggled to her feet. Ventnor slipped into the now empty panarium and Brigitta, leaning heavily on Dominique and Meath Boru, followed. Amana picked up her dagger from the floor where Dominique had dropped it and stood with her back to the panarium door, her weapon at the ready, facing the false wall. Shouts came from the other side of the wall. A crash made Dominique jump as he slithered down into the hole behind the stone oven. Loud pounding on the wall and bottles smashing set his heart thumping.

"Come on, Brigitta—I've got you." He staggered under her weight and put his arm around her waist, careful not to bump against her stomach. He and Ventnor, who cried out when he bumped his injured arm, helped Brigitta into the alley.

"Behind this wall!" a soldier shouted. "Harder!" Something heavy thudded against the wall, and breaking glass tinkled as more bottles and glasses smashed.

Meath Boru joined them, and Ventnor shouted to Amana. "Come! Now!"

Amana leaped into the hole and turned, tugging the stones into place behind her. She crawled out through the hole into the alley and heaved at the grate, pushing it into place over the false storm drain.

"It won't take them long to find the hole, once they start looking," Ventnor said. "Come on."

He started off down the alley, holding his bleeding arm close to his chest. Dominique and Meath Boru helped Brigitta, whose breath soon came in choking gasps.

"Leave me," she pleaded. "Go on—help Dominique and the kasyapa escape. Our future—"

A loud explosion pushed them forward and sent Amana, who brought up the rear, to her knees.

Ventnor choked back a cry of anguish as he looked back over his shoulder and saw flames licking the upper windows of the tavern. "Hurry. They will soon be searching for us."

The little group rushed to the end of the alley and Ventnor, his face streaked with tears, peered around the corner. He beckoned and they slipped into the shadows, keeping close to the building fronts and moving away from the burning tavern. Behind them, the orange glow grew brighter and they heard shouts and then the insistent *clang-clang-clang* of a fire bell.

Ducking into another street, they ignored the people who opened their shuttered windows and called out into the night, "What's happening?"

"Fire!"

"Ventnor's Tavern is burning!"

Beggar children, asleep in doorways, squirmed under thin blankets and piles of rags, trying to ignore the noises robbing them of sleep.

"We must get off the streets," Ventnor said. "We are too obvious."

"It's too far to the fishers and the boathouse," Amana said.

The four of them ducked into a doorway and looked back. They had now moved well away from the fire but the news of it was spreading quickly through the sleeping city.

"Amana," Meath Boru said urgently. "Do you know of somewhere closer where we could hide—just for the night. Brigitta must rest. We will be captured if we stay out here."

Amana didn't answer right away but nibbled her bottom lip, thinking. "Yes," she said finally. "Follow me."

"Wait," Ventnor said. "We are too many. I cannot help you with Brigitta—my arm . . ."

Tears glistened on Ventnor's cheeks.

"Ventnor, you can't—" Meath Boru started to say, but before he could finish speaking, Ventnor plunged back into the street and staggered away.

Dominique started after him but stopped when Meath Boru caught the back of his shirt. "Let him go. He is right."

"But where will he go?"

"I'm sure he will find someone to help him. There are many in Carnillo who are fond of Ventnor."

Though Meath Boru's words were confident, Dominique sensed both sadness and concern in his voice.

"We should go," Amana said quietly.

"Very well." Meath Boru nodded.

Amana emerged cautiously from the doorway where they had taken shelter and led them partway down the street until they reached a dark, narrow alleyway that stretched away between two buildings. They did not go all the way to the end, but instead turned into another tiny lane that wound behind shops and houses and took them deep into the centre of Carnillo.

CHAPTER

39

ILIATICA LERENTO

For five days and five nights the people followed the winding path into the mountains until Tara led them to the safety of the great cavern of Tulcha.

—Estorian folktale

Amana stopped at a wooden doorway set back in a thick stone wall. She pulled a large brass key from a pouch at her waist and slipped it into the lock. The door was stiff, but she put her shoulder to it and it swung open with a loud creak.

"Shh," Meath Boru said, glancing up and down the narrow alleyway.

Amana stepped through the door, gesturing for the others to follow. Once inside a large courtyard, Brigitta sagged heavily against Dominique and Meath Boru.

"Not long now, Brigitta. Soon you may rest," Meath Boru promised. Brigitta answered with a soft moan.

"Where are we?" Dominique asked.

"The Recitatorium, I believe," Meath Boru said. "Is that correct?"

Amana nodded and pressed her finger to her lips.

"The back entrance," she whispered. "Wait here." She darted off into the shadows at the far end of the courtyard. When her footsteps had receded, the other sounds of the courtyard seemed louder, closer. Dominique strained to see into the dark shadows behind a statue of a soldier on a horse, convinced real soldiers hid there. Every heartbeat sent a pulse of anxiety shooting through Dominique's blood. Struggling to focus on something other than his own terror, he patted Brigitta on the back and whispered, "You'll be all right. You'll be all right."

"There's a bench in the shadows," Meath Boru said. "We'll help you to it." Slowly, supporting Brigitta between them, Dominique and Meath Boru moved to a sturdy stone bench tucked between a flowering alipari bush and one of the courtyard walls. Decorated with intricate mosaic work, the bench was cold and hard, but it offered relief after their panicked flight from the tavern. In the centre of the courtyard, a fountain trickled over a series of stone ledges. The water sounds lulled Dominique, and beside him, Brigitta relaxed. A light breeze moved through the trees, swirling the scents of alipari and tinga blossoms around the waiting threesome.

"This way. The Grand Teller will help us."

Dominique jumped. He hadn't heard Amana return.

"Come, Brigitta—help is here. You don't have to go much farther." Meath Boru's voice was gentle but left no room for argument, and Brigitta struggled to stand, again leaning heavily on her companions.

Amana led them past the fountain and through an archway into a second, smaller courtyard. This one had a raised platform in the centre, surrounded by low shrubs. At least six varieties were laid out in a more detailed pattern than the crops in the fields beyond the city walls.

On the far side of the second courtyard a set of double doors stood slightly ajar. Amana pushed them open and the others followed her in. Dominique blinked as his eyes adjusted to the dim light inside a large room lit only by two candles set into recessed alcoves.

"Welcome." The woman's voice was deep, smooth, comforting, and strong, a voice to obey, a voice to believe. She had spoken only a single word as they entered, but the way she had said it, the way she carried herself, made Dominique think she was a woman who always said exactly as much as she needed to.

She was old, much older than Dominique had expected. Her pure white hair was pulled back and twisted into a braided knot behind her head. Deep lines radiated from the corners of her eyes and marked the places where her cheeks would fold around a smile, though she was not smiling now.

So this was the Grand Teller, Dominique thought—the woman everyone, apparently even Emberto, held in such high esteem. She glided past him as though nobody could touch her, floating across the room as if lifted by unseen wings. The Grand Teller beckoned as she went past and, without turning around, said, "Follow me."

"Where are we going?" Dominique whispered to Amana.

"Shh. It's not safe to talk, even here."

The Grand Teller led the group along several narrow passageways and up a short flight of winding stairs before stopping outside a locked door. Pushing a heavy key into the ornate lock she said, "You will be safe here for now." The door swung open and Dominique and Meath Boru helped Brigitta inside. "But it won't be long before they will look here, too." The woman bowed slightly and said, "My name is Iliatica Lerento. Welcome."

Amana returned the gesture with an even deeper bow. "Thank you for helping my friends."

Dominique followed the others' lead and bowed, not letting go of Brigitta.

"Never mind the formalities," Iliatica said. "Bring your injured over here."

Beneath a window set high in the wall, a sleeping platform stretched along the length of the back wall.

"The women may stay here. Gentlemen, there is an identical room next door, through there." She indicated a heavy wardrobe. "There is a latch in the bottom left corner under a pile of blankets. This wardrobe shares the back of another, exactly the same as this one, in the other room. Should the Recitatorium be searched, you may buy some extra time by moving from room to room."

"Is there access to—"

"Yes, Amana. I was about to explain. From the other room only, you can get to a secret passage that will eventually lead you all the way to a space beneath the Recitatorium stables. From there, it is easy enough to find your way back out into Carnillo."

"We thank you with all our hearts," Meath Boru said as he and Dominique helped Brigitta to lie down on the soft furs lining the sleeping platform.

Iliatica dipped her head again. "When Amana spoke of the kasyapa, I had no choice but to offer help." Her gaze flicked from Brigitta to Meath Boru and then settled on Dominique. "Welcome," she said. "And where is the bird, if I may be so bold?"

Dominique thought the Grand Teller's voice quivered a little. Amana handed the sack to Dominique and he carefully loosened the drawstring and called to Navina. The kasyapa bird's head emerged first, her scarlet crest unfurling as she took in her new surroundings. She crawled up Dominique's arm and settled in her favourite place on his shoulder.

"So, it is true." Iliatica could not seem to stop staring. Her lips began to move and Dominique realized she was telling part of a story.

And the boy was led to battle by the all-seeing bird upon his shoulder. The few who recalled the ancient truths saw in this boy their future, and in their future, a grand reconciliation. And so they followed the young prince's lead as he journeyed east across the sea.

Dominique shifted uncomfortably, wishing the others would stop staring at him, stop telling these stories about the boy and the kasyapa.

It was Brigitta who broke the awkward spell with a terrible moan. Meath Boru kneeled at her side. He examined Brigitta's wound and shook his head. "It was deep. No doubt the sons of boars dipped the tips of their blades in poison. Our magic is strong, but we need more of your healing drops to cure this wound."

Dominique nodded, feeling both honoured and unworthy of Meath Boru's faith in his abilities.

"Amana? You said you knew where the leranons are kept?"

Amana's nose wrinkled but she nodded. "I still don't believe—"

"It doesn't matter what you believe," Dominique said. "The leranons helped me once before. If I can tell them that I've come to help in return, maybe they will tell me how to get a little more of the healing potion." Dominique tried to sound convincing, but he wasn't at all certain the leranons would help. He couldn't even be sure that captured leranons would have any of the golden elixir with them. Brigitta rocked onto her side, raised her knees to her chest, and groaned again, her face contorted in agony. "We don't have a choice," Dominique said firmly, his hand reaching for Brigitta's. "We have to try."

"I don't know how many leranons we'll find," Amana said doubtfully. "I know the usual animal-holding pens are being used for prisoners who won't all fit in the tower."

"If the leranon pens are being used for prisoners, where have the leranons gone? Were they released?"

Amana looked at him as if he had lost his mind. "Release them? Do you have any idea how hard it is to capture a leranon?"

"Amana, where are you planning to take Dominique?" When the Grand Teller spoke, Amana's posture changed. She was no longer feisty and argumentative, her shoulders thrown back and her head cocked to one side. Instead, she bowed and lowered her eyes. Her voice dropped and when she replied, she spoke softly, in complete deference to her mentor.

"My intention was to take Dominique to the pen behind the east tower guardhouse. I have heard they keep leranons there for the guards to use. The enclosure is on the outside of the city walls and unsuitable for prisoners."

The Grand Teller nodded. "True. But reaching that enclosure would be far too dangerous—I can't let you go there."

Amana's shoulders dropped slightly, though she said nothing.

"Not everyone in Carnillo believes the leranons are no more than flying beasts of burden or creatures to be beaten into submission and used as mounts in battle." The Grand Teller smiled at Dominique as she said this, and for the first time, Dominique felt a glimmer of hope.

The Grand Teller moved to Amana's side and placed her hands on the girl's shoulders. "The leranons are gentle creatures at heart," she said. "But Emberto's men need us to believe otherwise, hence the stories of the beasts' brutality and stupidity."

At this, Amana raised her head, apparently forgetting for just a moment that she was on her best behaviour.

"But even you have said—"

"Yes. Even I have told stories, taught you stories, that

would be appropriate for telling in Emberto's court." The sadness in Iliatica's voice was unmistakable. "And now I will say only that there are other stories in which leranons are wise and gentle, fighting only when threatened or provoked." Glancing over at Brigitta she added, "But there is no time now for telling these tales. I must ask that you trust what I say is true."

Amana looked from the Grand Teller to Brigitta to Dominique. "Very well," she said, still sounding unconvinced. "Where else might we find a leranon?"

"Go to Ella Minato's stall."

"The herbalist on the barge?"

"Exactly."

Completely forgetting her reserve, Amana blurted out, "If anyone in Carnillo is going to help one of those creatures it would be *that* woman."

Iliatica smiled at her impetuous student. "Ella Minato might be rather eccentric, but her heart is good. She rescued a leranon from the burning pile."

"The what?" Dominique said, aghast. He asked the question even though he wasn't at all sure he wanted to hear the answer.

"The burning pile. Diseased bodies are disposed of in the burning square near the Gate of Liberty. Alas, the creatures deposited there are not always dead. Such was the case with this leranon."

"But Ella Minato lives on a barge on the canal," Amana said. "Her stand is on the deck—where could she possibly hide a leranon?"

"True, she lives on the water. Have you never been below decks?"

Amana shook her head.

"I suppose you have had no need to go below. You will see when you visit Ella tonight."

"She's not going to invite us in for tea—not in the middle of the night!"

"Amana, there is always a way if you know the right story. You know that."

Chastened, Amana lowered her eyes. "Yes, Grand Teller."

"Tell her I sent you. Then ask for permission to see the spirit of the lion."

Amana bowed. "Yes, Grand Teller."

Dominique patted Brigitta's hand. "We're going to try to get some more medicine," he said. "We won't be long." He turned to the Grand Teller. "We should leave now, while it's still dark."

Behind him, Brigitta struggled to sit up. "Don't move," Meath Boru said, gently pushing her shoulder back toward the bed. With some effort, Brigitta pushed his hand away.

"I have something to help them," she said. "Please—" Her face twisted into a grimace as she pointed at the roomy pouch she wore on her belt.

Meath Boru opened the pouch and withdrew a dozen small packages, each wrapped in soft, iridescent blue cloth.

With shaking hands, Brigitta felt the bundles, her fingers tracing hidden contours only she recognized. "Open this one," she said, nudging a package across the blanket.

Meath Boru did as he was told. Lifting the corners of the cloth, he leaned forward to peek inside.

"Oh!" Amana said. "It's so beautiful!"

"What is it?" Dominique asked.

Brigitta touched a wide bracelet made of hammered metal so thin Dominique thought light might shine right through it if he held it up to the light. Intricate designs had been etched into the metal, and six gemstones were embedded around a larger flat stone of pale marble. Tiny veins ran like rivers through the central stone.

"It looks like a piece of Ticabellan wrist armour," Meath Boru said. "Is that right?"

Weakly, Brigitta nodded.

"Beautifully made," Meath Boru murmured. "May I?"

Brigitta sighed and her mouth worked as if she wanted to say something but could not find the strength. Gently, Meath Boru picked up the wrist band and turned it from side to side so the candlelight caught in the gemstones and made them glow. He raised the piece to his cheek and closed his eyes as if listening through his skin.

"Ahhh," he said finally. "Warm magic in cold metal and stone."

Brigitta nodded and closed her eyes. "For the girl," she whispered.

Meath Boru hesitated for a moment and then placed the armour on the arm with which Amana wielded her dagger. "For you," he said.

"Oh, thank you!" Amana said. "It's beautiful." She covered the wrist armour with her other hand, her eyes shining.

"So long as you wear this, you shall be protected," Meath Boru added.

"No," Brigitta said. "The magic is more subtle than that. It will work only within sight of the boy as long as he has in his possession something of mine. But it is powerful. Use it to protect the boy."

Dominique caught Amana's nervous glance. "I will try," she said.

Once again Brigitta struggled to raise herself on one arm and, with great effort, selected a second item for Dominique. "Here. This is something you can use—an ampoule."

"Thank you."

Brigitta let her head drop back. Her chest rose and fell with short puffs.

Meath Boru lifted the length of golden chain from which a small container was suspended. Made of the same beaten metal as the wrist armour, the odd container was just a little larger and fatter than Meath Boru's rather plump thumb. At either end it narrowed to a cone-shaped point. A turquoise stone was set where the belly of the ampoule swelled to its widest. As Meath Boru held out the delicate vessel to Dominique, it turned slowly, glinting and winking in the flickering candlelight.

"Fill it with the leranon's healing oil. It will hold more than the small one you already have."

Dominique had to lean close to hear what Brigitta was saying. "The stories say that you will need as much of such a potion as you can carry."

Dominique reached for the ampoule and held it cupped in the palm of his hand. He expected the metal to be cool, but it was warm from being tucked so close to Brigitta's body.

Examining it closely he realized that what appeared to be a short, decorative neck at the top of the container was really a small cap. He unscrewed this and lifted the top. Fastened securely to the inside of the lid was a delicate silver stick no wider than a blade of grass but stiff and shiny. This, Dominique surmised, would be used to dip into the fluid inside. It was clever, he thought. He'd never have to worry about shaky hands or spilling even a single drop.

"Thank you," he said again, kneeling beside Brigitta and kissing the back of her hand. She sighed, her black lashes like death stitches on her pale cheek, her hands folded over her stomach as if she were resting blissfully and not in terrible pain.

"We must go now," Dominique said and stood. "Amana, show me where this Ella Minato lives."

Amana turned her wrist from side to side, still admiring the elaborate bracelet. "We won't be long," she said. "Thank you, Grand Teller. May we find a way to repay your great kindness."

The corner of the Grand Teller's mouth twitched, but

she did not look happy. "You will be lucky indeed to repay any debts you owe. Remember, your obligation is to the future as much as it is to the past."

Though Iliatica seemed to be addressing Amana, the whole time she spoke she looked directly at Dominique as if the message was meant for him alone. Self-consciously, he reached up to touch Navina, who still sat on his shoulder.

"Now, hurry, you two. You must return before dawn or it will be too dangerous to come here."

"Navina—" Dominique held open Amana's sack and Navina dove in once again. Amana backed out of the room, bowing one final time to the Grand Teller when she reached the doorway.

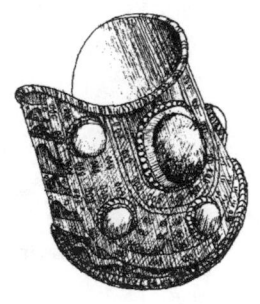

CHAPTER

40

SADRIAMO'S GIFT

You can't cut down a tree and expect the roots to flourish.

—Estorian proverb

They arrived at the canal soon after, and Amana scrambled down a steep ladder that led from street level to the water's edge. The herbalist's barge bobbed up and down, tugging at its tethers. A large market stand was set up on the deck, though its wares were covered with large sheets draped over the shelves. Amana hopped onto the barge, and immediately a dog started barking and whining below decks.

Dominique froze, panic-stricken, on the bank. The dog was so loud he expected a dozen armed guards to swarm the barge.

They heard someone say, "Hush, Alonzoro." The dog gave another muffled *woof* and then was quiet. "Who is there?" The woman sounded gruff and sleepy. Terrified at being left alone on the side of the canal, Dominique leaped onto the barge. This set the dog off again, and Amana drove her elbow into Dominique's stomach.

"Ooof! What's that for?"

The barge swayed from side to side as the person below moved around. "Who is out there? Quiet, Alonzoro. You can tear their throats out if they try to come in here."

"Please open the hatch," Amana said in a loud whisper. "Iliatica sent us." Silence. Dominique nudged Amana, perhaps a little harder than he needed to.

"The spirit of the lion," Dominique said, holding his stomach.

"We have come to see the spirit of the lion," Amana said.

A long silence was the only reply from below deck.

"Hello? Did you hear me?" Amana asked.

The hatch slid back but nobody appeared to greet them. Whoever was down below had not lit a lamp. "Come on," Amana said. "We can't stand out here all night. Someone will see us."

Even to Dominique it sounded as if she were trying to convince herself it was safe to descend into the darkness below.

"Go on, then," he said, hoping the woman had a tight hold of her vicious-sounding dog. "I'm right behind you."

Amana turned to face Dominique and backed into the hole in the deck, descending feet first down the ladder. When her head had disappeared, Dominique followed. The herbalist slid the hatch closed behind him, plunging the small space below into pitch darkness. Dominique held his hand up in front of him but could not see even the vaguest outline, it was so dark.

He heard the woman move around and then a wet nose pressed against Dominique's leg. "Ah!" he howled, leaping backwards and smashing his head against a low beam.

"Goodness!" the old woman said. "What are you trying to do to my boat?"

What about my head? Dominique thought, but said nothing.

A flame flared as the herbalist lit a lamp, and the cabin was suddenly cozy, a snug oasis in a city of stone.

"Forgive me for not being more hospitable—I was sleeping." She waved a wrinkled hand in the general direction of a cushioned bench.

"I must apologize for coming so late," Amana said.

Rubbing his head, Dominique ducked under a beam and edged back toward the ladder leading to the deck. Bunches of dried herbs hung from cords strung from one side of the cluttered barge cabin to the other.

Something about the smell, sharp and sweet at the same time, reminded Dominique of Bethusela's cottage in the woods where he had found shelter when he was first exiled from his tribe. She was a herbalist, too, and Dominique found this thought comforting.

"So, you have come to see the spirit of the lion?" The old woman reached for a loosely woven shawl and tugged it around her shoulders. She peered at Amana and asked, "Aren't you the girl from the Recitatorium?" She rubbed her arms. "I can't get warm. No matter how I try, I can't get warm. Do you find it chilly? Come here, Alonzoro. Make yourself useful."

The dog, a gangly black brute, hopped up on the bed at the same moment Ella Minato sat down with a sigh. Her hand went to his head and he squirmed closer, more like a young pup than an old dog already showing white at the muzzle.

"Sit beside me, there's a good boy, and I'll find out who they are. Ooh, it's so nippy this time of night."

Ella Minato's steady stream of chatter, Dominique suspected, probably continued whether or not the old woman had any visitors. "Who did you say sent you?"

"Iliatica."

"Not Emberto? Are you sure? You can't lie to me, or Alonzoro here will have your heads—and your arms and legs, too!" She chortled at her joke, her pudgy fingers clutching at her shawl, scratching behind the dog's ears. Dominique didn't find it funny at all but managed to force his face into a weak smile.

"Who sent you? Emberto?"

"No, ma'am. Iliatica."

"The Grand Teller," Dominique added.

Ella Minato leaned forward as if to get up and then settled back into her seat. Her shawl slipped and she tugged it back into place.

"Yes, Iliatica."

It was impossible to read the woman's expression. Dominique couldn't tell whether she understood what they were telling her or not. The dog's tail thumped and she swatted him playfully. "There's a good boy—you won't hurt a fly unless I say, right?"

"We've come to see if you have any leranon healing oil," Dominique blurted out. It seemed if they waited for the woman to ask why they'd come, Brigitta would be long dead, several dawns would have come and gone, and the city would lie in ruins.

"Healing oil? Oh, such a good thing for paws and chapped noses, eh, my lovely?" She kissed the dog on the nose and Amana hid a giggle behind her hand.

Dominique wished he knew the proper name for the golden healing liquid. "One of our friends was injured by Emberto's men. The Grand Teller said you knew about a leranon."

At the word *leranon*, Ella Minato shuddered and again she had to pull her shawl back into position.

"Now where would I get something like that?" she asked. "Maybe I don't even know what a leranon is. Maybe I've never seen such oil."

Dominique thought of Brigitta lying hurt at the Recitatorium. "Excuse me, Miss Minato, I don't mean to be rude, but I must have some leranon oil. My friend is dying, I think. She has a terrible wound. I have this to carry it in—"

He pulled the ampoule from inside his shift, and Ella Minato leaned closer to inspect it. "If you don't have any, then where—"

"A Ticabellan piece," the herbalist said. "Is that where you come from?"

"No. I am an Estorian. From the Bertolescu clan."

At this the woman leaned forward and squinted at Dominique until he felt so uncomfortable he pressed back against the ladder hard enough to feel the rungs jammed across his back. "Indeed," she said. "Indeed."

"Iliatica told us you had a leranon here," Amana said. "We don't have much time. We have to return to the Recitatorium before first light so we can take Brigitta the healing drops. And then, if we can, we have to find Ventnor, too."

"Old Ventnor? Of the tavern?"

Amana nodded. "The tavern is no more. They burned it down last night."

There was no need to say who was responsible. "Brothers of black hogs," Ella Minato said with a grunt. "Very well. Can you pay?"

Dominique raised his eyebrows and looked at Amana. "I have a few kinnels," Amana offered, taking a purse from where she had it tucked under her belt. "Will this be enough?" She counted out five silver coins and placed them in Ella Minato's palm.

"Hmph." She shrugged. "It will have to do. Come with me."

Ella Minato rose and moved toward the back of the barge. A solid wall seemed to indicate the end of the cabin. To one side was a small door leading to a narrow berth about knee height. Ella Minato crawled in and then disappeared.

Dominique followed, feeling his way along the wooden wall of the barge until he reached the bulkhead at the end. As he pushed on this, a trap door swung open and he crawled through the opening and dropped into a space beyond. He stood, carefully feeling above him so he didn't hit his head again. Another lantern sputtered to life as Amana joined him.

The three of them stood in what looked like a simple donkey stall. Bedded deeply with straw, the space was just large enough for the good-sized leranon to stand, turn around, and lie down.

Tears pricked at Dominique's eyes. "Ohhh . . ." he said, taking in the burns all over the animal's body, the wrinkled white ridges of scar tissue, the bald patches where no hair would ever grow again, the way the animal lay in the straw, not even getting up when its quarters were invaded by strangers. It was hard to believe this pathetic creature was the same species as the majestic beasts he had met in the wild.

But it was the same kind of animal: it had back legs like those of a lion, and where the hair had not been burnt off, it was tawny-coloured. Its skin was drawn tight over sinewy muscles, its back legs powerful enough to launch the flying beast into the air. The leranon's front half was very much like that of a horse. It had dark eyes spaced widely on an intelligent head, and protruding from its forehead was a single long horn. Tucked in close to its sides were two wings that Dominique knew were capable of unfurling with only a moment's notice.

This animal's head hung so low its velvety nose scarcely cleared the straw bedding. Instead of the mischievous grin of young Kyrie or even the wise, contemplative gaze of the older males like BellaMinka or Cornelius, this leranon's eyes were masked with a dull glaze, and this look of desolation, this lack of hope was the most difficult thing for Dominique to see.

"Sadriamo—these people have come to see you," Ella Minato said, touching the leranon lightly on the neck.

The leranon blinked, still getting used to the light. "Hello," she said.

The voice was soft, somehow familiar.

"Hello," Dominique said, excited to see the leranon safe from Emberto's clutches, but saddened to see the great creature locked away in the darkness, languishing alone. "My name is Dominique. I know some of your kind. I visited the leranons who live near the Cave of Departure," he said. "They helped me, let me stay in the cave."

The leranon lifted her head a little and then lowered it again so the tip of her long horn rested in the straw, as if even the effort of holding her head up was too great a strain. It struck Dominique that maybe he shouldn't have mentioned the others still living freely in the cave.

"I'm sorry—I—"

The leranon shifted in the straw, flexed its mighty back legs, and pushed to a standing position. Behind him, Amana moved away. "You speak from my kind is not bad. I must think me go back."

"You will," Dominique said, though he could not imagine how this could happen. The great beast's wings lay close by its sides, limp and lustreless. "Why don't you just fly away?" Dominique asked.

"Do you know nothing?" Ella Minato said. "They trim the wings so the leranons cannot fly."

Dominique recoiled. What else could the monsters do to a once noble, once free creature? He reached out to let the leranon sniff his hand. "Do they ever grow back?"

"Eventually. But very, very slowly," Ella Minato said. She turned to the leranon. "The boy here seeks aurum-curare."

So that was its proper name. *Aurum-curare.*

Sadriamo hesitated, drawing her wings in tightly against her sides. Dominique understood why she wouldn't trust him—why should she, in this city where every other person wanted to either enslave or kill the leranons?

"Please," he said softly.

"It's not right to force a leranon to do anything it doesn't want to do," Ella Minato said firmly. "After all Sadriamo has been through, it's just not right. You might have to go and find some other way to help your friend. I have some fresh estanchier leaves—excellent for treating wounds of all kinds. I could give you a good price, maybe throw in some tonic—you look pale."

Dominique wished the old woman would stop her chatter. He couldn't think clearly, couldn't find the words to persuade Sadriamo to help.

"Show them Navina," Amana said from where she stood in the shadows as far away from the leranon as she could get.

Dominique took the sack from her and reached inside for his bird. The effect was immediate and dramatic.

"A kasyapa!" Sadriamo said and rippled the tips of her flight feathers, a gesture that Navina answered with a ruffle of her own diminutive wings. Ella Minato was, for the first time since her unexpected visitors had climbed aboard, speechless.

"You are boy with kasyapa?" Sadriamo asked, as if by saying the words aloud she could convince herself that what she saw before her was no illusion. "Now me know why other leranon help."

Dominique didn't see why Navina made such a difference, but this time, when he asked, "So, will you help me, too?" the response was quite different.

The leranon nodded. "This I will do."

Dominique's heart jumped. "Thank you!"

"Have you place for to put in medicine?"

Dominique nodded and showed the ampoule that

hung around his neck. The leranon nodded.

"This will good do." The leranon carefully turned her head away so as not to bump the others with her long horn.

"Well, go on then, boy. What are you waiting for?" Ella Minato asked.

"What am I supposed to do?"

"I thought you knew the ways of the leranons," she said, her eyes darting suspiciously from Dominique to Amana.

"The leranons took the aurum-curare from a pool in the rocks. I thought it came from the stones."

"Hah! From the stones?"

"Boy is true," the leranon said, cutting Ella Minato's laughter short. "In cave we add aurum-curare from all leranons together in rock place."

Dominique felt a little better. But knowing he was right about how the leranons in the cave stored their precious healing fluid did little to help him understand where it came from in the first place.

"They have glands at the base of their wings, underneath," Ella Minato said matter-of-factly. "Only the females, of course. And they don't produce as much when they aren't living in the best of conditions—I try to get the best hay I can, but it isn't easy to sneak it in here. But there's no substitute for fresh, green grass, is there, Sadriamo? Show him—show him where the stuff comes from."

Sadriamo lifted her wings away from her body, revealing two small raised lumps, a bit like moles protruding from the skin. Beneath the wings the skin was hairless, pure white, and totally smooth except for the two glands.

"Not hard," Sadriamo warned. Gingerly, Dominique moved closer and unscrewed the lid of the ampoule. He pressed the lip of the opening against one side of a gland

302

and with his other hand gave the protuberance a hesitant squeeze. A golden drop appeared and fell into the ampoule. Dominique squeezed again, a little more firmly this time, and collected two more drops.

Sadriamo exhaled, and as she relaxed, the drops came more easily. After he had collected perhaps twenty drops, he moved to the leranon's other side and repeated the gentle harvest from the other gland. His container was not even half full when no more drops came.

"That is all," Sadriamo said. "Come in one more week and do again. More drops come then."

"Thank you," Amana said and stepped forward to stroke the animal's neck.

Sadriamo dipped her head and pushed her soft muzzle into Amana's hand. Amana smiled. "I didn't know," she said softly and rubbed the leranon behind the ears. Sadriamo sighed with pleasure.

"How will you pay?" Ella Minato asked suddenly.

"We paid you already," Dominique said indignantly.

"Yes. You paid me. But what are silver kinnels worth to a leranon? How will you pay Sadriamo?"

"There is nothing for to pay," Sadriamo said hastily.

"Kasyapa or no kasyapa," Ella Minato said as Dominique tucked Navina safely back into the bag, "you should not give the stuff away!"

"Yes. Must give for time to come. To help boy with bird."

"But—"

The argument went no further because just then a loud explosion rocked the barge. The dog started barking out in the cabin. Dominique staggered sideways and fell against the leranon's side. Ella Minato scuttled backwards and virtually dove back out into the narrow berth.

41

NECESSARY SORROW

The only mistake is to let one get away, for only the living tell stories.

—Campriano battle story

"What's happening?" Amana said, her eyes wide, her dagger already drawn.

Dominique had no idea. "Sadriamo," he said. "We will try to help you. Maybe we can take you away from here."

Sadriamo sank to her knees in the straw. "There is no—"

Another crash from up on deck, followed by a loud wail from Ella Minato, startled both Dominique and Amana into action.

"Hurry!" Dominique was closest to the way out and he scrambled over the berth and into the main cabin. The wild rocking of the barge had sent bottles and vials tumbling from Ella Minato's tidy shelves. Outside, shouts and screams made the hair stand up on the back of Dominique's arms.

"What is happening out there?" he asked, not expecting an answer.

"Where is your knife?" Amana asked.

Dominique snatched a knife from the table and leaped up the ladder onto the deck. It was hardly recognizable. The tidy stands had fallen over and the tethers holding down the cloth covers had torn away. A light breeze lifted the edges of the covers where they had come untied, and Ella Minato scurried from end to end of the deck, trying to scoop up as many of her precious herbs as she could before they blew overboard.

The frantic action of one woman scrambling back and forth on the deck was nothing compared to what was going on up on the road, where a bloody battle raged. Dominique watched in horror as soldiers and civilians fought other soldiers and civilians. The soldiers were well armed with swords, arrows, and clubs. The civilians seemed to be using whatever they could get their hands on. Some hurled rocks or bottles, others charged the soldiers with pitchforks and shovels, while others swung ropes at the horses' feet, trying to panic the animals. The tactic was working. Several horses crashed heavily to the ground, throwing their riders, who were then immediately surrounded by furious opponents. At the end of the street, new fires had been started and the air was filled with thick, acrid smoke.

"Go back below!" Dominique shouted over the din. The last thing they needed now was Amana getting any crazy ideas about going to battle herself, and he couldn't imagine that any herbs would be worth risking Ella Minato's life. "Ella Minato!" he shouted, and clutching bunches of dried leaves and long wispy grasses to her chest, the herbalist clumped across the deck and plunged below after them.

Down in the cabin, Ella Minato slumped onto her bench, weeping, and Dominique pulled the blanket up around her shoulders. Still gripping the herbs she had managed to salvage, the herbalist leaned her head back against the bulkhead, her jaw slack with grief. "The Battle for Carnillo has begun in earnest now," she moaned and then lost herself in a new round of sobs. Alonzoro hopped up beside her and pushed his head into her lap.

Amana nodded. "Emberto has never been so serious about eradicating all opposition. For as long as I can remember, we have told stories he wanted us to tell—of an impending invasion or a rebellion from within. That," she tipped her head toward the chaos beyond the hatch, "could be either, or both, happening out there. Either way, we can't return to the Recitatorium now."

"You can't stay here, either," Ella Minato said, choking back sniffles and hugging her dog. "I will be killed for certain if they find you here."

"We could hide with Sadriamo," Dominique suggested.

"There is hardly enough room back there—"

The barge dipped and swayed and the dog jumped to his feet, barking and snarling.

"Who is up there?" Ella Minato cried out over

Alonzoro's furious barking. Even as she pushed the dog aside and stood to slide back the hatch, she waved Dominique and Amana toward the berth and then turned to meet the intruders on her own.

Amana and Dominique leaped into the berth and crawled toward the bulkhead. They let themselves into the hidden hold and secured the trap door behind them. Crouching beside Sadriamo, they held their breaths, terrified they had not moved quickly enough. Any movement would set the boat rocking and give them away. Voices rose in the cabin, shouting to be heard over the dog's snarls and barks.

"What is happening? What are you doing here?"

"Quiet, old woman. Shut that dog up!"

"Quiet, Alonzoro."

"Have you seen any strangers?"

Cupboard doors banged and someone thumped the bulkhead alongside the berth. Dominique and Amana stared at the secret entrance to the hold. They had locked it tightly behind them, but would it hold if a soldier tried to batter his way through?

The thumping retreated.

"Go away! Get off my boat! You cannot just—"

A loud thump was followed by a second bang and Alonzoro barked again.

"Shut up!" one of the men shouted, and then the dog yelped before falling quiet.

Dominique's heart caught in his throat when Ella Minato screamed, a long, wailing cry so miserable he thought she would never survive her grief. "Alonzoro! You brutes! You monsters! My dog!" A tremendous crash shook the boat and another scream sliced into the darkness so loudly it seemed as if the old woman were right there in the hidden compartment beside them.

Amana reached out and found Dominique's hand as they stood, rigid, straining to hear what was happening in the main cabin. Another loud crash followed and then a thud shook the floorboards beneath their feet. Amana squeezed harder.

"Enough! She's an old woman—don't waste your time!"

"Fine. Let's go. There's nobody else here."

The barge swayed again and Dominique and Amana cowered with Sadriamo in the hold. Amana let go of Dominique's hand and pulled out her dagger again.

"I'll come with you," he whispered.

Together, they eased open the trap door and listened. Outside, water lapped gently against the sides of the barge, and farther off, Dominique heard running feet, shouts, and screams. But inside the barge he heard nothing.

A single lamp still burned in the cabin. At first, Dominique didn't see where Ella Minato and her dog had fallen. For a wild moment he thought they might have escaped.

"Oh, Dominique," Amana said and tugged at his sleeve.

Dominique saw them then, Ella Minato's crumpled body, a gaping wound across the back of her neck; the dog sprawled across the rough wooden planks of the cabin sole where he had fallen, mid-lunge, as he had leaped at his mistress's attackers. Dominique dropped to his knees and unscrewed the top of the ampoule.

"Dominique—don't." Amana kneeled beside him and very gently touched his hand, stopping him from using the golden potion. "Don't waste any," she said softly. "You don't know when . . ."

Reluctantly, Dominique resealed the cap and let the ampoule hang from the chain around his neck. He closed his eyes and leaned forward until his forehead rested on the cabin sole beside Ella Minato, tears hot on his cheeks. It was true. A week was a long time. Anything could happen before Sadriamo would be able to give them more aurum-curare.

"Dominique—we can't stay here. They might come back." Amana lay her hand on his back and moved it in slow circles. "Dominique. Come on."

"We can't leave Sadriamo," he said, sitting up and wiping his tears with the bottom of his shirt. He thought Amana might argue, but instead she turned and crawled back into the leranon's stall.

Sadriamo collapsed to her knees when Dominique told her of her protector's death.

"No, no, no," she said, shaking her great head from side to side. "You go," Sadriamo whispered at last. "You no can stay here."

"We can't leave you," Dominique said.

"We'll try to hide you somewhere—take you somewhere else," Amana insisted. "But how can we get away—the streets are filled with soldiers. Half the town is on fire."

"She has small boat," Sadriamo said.

"Do you think we could get away on the canal? Is there any way to sneak out of Carnillo on the water?" Dominique asked.

Amana shook her head. "No. There's nowhere to row even if we could sneak out past the guard towers. But we might be able to get to the wine merchant ships."

Dominique tipped his head to the side. "How? And what good would that do?"

"Emberto will never allow the wine shipments to be halted. The ships travel to and from Pettela nearly every day."

"Pettela? On the mainland?"

"We can try."

Sadriamo nodded her head. "You try."

Dominique moved to her head and said, "We can't leave you here."

"We can't take her, either. Leranons are not allowed to be free here in the city."

"I know that." Dominique took a step back and gave Sadriamo a long, hard look.

"What are you thinking?" Amana asked.

"Go and bring me the blanket—the one from Ella's sleeping bench."

"But why? What are you—"

"Go. Hurry. It will be light soon."

Amana slipped away and returned in a moment with the blanket.

"Help me put it over her back," Dominique said.

The two tugged the blanket up over the leranon's wings and spread it over her back. It fully covered her back, wings, and leonine hindquarters.

"If one of us rode and one of us walked, we would look like travellers with a donkey," Dominique said.

Amana answered this suggestion with a snort. "A donkey with a horn! I don't think so."

Sadriamo looked at Dominique with a peculiar mixture of sadness, fear, and resignation, and with a sick feeling, Dominique knew what he had to do. He reached out and gently touched the base of Sadriamo's horn.

"Will it hurt very much?" Dominique asked.

Sadriamo nodded. "Yes. But you have collected enough healing drops that I will survive the wound."

"You can't be serious! You aren't going to cut off her horn, are you?"

"What choice do we have? If she stays here, she will starve. If we release her, she will be recaptured or killed in the streets. You know how Camprianos feel about leranons."

Amana looked down, suddenly very interested in the design on the hilt of her dagger. Dominique turned his attention back to Sadriamo. "Will it hurt you in some other way? Your magic . . ."

Sadriamo sighed heavily. "I stay, I die," she said. "No horn, no ever get mate. But dead no get mate." Her upper lip wrinkled as if she had tasted something unexpectedly bitter. "You want me to come, then take horn."

"Give me your dagger," Dominique said softly to Amana. "My knife is not big enough."

Steeling himself, he took the dagger and stepped closer to Sadriamo. "I'm so sorry," he said.

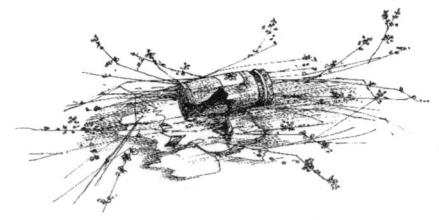

42

SADRIAMO'S SACRIFICE

The old man added his wife's story stick to the fire and watched the sparks spiral up into the night sky, taking her stories with them.

—Estorian story

Sadriamo lowered her head and closed her eyes. Dominique began to saw at the horn. It was surprisingly soft and he cut through the tissue, continuing despite the blood and Sadriamo's deep moans of agony.

Amana stepped forward and held the end of the horn so it did not tear away from the animal's head. Dominique gritted his teeth and kept cutting until the incision was done. The very second the horn was separated from Sadriamo, Dominique dropped the dagger into the straw and unscrewed the top of the ampoule. He applied healing drops all around the outside ring of the bloody wound and then worked his way in a spiral until he reached the centre.

"There," he said, watching the golden fluid soak into the horrible place where her horn had been. The bleeding had stopped already and Sadriamo leaned against him, her eyes still closed.

A loud *boom* followed by loud shouts and running feet up on the street startled them all into action.

"Can you fit through there?" Dominique asked, doubtfully eyeing the opening to the berth. Sadriamo stepped forward unsteadily.

"Yes. Go. I come in this way. I go out this way."

"Wait," Amana said. "Give me your name ring."

"Why? We don't have—"

"Give it here."

Recognizing the fierce, uncompromising look on Amana's face, he reached down and unsnapped the wooden ring from his ankle. Without asking permission, Amana took his knife and deftly carved two circles, one inside the other. She rubbed her little finger in the blood on the base of Sadriamo's severed horn and then coloured the outer circle. "It will look faded when it dries," she said, looking around the stall.

"What do you need now?"

"Something black."

"What about the lamp?" Dominique suggested.

Near the top, the inside of the oil lamp's glass had been blackened by smoke. Amana cut off a corner of Sadriamo's blanket and, being careful not to burn herself, wiped the glass, then rubbed the blackened blanket over the inner circle. She had to repeat the process twice more before the circle was dark enough to satisfy her.

"Let's hope that works," she said. She looked critically at his dark hair. "It's a good thing Ventnor's people dyed your hair."

"What are you—"

Another explosion rocked the barge.

"We must go now," Amana said. "Go, Dominique. You first, we'll follow."

Dominique shuddered as he made his way back into the main cabin. For a moment he looked at the old woman lying on the cabin sole. Then he pushed the body of the dog closer to the herbalist, lifted Ella Minato's arm over her old companion, and tucked her shawl around them both.

He turned in time to see Sadriamo pulling herself awkwardly along the berth, Ella Minato's blanket still tucked firmly around the front of her folded wings. The leranon lifted her head to avoid looking at the fallen bodies and went straight toward the ladder and hatch.

"Amana, do you need to take the coins back?"

"I have another pouch," she said, "but yes, that's a good idea."

She retrieved the five kinnels, then climbed the ladder and poked her head out of the open hatch. "They're still fighting out here," she reported to the other two waiting below, "but a little farther along the street. Sadriamo, where is Ella Minato's rowing boat?"

"Tied at back of big boat."

Amana climbed right out of the hatch and disappeared onto the deck. The barge dipped and swayed as she moved around and then they heard bumping noises and a soft scraping sound along the outside of the hull.

"Dominique," she whispered when she returned to the hatch.

"Go on, Sadriamo," Dominique said. "You go first."

Sadriamo raised her forelegs and stretched upright so her head and the front half of her body stuck out of the opening. Beneath the blanket, Dominique saw her huge hind legs flex and tense. She took a deep breath and then leapt upwards.

Dominique took one final look below and blew out the lamp, hiding the ghastly sight in darkness. He wished he'd had the chance to say thank you, but as in the story of the fisher El Madrical, who never told his wife he loved her before the tidal wave swept him away, it was too late now. "Goodbye," he said. "Thank you."

43

FLIGHT

If you open your hands, the bird will fly away.

—Campriano proverb

Amana stood in the rowboat and reached up to hold onto the toerail that ran all around the deck of the barge. "Hurry, Dominique," she said. He hopped down into the boat beside her and steadied the flat-bottomed craft so Sadriamo could jump in. It sank dangerously low in the water with her added weight, and Dominique nervously eyed the black water of the canal to see if it would actually come over the sides.

Amana pushed away from the barge and slipped the oars into the water. "Sit up front," she whispered to Dominique. "Tell me if you see anyone. Anything."

Amana hauled on the oars and guided the boat to the shadows along the base of the wall at the far side of the canal. Flames licked the rooftops of several buildings directly opposite. Though the fires cast extra light on the dark water, the people in the streets were concerned only with saving their homes and businesses by throwing bucket after bucket of water at the flames. Fire bells rang all over the city. Cries of terror rose from the streets, drifted out of open windows. The three in the boat were paddling away from the worst fighting but, Dominique realized, Brigitta would not be able to go anywhere. For her, escape would be impossible.

"We have to help Brigitta!" he said.

"We can do nothing for her," Amana said. "The Recitatorium is about the safest place in the city." She pulled steadily on the oars. "Sit still. What are you doing?"

Dominique pulled Amana's bag away from her and reached inside for Navina. He set her gently on his knee and then reached into the bag for the small vial the leranons had given him in the cave. Carefully unscrewing the top of the vial, he dribbled a few drops into it from the ampoule.

"Dominique, stop! What are you doing?"

Dominique ignored her. "Quiet. Someone will hear us," he said. Amana kept her protests to herself after that, though she rowed even faster, obviously furious. He tugged a length of thread from a seam inside the sack and fastened a crude harness around Navina's chest. When he tucked the old vial into the harness, though, Amana couldn't restrain herself any longer.

"Dominique, you aren't going to—"

He did not wait for her to finish but cupped Navina gently in his hands, raised her close to his lips, and whispered, "Find Brigitta. Then find me."

"No!" Amana said. But it was too late. Dominique had tossed the bird into the night. Her wings had to beat harder to lift the extra weight tied around her chest, but she managed to rise and flew away from them.

"That was so stupid," Amana said. "You don't expect her to find us again, do you? What a waste of the medicine. You don't even know that she will take it to Brigitta."

"Shh," Dominique said and pointed to a bridge over the canal. Two horsemen trotted across, swords drawn, shields at the ready.

After that, not another word was spoken in the boat. Dominique thought perhaps they would join the fishers in the boathouse, but then Amana turned and rowed out into the middle of a small anchorage. Completely surrounded by the city, the bay was like a market square on the water, filled with many ships of all sizes.

Several of the largest vessels lay at anchor in the very middle of the basin. This, it seemed, was where Amana was taking them. As they drew closer, Dominique could make out the pale moon faces of guards lining each deck.

"Who is that?" one shouted over the railing of the closest ship.

"Lady Amana of Emberto's household," she said. "Is Captain Ipsilon aboard?"

"Aye!" A shout brought the captain to the rail. His hand on the hilt of his long sword, he leaned forward, holding a lantern aloft.

"Lady Amana—what brings you here?"

CHAPTER

44

NĀVINĀ

*Of all the children, the boy with the ability to see far
beyond was the only one of the clan to journey safely to
the other side of the ocean. And, oh, the stories he told
when he returned were marvellous!*

—Estorian story

Dominique's fingers gripped the seat in the bow as if
they would never again let go. Had Amana completely
lost her mind?

"Emberto says that for your safety and the safety of
your crew you must leave the city immediately."

"Is that so? We were considering joining the—"

"No! He requires your service in another matter. I
have here his nephew from the palace. He is too young
to fight but must be saved."

Dominique hunched down, trying to look as small as
possible.

"Emberto has disguised his nephew as a poor peddler—you see his donkey?"

"Aye."

"Emberto said that of all the wine merchants, you
alone could be trusted. He also said your ship, *Search for*

Gold, is the fastest of all the wine fleet and must not be lost. Lord Emberto will reward you well," Amana said, jingling a pouch of silver kinnels.

"Pass up your name rings," the captain said.

Glad for the darkness that hid his shaking fingers, Dominique unsnapped the wooden ring from around his ankle and handed it to Amana. She stood and passed them up to one of the sailors. If the captain noticed that one of the rings had been altered, Dominique knew their journey would end immediately. He concentrated on the even grooves of the planks in the bottom of the rowboat.

"Very well. Men—help them aboard."

There was no chance to celebrate. Immediately two sailors lowered a sling over the side and first Amana, then Sadriamo with the blanket still covering her back, and finally Dominique were hauled over the side of the ship. Amana and Dominique reclaimed their name rings and the captain started shouting orders.

"Raise the anchor!" To another crewman he said, "Take the beast below."

"No," Dominique said.

"It is well and good, your grace," Amana said quickly. "I shall sleep below and tend the creature. As a servant of the house of Emberto it would be my honour." She bowed deeply and it was all Dominique could do not to grin.

"You, too, must go below," Captain Ipsilon said to Dominique. "Show the boy to my quarters."

"Sir, with respect—might I stay on deck?" Dominique dredged up every shred of knowledge he had about infusing emotion into a good story and said, his voice quavering, "I don't know when I might see my uncle's city again." A seemingly heartfelt sob caught in his throat, surprising even Dominique.

The captain puffed out his cheeks and scowled down at Dominique. "Stay out of the way."

"Yes, sir. Thank you, sir."

But the captain had other things on his mind. He spun on his heel and marched aft to take the helm, bellowing orders as he went. Amana and Sadriamo followed a sailor and disappeared around the far side of a low deckhouse.

In response to the captain's shouts, men appeared everywhere, blinking and rubbing the sleep from their eyes. They wasted no time and were soon scurrying about on the deck, climbing up into the rigging, hauling on ropes, and peering aloft as the sails unfurled and filled.

Careful to stay out of the way, Dominique found a place to sit between two barrels lashed to the deck. Slowly, the ship began to move.

"Come on, Navina," he whispered. "Hurry." He tipped his head back and stared up into the rigging of the ship. The barrels were located toward the front of the ship, near the base of the third mast. It rose dizzyingly above him and, though they were moving slowly, seemed to be tipping backwards. It took a moment for Dominique to realize this was just a trick of the eye and that the mast was not, in fact, toppling over.

He noted every detail of the handholds jutting out from the side of the mast, the rigging, the sails, still mostly furled, the men moving about like spiders in a giant web, the triangular flag of Emberto fluttering high above. Dominique didn't move until his neck ached and the ship passed through the open sea gate and left the City of Carnillo behind.

Dominique stayed where he was until he saw another image in his head, one of a wide stretch of sea and, far below, the *Search for Gold*, now under full sail, cutting across the ocean toward the east. It was only then, when he knew Navina had spotted them, that he moved to the front of the ship and stood at the rail, watching the waves peel away in ripples from the bow.

Gripping the rail, Dominique braced himself as the ship climbed up and over each rolling wave. A stiff breeze blew on the open water, riffled through his hair as he searched the lightening sky. At last a flutter caught his eye and he swirled around. A bird far above the ship beat her wings furiously, and Dominique's heart rose to meet her.

Navina dove, plummeting toward Dominique so fast he gasped—surely she would miss and fall into the sea!

At the last moment, Navina spread her wings and tail feathers and reached for his extended arm with her feet. He pulled her close and checked quickly to see if anyone had noticed her landing. He let out his breath: he was alone on the foredeck.

"You found me," he whispered, barely able to speak. The vial was still tucked into the makeshift harness. Dominique tugged it free and shook it. It was empty. "Were you in time?" he whispered, lifting Navina so close to his lips that her delicate feathers lifted as he breathed. "Did you save her?"

The bird ground her beak and cocked her head to the side, inviting him to scratch the back of her neck.

But from somewhere deep inside, anger boiled and churned and rose like bile in his throat. "Why can't you tell me what I want to know?" he shouted.

Navina peeped and hopped onto the railing, her wings flitting out sideways as she struggled to keep her balance.

As fast as it had come upon him, the bitter rage subsided, leaving him numb, guilt-ridden, queasy. "I'm sorry. I'm so sorry."

He offered his hand again and Navina climbed back on, her delicate feet gripping his thumb. Dominique shifted against the rail and felt the metal ampoule against his chest. He tugged it free of his shirt, moved Navina to his shoulder, and turned his back to the wind. He squatted down, protecting his delicate work from the gusts and the sea spray they chased onto the deck. Carefully, he transferred the rest of the leranon's oil into the small vial. He could replenish his supply. Those he had left behind—Brigitta, Ventnor, Toranosco, Breska— could not.

Working quickly now, he slipped the vial back into Navina's harness and touched her lightly on the head.

"Go find Ventnor and the others," he told her. "They need as much of this as you can carry." He choked back tears and turned his back on the railing where the glorious bird perched, his thin shoulders hunched against the wind, against the misery of what he was doing.

A long time later, when he finally forced himself to turn around, Navina was gone. He wiped his eyes, straightened his back, and fixed his gaze forward, toward the east. The sun, a radiant disc of burning rose, crept into the sky, drawing the ship and her passengers ever farther from the City by the Sea.

ABOUT THE AUTHOR

Nikki Tate has written more than a dozen books for children. She lives on Vancouver Island with her daughter, Danielle, and a menagerie. Inspired by storytellers through the ages, Tate created the world of the Estorians where, she admits, she would like to live some day.

Tate is a much sought-after performer and workshop leader who is entertaining, inspiring, and informative. Each year she speaks to thousands of schoolchildren in the United States and Canada about writing and storytelling.